Caged Ocean Dub

Glints & Stories

Dare Segun Falowo

Android Press

Published by Android Press
Eugene, Oregon
www.android-press.com

First Printing, 2023
Cover Art by Justine Norton-Kertson

ISBN: 978-1958121276 (paperback)
ISBN: 978-1958121269 (epub)

Permissions:

"Oases" – originally published in *Klorofyl* (2015)
"Eating Kaolin" – originally published in *Omenana* (2021)
"Sonskins" – originally published in *Baffling Magazine* (2021)
"Ngozi Ugegbe Nwa" – originally published in *The Dark Magazine* (2020)
"The Visions of Atanda Ekun" – originally published in *Saraba Magazine* (2014)
"Kikelomo Ultrasheen" – originally published in The Magazine of Fantasy and Science Fiction (2020)
"Vain Knife" – originally published in *The Dark Magazine* (2018)
"The Fields of Abete, Iwaya" – originally published in *Professor Charlatan Bardot's Travelogue* (2021)
"Convergence in Chorus Architecture" – originally published in *Dominion: An anthology of Speculative Fiction from Africa and the Diaspora* (2021) *Published in Italianas Convergenza nell'architettura del coro* by Zona 42.

Contents

Introduction

For as long as I can remember, I have always been curious about the strange, the weird and the otherworldly.

I believe that who I am today is a being shaped by these glimpses into a beyond, through first-hand experience, via my luck at having a mind sensitive to this otherness.

These sensations that there is something more out there, beyond the surface of concensus reality, stirs up something in every human being. In their quests for God, in their superstitions and in their arguments about what is real and what is only just shadow, false skin.

My work as Dare Segun Falowo has been a semi-direct investigation through my intuition and my imagination into worlds where that which is unknown collides openly with that which is believed to be the only reality.

These stories were collected from over a decade of deliberate work. Some are faintly inspired by experience and others by a hunger for experiment and play. The very rare ones fell out of my hands seemingly without any typing at all.

I am honored by this occurrence called "Caged Ocean Dub", so grateful to the cosmos (and the editors) for allowing this collection of texts in glints, pieces and episodes across times and spaces that I've drifted through, become a wholeness.

Enjoy your beach.

D.S. Falowo. Ibadan. 2023

I. Hungers

Akara Oyinbo

On the sixth day of February, in the year that they declared all the Nigerian houses be painted white and grass-green, Mrs. Lola Joy who lived in the largest house on Ada Goodness Street choked on wedding cake and died.

She lay stiff on the black rug of her mansion with a smile on her face. The cake had been really good.

At the moment of her death, she was forty-nine years old and a busy mother of three children; Fortune Joy, Justice Joy and Joy Joy. She had been a stern mother in her lifetime and her ability to mix cake batter whilst doing other activities such as: breast-feeding, frying fresh fish or dodo, counting the beads of her glow-in-the-dark rosary, driving a bus with her newborn twins in elbow etc. was quite remarkable (until the electric mixers came from Japan to relieve her of a bit of pride and a lot of pain).

She had married Emenike Joy of Joyous Song Records, three weeks after they had first crossed elbows to drink chilled Star together on a hot Lagos beach under silky moonlight.

She fell in love with the exuberant Igbo man fiercely and moved into his home, where she began to bake even more fierce-ly. She had run the Joy Joy Joy Bakery from the kitchens of all their four homes in Lagos.

Twenty years after she had baked her first cake, a droopy muf-fin in an oven made from a heated pot filled with dry sand, she had eaten her last; a buttery fruit cake, whorled with cream and held with honey.

She had learnt to bake at her secondary school, Our Lady of Blessed Grace, under the tutelage of Sister Persistence; who loved to wear lipstick, drink of the sacrament and play card games on Sunday nights. Sister Persistence had strong pliant fingers and a quick tongue with which she dispensed her knowledge. The girls would gather round in their light blue habits, ironed and perfumed to perfection, with faces that beamed with an absence of mind, and watch as she plucked round heavy cakes from the ugly black oven, clutching their rosaries like they were praying with all their might not to fall into the pits of Hell, which they knew in that moment, would smell like cake.

Lola Joy, then known as Sister Peace, often felt her mouth water alongside her sisters' as they watched the cakes cut up and sent to Mother Superior's office. She could feel an almost terrible power in the way the cakes called on primordial hungers through the nose, and she thought once; maybe it was cake and not bread that was Christ's flesh, and Sister Persistence had gotten a hold of the recipe from the Passover.

She knew that if she took proper notes she would be able to eat all the cake she wanted once she left school and had enough money. Sister Persistence always gave them small creamy cubes at the end of class and they would testify that her baking skills were divine, sent from the bosom of Jesus' Mother Herself, confirming Sister Peace's suspicions.

Joy Joy, teenage heiress already adept with a rolling pin and scary good at icing sculptures, found Mommy asleep on the carpet when she came in from school. Mommy always complained that the carpet was too soft and encouraged a boneless idleness in the family.

Joy Joy was humming along to the vulgar Nigerian pop that often ran through her mind like a narcotic, escaping from her lips in uncontrolled bursts. Her mother always explained to her that the Church was against her taste in such ghetto musics, often vocal about how much she believed they attracted demons, and randy teenagers who smelt of old marijuana and sweat.

Unaware of her mother's true state, Joy Joy eyed the cake that stood on the table in the parlor and the knife that lay by it, shiny surface fuzzed with batter and icing. She slowed down into tiptoe and pulled herself up to the front of the cake with stealth, a domestic Jane Bond. Her nose was instantly filled with the rich creamy cloud that came with freshly baked Joy Joy Joy cakes and made most humans lose control of everything for a few moments, the thought of a slice being quite destabilizing.

She picked the knife, cut a large dark wedge, edged with cream and dripping honey that begged to be licked, and ate it over her mother's dead body.

Busola Orange Juice

The emptied bottles of this drink are labelled by the use of strips of white exercise-book paper cellotaped to used eva water bottles. Handwritten with a fading Bic in overt cursive is "Busola Orange Juice".

Those who have bought and tasted of this juice say the girl who sold it to them is a slim thing of about twelve. She is blacker than wet roads and too quiet for their liking. The men who tried to touch her inappropriately as she bent down to pick up the juice, say their hands had barely come close to her waist or yansh when they felt a sense of doom lift their stomachs. It was, they say, as if their entire beings were warning them that they were about to put their hand inside a pit of snakes. One woman who thought Busola beautiful enough to be her housegirl had put her palm on her shoulder and experienced the feeling of leaning too far into an empty well.

Busola sold her curious drink to exactly a score of Lagosians.

The contents of the bottles were a furious shade of orange and this was exactly what called the eye of the customer to it as she walked rather slowly under those peculiar heatwaves in Lagos that blurred the vision, toasted the flesh and dried the soul. Packed in the danfoes, sweating and stinking like old sardines, some called to the gentle girl who wasn't even advertising what she hawked with loud calls.

She seemed to simply be walking down the road like she knew it would never end.

On collecting the bottle of reddish orange liquid, they saw the handmade label and instantly deemed it too dangerous to ingest. They looked at Busola waiting under the sun for them to make their decisions. Her eyes gazing far off into something.

She looked like a statue that had no need to work, who would profit more from simply standing still in an unseen corner forever frozen, diving fathoms into her own soul without any urge to surface. As they were looking at her, they realized just how *cold* what they were holding was and without thinking, they all admitted to this, drinking it like their lives depended on it. It was that cold. They said it spoke to their throats, calling them to unscrew and drink.

Busola Orange Juice is refreshing and cool to the sun-parched dungeon of the belly. When it touches your tongue, its razor sharp tang make spit explode across the entire digestive tract, then, the delicious juice follows and nourishes with its rich heft, bringing to mind an avalanche of oranges crashing onto a stuck traffic jam.

After the first three gulps, you know who she is. Busola Aro, ex-wife of Commisioner Aro, that giant of Nigerian Agriculture. She, his wife since thirteen, locked inside a three-tiered palace of marble, alone with the chef and the dog and a vast grove of fat blood oranges. In his mind, Aro had loved her. To himself, he kept her safe from harm, safe from the acid of the public eye. He had three other wives to bear him children but she was his Bus-Bus. His very own innocent beauty. A statue to grace his tenth house with life.

Busola had lived there till she turned twenty, tending to the grove of blood oranges when she wasn't dreaming or crying. Once, while Aro hadn't visited in over two years, she made love to one of the gardeners under the night sky. When Aro returned, he found her heavily pregnant. "Why did you do it?" He had asked, furious and twisting around the room in his black lace agbada. Busola had no answer. She only knew she wanted to keep the child. She rose from the bed to beg. The room was lit by one faint white bulb. Aro shot her ten times. In the head, the throat, the heart and the child. He buried her corpse beneath a baby orange blossom and vanished into the night.

When Busola rose out of the moist earth three months later, she was twelve again and her unborn son was unable to come along with her. The palace was empty and in ruin and the orange groves overgrown. She found that she was unable to leave the palace. Every sunset finding herself back beneath the grove every time she tried to run away. She began to make orange juice to sell from the fruit of the tree under which she had been entombed, walking only as far as her buried bones would let her to sell her handmade tonic – a big bowl was chilled by one tear.

After they took the final gulp which made the empty bottle dent with a loud pop!, the consumers found their cheeks streaked with tears and the centers of their hearts sweetened by her sour, bottled dream and the place where she stood before they placed it to their lips, empty.

Oases

I

Yesterday, Fatima birthed twins. Ma and Rafat played midwife.

Umaru, Baba & I stood outside the large tent with the sheep and spooked camels as her screams filled the cool starstruck savannah. After many sweaty hours, just as the dawn rose pink like insides, Hussain and Hassan were born.

Baba killed a large brown ewe and roasted her over an open fire with pungent leaves and peppered spices. Ma poured out some sour fura de nono to cool our tongues as we watched Fatima and Baba blush over the naked velvetskinned babes in the crackling morning fire.

Fatima glowed in her pale blue kaftan and Umaru sulked because his Baba time had become cut dangerously. He was the oldest and often sat with him on the soft furs we used to welcome guests with back home -- they always drank, chewed, spat and talked in rumbly man tones.

Rafat, Fatima and Ma run whatever open spaces we settle in and are either salting meat, plucking herbs or weaving smooth jute blankets at all times.

I often stargaze in trees or on warm rocks as predators slink through the surrounding night. Sometimes, Umaru finds and lays beside me, we chew salted meat in silence after a few brother-ly questions. Then he vanishes into the yellow heat of the coming desert to look for oases.

We are in our sixth month of finding a new home away from the sudden flame and endless smoke of the North. Dry pale grass fields have given way to baobab-studded stretches of red earth, the sheep have become steadily slimmer and Ma and Rafat's warm honeyglow from Kano has given way to a dry smoothness.

Baba and Umaru look the same; tall and longlimbed and dark like old wood. Baba won't age, they say he's sixty years old but he looks thirty. My hair now grows slower. Umaru says Baba didn't run away from the bombs alone, he's chasing something lost in the heat ahead.

When she was pregnant, Fatima was a constant source of bliss and smiles, even on the coldest nights she glowed. Now, she has fear and fatigue in her eyes as her baby boys suckle loudly at her breasts every morning.

II

At the edge of the Sahel, Umaru finds a grove of orange trees with white flowers that scent the hot air. They are the only vegetation in sight -- ahead, the desert sprawls.

Their green branches embrace the worn sides of the tent and hold juicy oranges the size of Hassan's skull. We spend the night eating them and passing the babbling citrus-scented babies around and talking about Kano. The wind whispers and howls around our ears. Fatima is flanked by Ma in her always white shawls, and Rafat whose sleek head nods as her nose ring glints and her light voice rises passionate.

They miss their friends and sharing new laali and recipes. The constant movement exhausts them, they hope we can stay here for a while. Baba is talking about water to Umaru and I. If we can find clean water and stay close to it, protect it, use it well, we could stay alive forever. Baba has had too much wine but Umaru agrees.

I keep staring at the streaking indigo sky, feeling the chill night wind sweep in from the Sahara over my shoulders and lift the edge of my father's dark blood turban again and again.

The desert sand barely glows as it rises in dust skirts over dunes and ridges into the cold clear air. The sand is finely scalloped where the wind runs over it.

There is a freedom here unlike I have ever felt.

That last day in the city, when Rafat had come to pull me away from Badamasi's soot-colored hyena puppies, saying Baba was suddenly travelling with his whole clan and there was no time to waste, I had no friend come bid me goodbye.

Only a gaggle of young mournful women in shifting gowns came to aide Sanusi, Sakinah and heavily pregnant Fatima on their sudden self-exile, their tapered fingers curled with henna flora had stroked shoulders in overt sisterhood.

Here I am not my father's too-thin runt -- I conquer trees and quicksand and hop over snakes, when I run barefoot across the hot sand and look up, the sky falls open.

The babies sleep, then Fatima and Rafat take them in and don't come out anymore. Ma yawns last and strokes Baba's left shoulder before going in to curl on her bed of silken pillows. I lie back and look onto star studded velvet, listening to Umaru now talk about water. "We barely have a drum full. There are rumors of thirsty pirates hunting for water with rabid dogs." We can't stay in this sweet smelling calm beyond tomorrow. Baba sighs melodiously and I hear him gulp more wine.

III

Our throats are dry and our tongues no longer faintly orangesweet when we suckle on them.

Umaru leads the line, Ma and Rafat flank Fatima and the twins on camel, draping them in muslin. The wind sends sand into every nook of our bodies. Our eyelashes are encrusted with rejected grains.

I am behind them, Baba is behind me, his turban pulled up to his eyes. We all walk slowly, our sheep have been let go and only the three camels remain.

The sun is high and bleeds violent orange heat across the sky and onto our backs. It peppers and burns the exposed skin of our arms. Baba covertly hands me some wine and I lap at the near-empty hide bottle for a moment of cool tanginess and it doesn't come.

My handstitched vest has drunken up my sweat and that has been soaked up by the sun. My tongue is beginning to crack, lips are rough with little sores, my smooth brown skin is peeling in places.

My eyes dance in my head, my limbs are filled with a hot sludge, my belly is screaming.

I stop walking and fall to my knees, the sky and all the undulating hills of fine gold sand spin. I hear Baba shout "Sanusi!"

& then I see the white ghosts, taller than everything around, staring parched from dried skulls, surrounding us, glinting in the ruthless sun.

Eating Kaolin

I

Many years after the incursion of the pale man onto West African soil, Mary Ogene in Omahia, newly pregnant and ravenously hungry went missing for three days and did not return the same. In the extended absence of her husband, she had been seeking the crunch of kaolin against her molars and the subsequent stillness of her rumbling stomach after.

II

Mary Ogene had walked out of her township, through a rapidly changing world, past men building a bungalow for the new Warrant Chief Nwankwo, who had started walking around telling the women of Omahia that they would have to pay something called market tax based on how much of the new money they were making off exchanges at their market stalls.

Some of the women in Mary Ogene's neighbourhood said that the Warrant Chief had wanted to enter into their huts and count their clothes to gauge how much they were worth, before he threatened that his boy-boys would return to collect the money that they owed to the Governor-General, or else.

No husbands were found to defend them from the harsh demands of the New State, through the Warrant Chief and his lap dogs. Their men were the ones clamouring for work under these new gods, pale as weathered bones, with their gifts of a salvation, its Bible, mirrors and starched-cotton servant uniforms. Mary Ogene's husband, Jude, had found work serving as a gardener for a Chancellor, deeper in the heart of Aba.

He was barely home.

The simmering unrest across the East of the yet-to-be-amalgamated country rose gradually as the pale man and his domineering ways seeped into the body of their old world, which had been crafted and handed down through mouth, divination and craft from Mary Ogene's ancestors.

In the old world, women were left to work the engines of both home and society without any questioning or control from the men they shared the world with. There was no creed or suggestion about only doing certain specific things in the world (like staying out of community affairs to man kitchens and market stalls) because one was born physically as a woman, or a man. There was a freedom to continuously attempt tasting life anew, regardless of what one carried between their legs.

Now, the invaders with their moustaches like yet-to-be-roasted caterpillars had come into their midst with holy words of submission and their men had changed, become hollow tools and violent mouthpieces. They were trying with caged fury to take away the freedom and power the women wielded under the old world in the name of the god of the new world.

In the name of his Son.

This unease in the air was why Mary Ogene went to look for ancient riverbeds, their banks rich with white deposits of chalk. The world was changing too fast. It made her baby seem to tangle itself up inside her. The men and their adoration of these new visitors was turning trusted tradition upside down. Left seemed to have become right now, and right, left.

She walked behind the market, avoiding her friends and her relatives, hiding her face. Mary Ogene quickened her steps once she was out of Omahia, past the seized farmlands filled with men in strange cloth, digging for something they would never find.

She walked deeper into the forests that fringed the town.

Her child was only faintly beginning to do the swim and kick, and it felt like the unborn one knew something was coming. Mary Ogene's heart would occasionally fly into rhythms unknown, her stomach would tighten and her spittle dry, as she sat in gatherings with women who could see ahead, to a heavier curtailing of their old freedoms.

They complained of the shortening of market days, and the curfews that had trickled in until they were no longer allowed to move at night or before dawn which was when they most needed to rise and greet the work of the day.

The women were then reminded of the guns and the rock-faced men carrying them under authority of the Governor-General. Someone offered, "We should carry our own weapons!" and was met with fiery debate.

Mary Ogene was silent during these meetings, gazing into nothing, hand on her belly wondering if Jesus Christ, the saviour whom her namesake had birthed, would want such conquests done under the cover of his blood.

After she was out of reach of the sounds of the town, she turned left off the path that would lead to the next community and began to trample forward, pushing down the undergrowth quick with her bare feet.

She used trees that could as well be friends, and bushes ripe with flower to find her way to the hidden chalk rivers that her great-grandmothers had dug kaolin from.

She knew where to dig and reach into the warm heart of the earth to exhume chunks of this pure chalk, sometimes streaked with red or with sky blue. It was good to eat for the upset stomach, and for thin blood, and for when there was too much heat in the face and it felt like one's head might fall off.

As she picked across the riverbed, Mary Ogene stood to her full height and looked downriver to find herself standing exposed before a strange sight.

Her body trembled as she grasped her belly and bent down to hide behind a wild berry bush, heady with a too-sweet fragrance.

Spit pooled in her mouth.

III

The white-skinned people and their workers (who were once brothers to Mary Ogene, though she now found them as untranslatable as their masters) were gathered around a large area that couldn't be where Mary Ogene had come to so many times, she could find it in her sleep.

It couldn't be.

The very earth looked to have been in a great battle with something that had no grace. Watery mud mixed with raw chalk, blood in pap. The narrow white river had been blown wide by hoes and pick-axes and a structure that towered yellow and clawed behind the small men who stood around it.

Mary Ogene had always known the deposits were deep and rich, because sometimes the women came with large baskets and left only after they had overflow of kaolin, without disturbing the way the river looked.

Before, this.

Now she saw how they had been blessed beyond her imagining. How Ani had indeed given them a gift to be used for generations. A gift now plundered.

The structure carried a heap of white chalk in its claw, which hung high over the men and their hard bowl hats. There was another person moving in the middle of the men, carrying blue water that gleamed with sunlight in a glass.

The glass was odd like everything that had followed the pale people into Igboland. The person shook the glass, raised it to the sun and shook it some more. The diggers were resting, glistening ebony in the sun, their backs against mounds of exhumed kaolin.

Mary Ogene decided to approach quietly. She needed the kaolin more than the ways of this new world could scare her. She crawled downhill until she was close enough to see that there was a man inside the structure with the claw. He had pale skin too.

She could now hear the voices of the pale men, excited and hungry, like they had just found gold. She moved closer. Someone said something something Queen. Mary Ogene knew that word because they always said it whenever they came around to talk to the people of the land about accepting Jesus Christ.

She moved closer and then, at her feet, some kaolin flung far by their plundering. This one seemed to glitter and had the most vibrant blue, yellow and red streaks, clean mineral lines in the center of all the dusky white. She could feel it against her tongue, almost. The crumble as the chalk fell apart in her mouth and dissolved into a muddy mess at the back of her throat and then all the way down to her troubled stomach, to soothe her unborn's dreams of strange, fiery tomorrows.

Mary Ogene grabbed at the kaolin lump quickly. Too quick. Her motion made the bushes around her rustle aloud and then all her once-brothers were alert, bloodthirsty and awake from their sleep; hungry for some bush meat, while ready to fight any intruders.

The white men stopped all their motions and the woman who had been carrying the blue water in her hand, hair like cornsilk all the way to her back, who wore a shirt and shorts like the men, shouted up, tearing the air.

The men moved quicker then, as if prodded with hot irons, gathering into a pack to surround and attack the infiltrator, but the small dark woman in the blue-green wrapper with hair woven down from her temples to her chin was no more there.

IV

Mary Ogene didn't know how her feet flew so fast.

The foliage of the forest blurred in her periphery, into something like water, until she felt she was swimming.

Wind rushed fast past her ears and cold through her wrapper. She was sure she could hear her brothers' voices barking behind her. *Jide ya! Jide ya!*

The kaolin in her fist was the size of a very large snail and she didn't let it go.

Not when she stumbled and her entire body flew forward, still running so quick, nearly shattering her jaw on the rough trunk of a mango tree. Not when she slowed down, righted her body and continued to run pathless in the green, thorns and branches nicking her calves. Not when she saw them surrounding her, slipping out of the blurring forest like free fish.

They were many. Their lithe backs surrounding her, spotted yellow and black. Their streaming bodies were lean and quick as they ran alongside her small tiring body.

The leopards seemed to be guiding her and in her fevered daze she followed. She didn't want to stop, or try to escape them. She followed, excited and mesmerized by this delirium that seemed to have been born of her fear.

Sweat was slipping under her lids when the path she ran through with the leopards ended in a dark copse. The ones ahead of her didn't stop running. They slipped between two dead trees, sheathed in curtains and excitations of moss.

Mary Ogene's heart was beating too fast and she could feel the exertion begin to bear on her body. Her gut lifted. Was that burn in her sternum a sign that her baby was about to come up through her throat?

She didn't stop running.

She could feel their heat close to her pumping thighs. Three leopards on either side of her. The kaolin in her sweating fist. Woman and feline all rushed through the gate between the trees, before Mary Ogene's body fell slack and all turned night.

V

There were voices outside the oily night she was suspended in. She still felt the kaolin in her loose hand.

They spoke Igbo as they lifted her onto a softer land;

"Where did she come from?" "Nwaikwu, look at her belly!" "Chineke!"

"What is happening to our land? What could have brought someone like her running through here so fast? Without fear."

"Fear is blind to itself."

Clean water fell over her face and chest. Sweet smoke swam into her nostrils as a quiet soothing susurration filled the air, like song from the throat of an unusually large bird of paradise.

Mary Ogene sensed a parting as the voices faded away.

"The rest of us at least got to wait at the gate, to decide and gather courage to pierce the veil." Warm bodies lowered themselves around her, their velvet fur soothing and comforting.

"You can open your eyes." A bigger voice spoke above those whispering to themselves.

Mary Ogene did as she heard. There was a very tall woman draped in white lengths of silk crouched beside her head. She was beautiful among the women and leopards who stood around looking on toward Mary Ogene, like a bird of paradise is beautiful among the trees, her skin refined as new earth. She put a cool palm behind Mary Ogene's head and pulled her up to sit.

Mary Ogene remembered her unborn as she felt the fullness of her belly again.

"What led you here?" The tall woman asked. Mary Ogene looked around at her sisters from Omahia, who looked to her, clothed in a regular array of patterned wrappers and blouses. Some had their coin purses tight beneath their armpits still. She saw now that they had no black in their eyes yet the tall woman's eyes were normal and spring-clear.

"I went to the river to get some fresh kaolin. There were some people there. The pale man and some of our brothers... they destroyed the river. The brothers gave chase when they heard me moving through the bushes, and then I ran, without looking back, and then..." Mary Ogene gazed at the leopards, who looked to her with what seemed like certainty. "...I am here."

"I got chased from the river too." A woman standing with a child fastened to her hip said. Mary Ogene couldn't tell if she was looking at her as she spoke. "They've been there many moons now, seeking hard for what is already before them. Mmiri says they're trying to steal the medicine inside the kaolin and so they broke the river open in search of the purest crumb."

The tall woman stood, and Mary Ogene feared her head would break against the branches of the trees that formed the grove. She was a half-giant. The chunk of kaolin that had filled Mary Ogene's palm was carefully held between three of her fingers.

"We are Mmiri. Preparing with your sisters for war. The visitor has just begun to take from the land. They will continue to seek more power, more medicine, more fuel, more bodies, until the land is emptied like an eaten snail." She said, "Rise to your feet and see what we do."

Mary Ogene felt her body flood with strength as Mmiri spoke, a warm prickling rushing into her back from her toes and fingers. She rose up, resting her elbows on the silent leopards' sides, who also stood as soon as she did.

The grove stretched far into a faint-lit night. The low light came from fires burning at the ends of staves, held by more women from the villages in and around Aba. There were more than twenty of them and around their feet, by the light of the held lamps, even more women knelt, working firmly at something in the earth. They beat and ground and threw water and fire against these pits that they knelt by. Into the earth, their arms disappeared to the elbow, coming out sluiced and wet, slipping in over and over again.

Mmiri was ahead, walking in some other grace, almost at where the women worked the earth. They stopped moving. Mary Ogene realized they were standing so that she could catch up with them.

She pushed herself forward, after the women and leopards behind Mmiri, rustling the bushes of the grove.

Within the pits, Mary Ogene could see nothing but swirling reflections of firelight on breaking water as the women worked with silent grunts. She walked faster until she stopped where Mmiri stood sentinel over a pit, worked at by four young women.

They had stopped pushing into the thickening waters and knelt back, to observe it coagulate, gurgle and swirl in on itself.

Their eyes remained clear of human sight, but they watched the contents of the pit as one would watch a waking child.

Before Mary Ogene's eyes, the pit erupted with brilliance and a grown leopard leapt out. Fiery fur slick with the shine of its earthwomb. It had its head lowered in tension, slipping on its paws as it looked around at its new surroundings.

All the women around who saw its birth, went down on a knee and bowed softly to it. The other leopards walked over and began to lick and paw at their sibling.

In the near distance, other women continued to work at their own pits without breaking concentration.

"Join us, Ogene." Mary Ogene looked up and her breath went small in her chest. Mmiri now stood in triplicate, a sudden monument amongst the leopard pits. Each half-giant had slight variations when looked at with more intent, but Mary Ogene didn't have the clarity at that moment to look with intention.

"Your sisters woke us up for a reason. Something is coming and its power will be blind." Mary Ogene found herself flush with heat, flustered by all that seemed unreal continuously revealing itself to her. She wanted to go back to where she was before all this began. Back to the dry stall, the empty house without Jude for days. Always cooking and eating pots of food alone. At least, she was invisible under the roof of a husband, forgotten, except when the women were returning home in the evenings and came to offer greetings to the unborn one she carried.

"Build leopards with us. We are many and will be more. Give to us of your weaving."

Mary Ogene considered going against herself and her place in the world as a wife and soon-to-be mother. One of Mmiri broke from where they three stood tall and white amongst the women building leopards and the women carrying light.

Her hair was liquid coal and flowed pure as waterfall from a knife's edge. Her serpent twined left arm lifted. Up to brush her fingers against Mary Ogene's cheek. To bring Mary Ogene to see.

VI

Nwakaego and Ogechi had lived together since both of their husbands died in the same hunting accident. They watched over each other's child and provided care and food for their little family by pooling together the resources they got from sales at their individual stalls in the night market. They had united in home and hearth, in a bid to prevent their brothers-in-law from attempting to marry them, to inherit them via family, as material property.

No one cast a wary glance towards them, when Ogechi moved her daughter, Somto, and their belongings from the small hut they had shared with her hunter-husband into Nwakaego's larger house.

They mourned and comforted each other at midnight, in silence and warm embrace.

Warrant Chief Nwankwo had always looked askance at the widows and their open affection for one another. He believed they should be under men who could handle them, not pretending to live in a world without a need for their virility.

Thrice, he and his boy-boys had accosted Ogechi on her way back from the night market, way past the hour that splits the day. They had threatened her with imprisonment all three times, and she had stopped arguing to spit on the floor and look into their drunken eyes till they could feel a bitterness stain the roofs of their mouths.

They had let her go.

Each time Ogechi walked away from him, Nwankwo decided it was better to treat the issue at its tough root, than to bruise its dangerous fruit.

He began to send his boy-boys to ruffle Nwakaego's feathers. They yelled at her to pay her market tax, from the doorway where the four of them stood when she refused to answer to their knocks.

They did this for three days then stopped.

The last time they came to visit Nwakaego – who was no longer able to walk to the market and back because her right leg had finally decided it would only work when it wanted to – they lit a battle spark.

Instead of knocking or calling names, the boy-boys, teenagers with a broadening taste for power, force and violence, broke through the door.

Nwakaego was asleep, and the home was being watched by Somto, and Nwakaego's younger son, Chinedu. They were playing a game of hide and seek when the door broke to pieces and three shadows rushed in after the sudden daylight.

Somto, stunned, stayed where she was. All she thought of was how Chinedu's curiosity would lead him out to see what was happening.

"Show us your property. All your items! Clothes, shoes, farm tools, kitchen tools." They spoke the Queen's English, heavy with the drag of mother tongue. Nwakaego was slowly sitting up from her rest in the hosting room when one of the warrant officers grabbed her by the arm and jerked her to her feet.

She groaned, "What do you want?"

"The Warrant Chief demands you pay your market tax today. Last day or else you will go to the new prison. We are to take you there ourselves."

"I do not belong to your market tax group, because I closed my stall and ceased market visits several moons ago. Soon after your tax began."

"Well, let us count what you have and we will tell you what we want in return." Nwakaego watched as her and Ogechi's belongings were thrown around in heaps.

Old clothes, and hiding clothes that were supposed to be surprises, and underclothes and eye paint and unsolved bead clusters. Nwakaego's flat wooden carvings flew through the air to land on the hard mud in front of the house with a sharp sound.

She flinched. Everything ached and Ogechi was nowhere to be found.

"And you will pay us a husband tax, or else you will explain why you have been living alone with another woman since two New Yam Festivals ago."

Chinedu screamed; play or fear, Nwakaego did not know. She found herself out of the loose grasp of the warrant officer, and the intimidating circle of two that they had formed around her, walking before her feet moved.

As Nwakaego walked towards the front of the house, Somto appeared out of the nowhere she had hidden in and ran out of the door to leap at the warrant officer who was holding Chinedu's wrist too tight and dragging him low across the rough earth.

The day was clear, slowly tipping into evening.

Mother joined daughter of friend and they rained their fists hard on the officer's neck and stomach and back, pressured his fragile bones until he slid to his knees and began to bleat.

Chinedu broke free and ran off, away from the suffocating grip of the officer, zipping away in his yellow shorts and big singlet into the open field of forest-swallowed huts and farms that lay beyond Nwakaego's town-border house.

Nwakaego shattered a piece of rotting firewood across the officer's shoulder and he fell instantly, and began dialing up the volume of his shout. At the sound of the officer's cries, the other two officer boy-boys emerged from the mild destructions that they had been tasked with inside the house.

Nwakaego and Somto had their colleague down on his face. He was barely awake, slowed down by the agony in his shoulder. The girl sat on his back, now hitting him half-heartedly as she came to notice the absence of Chinedu. Nwakaego screamed furious curses at the men who approached gallantly to save their injured colleague. She limped backwards, throwing the remains of the firewood in their faces with one arm, and with the other tried to shield Somto from their fuming bodies.

The boy-boys fell on them.

She wasn't fast enough. A kick sent all the air out of her ribs and made a sharp current of pain rise up her spine. She found herself prone with no memory of falling. From where she lay on the ground, she watched an officer kick Somto hard, square in the stomach. She flew briefly through the air to land on her back.

The boy-boys moved around their colleague, slowly trying to lift him up.

The girl tried to move but was clearly dazed. As Nwakaego watched the daughter she was learning to call her own struggle against hurt, Chinedu emerged from within the dying villages, to kneel beside her.

After him came Ogechi. She moved careful as always, like her back ached. Her shoulders were burnished by the sun and her thighs guided creatures that made Nwakaego sit up and try to run back into the house.

Some of the leopards that lurked around Ogechi's knees as she walked towards Nwakaego broke into brisk runs, slingshoting their bodies and dragging the retreating warrant officers to the dust, in the time it took Chinedu to help Somto back to her feet. She remained hunched over and he led her to lean against a tree.

Ogechi pulled Nwakaego to her feet and held her close, dusting her back and hair of sand.

A crowd more than leopards had followed her.

Other women walked towards them, emergent shadows in the foliage, guiding more felines across the open ground with their hands and legs. The beasts barely rustled the undergrowth as they poured from within the deeper forest herded by the women who had made them, sometimes disappearing where light and shadow made a pact with their fur.

Nwakaego gasped as the first half-giant broke into sight ahead; a dense wraith, pure silken body taut in the wind. She leaned away briefly from Ogechi's hold, to look into her eyes.

The procession continued as the other two aspects of Mmiri came into view mere meters behind the first. The leopards continued to slip through and beneath the overgrowth like strange gulps of hot water. The women walked proudly among them, eyes emptied.

"What is happening?"

"Nwankwo has declared war. He sent his boys as far as they could reach and his damage is done. Now, we're taking it back to their masters all the way in Aba, but first we need to gather strength."

Nwakaego looked stunned. Somto, still holding her stomach tenderly, held Chinedu's hand beside them and watched as the leopards, the women and Mmiri filled their compound and spilled onto the overgrown fields that had been thriving parts of the town, before they came hungry for power that was not theirs.

"We're going to sit on him, Nwakaego. Come with us." One of the tall spirit, Mmiri spoke. The nearest woman approached

Nwakaego and Ogechi with a calabash filled with thick white paste, kaolin crushed and wet with saltwater.

They began to draw lines down their skulls, towards their chi and the chi of those who had walked before them.

VII

To sit on a man, you should know when he will be at home, not lured away by work or palmwine or some young maiden by the water. After you are sure he will be around, visit him at home with your sisters, the one hundred and one leopards they have built with their hands, and the water spirit that brought it all to pass.

Sit.

On the low stools and rocks and buckets you have brought. The best time to sit is at night, because by morning he will wake up full of dreams of your voices and the pressure of your breathing, and visions of his errors that you have slipped into his mind through his nose.

He will come outside and shout. Threaten violence to his sitting wife. He will not see the leopards. You will shout back in rhythm and suddenly switch to the singing. Taunt him until he begins to break things inside his house. Call him his names: worthless, devil, pig, fool, coward. For that is the plight of those who try to rule the world away from the eye of the woman. Those who try to turn blind power against her.

Nwankwo will shoot his gun into the air. Do not scatter. Lean against the leopards as you arrive and join the growing sit. As morning approaches your numbers will have quadrupled.

The women will see the leopards and Mmiri and sit among them, beside you. They will eat kaolin and make masks of their thunderous hearts with its milk.

The officers hearing the distress call of their brother's bullets will come, bearing more bullets. They will loose their death into the crowd like rain and the bravest of your sisters will drop to the ground, emptied.

The leopards will fly at the men and tear them limb to limb, even as they are beaten back into inexistence by red hot bullets.

You will break down his house, push it down with the crux of your shoulders and trample on the mud walls, until a red cloud rises around you.

VIII

The Women's Rebellion broke across the claimed world of the pale man in an ocean of effervescent anger.

Woman, leopard and water finally breaching the binds to their freedom, devoured everything that came up against them. Sweeping the streets and adding more and more women and waters to their number until their sound across Aba was a virulent roar that set its hearers running for no reason at all.

The pale man sent his soldiers, as the women and their unseen ferocity stood barricade against official vehicular motions on Main Street. Boldly denying order to this new Queensland, and also asking to be free from its demands and unnecessary weights.

No more market tax. Let us be as we are. Free to make and know, to buy and sell and grow.

The women swung clubs made out of fallen tree against coward soldier's skulls. They threw rocks that were once pieces of the houses of offending men, which exploded in bombs of red dust, and they spat, streams of warm water that became lasers of yellow-red heat, scalding through the hard hats and burning the aiming arms of the soldiers.

Mmiri drowned the woman in sweat, cleansing her sight with salt. They gave her aim wings, and made her rage a river that knew where it was going, a river that seared its banks with fires unseen and cried with the voices of a thousand women aflame.

As their comrades screamed and fell to the slow ammunition of woman and spirit, their scattershot came like rain, gunshots, wounds, rending the afternoon.

IX

Mary Ogene, who had assisted in the birthing of more than two dozen leopards from the pits in the earth, sat in labour on a thick mat of fresh banana leaves, in a circle of kaolin-lined women who breathed as she did. Panting with her. Deep breaths as her spasms seized and returned, pushing hard, increasing undulating pressures around the gravity of her being.

She felt she could split a universe with the grind of her teeth.

They would split the universe together with the grind of their teeth, bring enough pressure to make diamonds into aged kaolin under their gums. Enough pressure to smelt a life.

They could split the universe together.

It was their ordinary work. To shatter blockage and free time. The rooster is birthed first in an egg. They will do it again. They will dissolve their strength into an elixir and give to the one alone.

X

Mary Ogene splits the universe, alone. The leopards dwindle in number, melting into strips of sunset. The keen cry of the newborn stretches pure through the air.

XI

After choosing from an offering of knives that the women lay before her chest like sharp tongues, Ogechi cut Agwu free from Mary Ogene and bathed him in water from a dissolving Mmiri's heart.

He was anointed in kaolin, and promised a world, away from the one which thundered with violence and spite around him as the women and their companions marched onwards, their fury a new blade aiming for the throat of the pale masters whose homes were in the near distance.

He would be spared, they prayed, from the death harvest of any future wars, and his only roars would be to cry joy.

October in Eran Riro

I

Appetite

You are so angry, you might kill Monday when you find him.

In the danfo, you try to hide your face. The clothes on your back are dirty and beginning to crumble and tear with every harsh motion of the crowds around you, and in the streets of Lagos, every motion is harsh. You breathe deep and press on your sternum to push back the welling of an abyss.

You are wearing Monday's old clothes, and they hide you. The money you had borrowed from the cobbler next door to Mama's shop is going to finish when you climb down from this bus in Surulere.

Your thin body is hard with weeks of hunger and your hair has followed too, gotten like untamed thatch; uncombed and unwashed and knotted until it has a life of its own, metamorphosing with every turn of the pillow. You have no bag, no purse, no phone, no earrings or sunglasses or hat. Just your brother's old clothes and the name of his...church.

The conductor lets you out into a sunset that seems to want to restore the decay of the city around you. Everything is burnished with rose and edged with gold. You walk into the night, quickening its fall with your arrival as you ask the fifteenth person you pass,

"Please. Where is Eran Riro?"

"At the end of this road, enter that narrow path above the gutter and follow it till the end, you will come out on Williamson. You can't miss it. Big red sign."

"Thank you."

You drift away from that man, his kind face and sad eyes, and on towards the end of the street. You walk hard and linear, like Monday and all the men you have seen people respect, pushing your shoulders up and swinging your arms like guns.

The people in the unnamed zone you are walking through are busy in their night-time wrappers and face masks; smoking, eating, drinking, stuck in boy-meets-girl. They pay you no mind. You slip into the slit between house wall and fence. You toe beside the gutter with Monday's boots, past soft moss and slippery spirogyra until you fall out into Williamson.

The street is ordinary, not smooth enough to be a major road but also not completely empty of traffic. Drunk okada men zoom past, celebrating Friday night decadence. You tip toe in the surprisingly light boots to the other side of the street.

You immediately see that you are now on the wrong side. You were on the right side before. Just a few hundred meters down the road is a long glowing wall of glass, smeared in ripped posters, lit from within by giant light bulbs that look like suspended ostrichs' eggs.

You walk on the wrong side. The blue and white lighting of all the other shops around, who sell wall fixtures and bags and haircuts, pales next to this incandescence. You move closer until the name comes into view, a red plastic neon sign hovering above the doors.

Eran Riro.

The name that wouldn't leave your brother's mouth whenever he had the chance to talk about anything relating to food. And it didn't help that you all loved to talk about food. Cooking was rare as a prayer in the shop, before Mama fell ill and Monday slipped away into eating out and compulsive lying as a way of coping.

Your mother said that your great-grandmother's grandmother had learned how to cook from the spirits. Hence the surname of your mother's side, Abemise. Almost every woman who followed down the line was born with the mark that the spirits had gifted that first woman, nestled beneath the phalangeal bones of the left hand, a flat, concave hardness that often burned: *olowosibi*.

You have it inside your hand; and it used to burn so fiercely whenever you cooked something that you knew would be superior, more delicious than your usual skillset could produce. It also burned when you touched bad food and when Monday would start to talk about how the food at Eran Riro should be studied in culinary universities worldwide. How it was so good that even though the portions they served were minimal, the satisfaction derived afterwards was beyond any law of economics.

"No woman cooks behind the walls of Eran Riro," Monday had said, "but God Himself."

You used to literally clench your fist and bite your tongue, not wanting to start a fight with him for coming to detail his feeding adventures to the ill mother you share. Mama was sick with a throat infection that made her sob when she made to swallow, and when Monday talked about food to her, she smiled as if in irony.

She was no longer able to eat solids, only water and juices and pap. His enthusiasm seemed to help her remember what taste once was, until he stopped coming to talk to her.

You see Mama wither and expire over and over in the back of your head. Monday's absence burns black.

Your olowosibi burns with pins as you cross to the other side where Eran Riro shines hot and loud, and walk towards the double doors from which a fully sated man emerges with the hard rind of his potbelly gleaming. He picks his teeth and belches and looks at you with a warm absence in his grey eyes, a rolled newspaper under his thick arm.

You stand at the receding doors for a moment bathed in ice-cold air and aromas you had long forgotten existed, the coolness streaming over your skin. Something pepper-buttery slips up your nose, making your hunger extend fang.

After months of eating only sweet potatoes and water to save money so that your mother could at least have an intravenous anesthetic, you are ravenous. Not as much as you were last week when you pushed the earth over her body down in the canal behind the fortress of the shop, but close.

You move in. There is a smattering of people eating on low benches and tables of polished wood. Some rattle off their orders, standing at the glass-framed serving counter

White rice. Ofada. Dodo. Two pomo. Dodo. One egg. Jollof two hundred. Dodo. Coleslaw. Pounded yam. Egusi. Turkey. Dodo. Beans. Abula. Ogufe maarun.

You turn towards the counter with no money in your pocket, walking like a thief, drifting slow towards the warmth and chatter. When you reach the counter, you face a tall woman with thick arms and skin like fresh amala. She looks at you like she knows. That you are wretched. Refused by the circle of fate and cast into this moment to suffer. She picks a plate in the universal gesture of, "What do you want to eat?"

You keep staring. Other Soft Girls have come to hang behind the tall woman. They are whispering. She just stands and stares at you with that look in her eye. The plate has a fish painted inside it, iridescent blue and bent.

"What do you want?!" A new Soft Girl has joined the group and her voice is one of those too-loud ones. The line is empty. You forget about Monday. You forget all words. Everyone else is already eating at the tables or gone.

"Hey, ode!" She shouts and pushes her eyes out of their sockets in mimicry.

You startle and run. Picking up the folds of your hunger like a cloak, you push past the glass doors and dart down the road, away from the harsh lights of the buka.

When you come to your senses, you are bent over your knees, panting breath like iron in your chest. Eran Riro is still in sight but on the other side. You are looking at the back end of the building that houses the buka over the lip of the fence that you lean on.

This should have been the first and only way.

You climb up it and stand. It is dark on this side of the fence. No streetlights working around the area, but there is a sharp orange glow and shadows moving in front of the large warehouse that sits behind the buka. Several motorcycles stand in the bush that covers half of the compound, riding nowhere in the tangle of creepers and bent branches.

You reflexively crouch, amphibian.

Toast

You drop six feet down and start to quietly tear through the field when you hear an odd sound. There are scurrying movements in the undergrowth, but that's not it, those are probably lizards or rats. You walk forward again, trying your best to not rustle the leaves too loud. It happens when you move. You realize the sound is coming from beneath your soles. A low crunching, like stepping across broken glass.

You bend and look at the hard white particles that carpet the undergrowth and rise into ridges and mounds under the tires of the motorcycles that are hiding you. You scoop some up and peer close as your nose will allow – crushed bone. You sigh at your heart-rate. What did you think it was?

Let it fall from your palm as hard snow.

You push your lean, weak body past the motorcycles into the low stained-orange light that beckons. High up on the ware-house wall, a thin fluorescent tube casts its light. Beneath it is a door, tiny in comparison to the rest of the building. It's like something Alice would encounter.

A man steps into the light with an automatic rifle at his shoul-der. His face seems to be a permanent frown of rage. He moves to you with a grunt, his muscles rippling under black lycra.

"Who are you?" He asks, so sure of who you are not. He's wearing black shell glasses and his jeans are tattered from overuse, not for style. There is something gold gleaming at the angle of his waist.

"I dey find Monday." You say. The pidgin is supposed to make him see you as streetwise. You stand, still angular, thinking about boyness and the freedom to be wild and rough and fearless. The guard looks you up and down.

'Monday no dey here! How did you get into this yard? You are not staff."

You shiver as his eyes search yours. A door opens and there is a bloom of sound, sparse voices coming from the doorway behind him; a kitchen in process. Metal and glass and Formica in percussive discussion, hot oil and fish cheering as they came together, gurgling boiling rice spilling onto the heat source.

You are finally here.

You collect your head and move closer to the fuming obstacle in your path. You think maybe if you touch him, or get him to really look into your eyes and see how lost you feel, he'll soften. You can't imagine running away now, backing down, fleeing back to the streets where nothing waits for you. You begin to beg.

"I said there is no one here." You move even closer, his body is hot with some wildness. "Please." You say, desperate for some answer, for any kindness. "Get. Down." He whispers harshly as he hits you in the temple with the base of a gun, gold and new.

Catfish Peppersoup

You come to in the center of a court of sorts. There is clean white light pouring from a series of fluorescent tubes behind them. You are in a corner of the kitchen and the aroma of frying, boiling and roasting foods makes your stomach curl into itself.

Three people are leaning over where you lie on a pile of table-cloths. It is like scenes from a birth. Everybody you can see is wearing something red.

"She's breathing." One of the women says. There are two women: the one kneeling before you plus one standing behind her. There is a man built like the one from the gate but shorter. He is wearing a blood-spattered once-white t shirt, elastic over his biceps. He has no glasses and you at once see something tender behind his wide eyes. He is holding an axe.

"Where are these children coming from? They're like cock-roaches at this point, at least one every month." The standing woman who seems quite tense, says to her colleagues.

The kneeling woman is moving across your body efficiently, checking your pulse and breath like a nurse, even though she is wearing a touch of the same red silk or cotton as everyone else. "Can you hear me?"

You ask about Monday as you did at the gate, showing gulli-bility. The standing woman laughs. The women have the same shiny hairstyle of thick fingerwaves, like helmets on their heads. On top of the hair are frail hairnets that will crumple into ash lumps when removed.

"Keep him? Her? Keep it in Holding, while I go and get Madam, abi? How did you wander into this compound of all places?" The woman standing and looking at you with new venom in her eyes says, speaking with the cruel authority of one briefly in charge.

"My brother eats here a lot." You say defiant. Several bodies move with silent precision behind your interrogators; chefs clad in starched white, pleated hats tall as wedding cakes.

"He couldn't stop talking about how delicious your food was." You erupt. "How he shouldn't feel so satisfied! He never stopped talking and praising this place. He used to call it Church. Church!. I believe you guys give your customers something to -."

A slap explodes across your cheek, from the kind-eyed Butch-er. Your face rings with the heat. You may have bitten yourself.

"Holding. No need to even call oga." The tall stern one with the voice like a blunt cutlass says with instant finality and walks away from the corner to rejoin the motions of the kitchen.

They grab you to take you to Holding.

You hang between the two boys who have appeared out of nowhere, sailing through the architecture of the kitchen nestled deep inside the warehouse. Wide, segmented and perforated walls of steel and then wood and beaten steel again. The gut of a super-efficient machine. The women who seem to have forgotten your fate so suddenly, move in a slow dance as they sear flesh that smells like salvation to you.

Your hunger sends you raging and you begin fighting the boys who hold you.

You grapple as the motion of the large kitchen stills. The chefs you had seen in white are young women and men, working in couples behind each of the two women who just left you. They don't even flinch as you tussle. Washing, rinsing and chopping with utmost concentration and an air of perfect quiet.

The woman who knelt before to check your head is a few meters away, watching and slyly she announces to someone in the room, "Paloma! We have a live one."

The harsh woman who could have been the leader turns from a wide board covered in chopped tomatoes, their insides splattered across the marble. She looks at you and laughs an empty laugh. She's thick and her skin glows, neck strung with a heavy gold necklace.

Distracted you fall. Hands grab you around the knees. They drag you to the end, past a platter of the largest roast you have ever seen in your life. The meat is dark brown and glazed, surrounded by rings of caramelized onion.

It sizzles and that scent rolls over you, making you struggle again, your mouth flooding. The sensations that follow in your belly make you growl and lunge for the meat.

They put you in a cage.

Dundu & Pomo Alata

"Child. Omo. Wake. Ji."

The voice is soft, a whisper that slithers between iron into the cage until it feels like she is sitting right beside you.

"Bring your hand."

You stir awake, trying to figure out where you are, and she is already reaching between the math-grid of the cage to take your left hand in both of hers. She rubs and the olowosibi glides under your skin, a slippery disc under muscle. You wince.

"Pele. Marcus, come open the cage. This child is valuable. Where did you find her and how long has she been here?"

The Butcher comes forward, you can almost hear the heft of his body under the jingle of keys. He bends towards the grid. The cage is five feet tall.

"She looks very worthless to me."

"She has the gift of the spoon. Take her out of the cage. Did you people beat her up yet?"

"It's called 'Holding', Aunty. For trespassers. And no one has touched her. She should have known there would be trouble before trespassing on private property. If Oga stresses me about this, it's your name I will call."

Marcus complains as he reluctantly moves. In the strange light, you can see the Mama, a lump of white and blue cloth, kneeling before you. The Butcher, Marcus, finally looms, meatfaced. The cage jangles and his large arm reaches in to pull you out. You scuffle, wanting to climb out yourself.

The dregs of dignity are better than none at all. He lets go and you win.

Mama takes you into a room, like something lifted out of your hostel from when you were a boarder in Junior Secondary School. It is completely dark, except for a light in a small corridor at the other end of the wide room, spilling deep yellow across the floor. There are fewer bunks than in Funlola Memorial Girls and the sleeping bodies are under repurposed table cloths, red and white like petals on charred ground.

You hold onto Mama. She smells like goodness, all layers of old milky fat and caramel garlic. Her bones are long, seemingly breakable, beneath the white and blue cloth that she wraps around her middle and also ties wide around her head. She lets you see her own olowosibi. You rub it and she snatches her hand away, tickled.

"Stay here, sleep here. Tomorrow I will bring you dressing." She disappears into the night. You lie on a bunk that is farthest from any of those sleeping. Someone mumbles and another changes sleeping posture. You lift your back and the metal spring beneath you creaks like a gun in the night. You stay there statue-still, wondering what has brought you here truly. You know Monday is nowhere near.

∧

After your father, Mr. Lanwa died in that accident with a bad batch of Paracetamol, your family crumbled. Like spoiled meal. His family took your house, the cars and the biscuit factory and you ended up getting spit in your eye from Uncle Lanre screaming at you to pack your whore of a mother out of here now.

Mama had slapped him hard, and immediately you, her and Monday had been evicted from the premises by the same gateman who used to steal your CapriSun when you were a child and no one was looking.

For shelter, you ran to the shop where your mother also stocked and sold provisions , School stopped and so did all the sweetness that came with having money. You wonder if your blindness to your cocoon of wealth and security was what made the lifting of the veil hurt so much. Is what makes it hurt so much.

You found out you got nothing for being poor. Mama got nothing for being a poor businesswoman, saddled with two older teenage children, struggling to sleep on the thin mattress in the night, calling his name.

The crinkle of provisions subsided.

First the ice cream. Then the special biscuits, including a last box of Lanwa's Small Vanilla Cakes that she cried selling. Finally, Milo and Peak and the Dangote range of foodstuffs. The fridge and the popcorn machine. The returns outweighed the gains until there was a sudden emptiness.

Mama fell ill. You started to fry dundu and akara, and that worked for a while, the symbiosis of you and your mother's work in the world. She stayed alive, a ghost in the doorway of her shop, keeping watch over you as you did over her.

You quickly discovered what you did to be no work at all. Real work should bring sustainable wealth, not keep you fingers-hanging over a canyon of penury.

The crumble finally stopped. An exact decade after his death, she followed.

Where was Monday in all of this? Awayaway. As he always joked. Away, away. Twice to increase distance. Now you have gotten away too.

You always knew it would twist in the middle.

Start again.

Small Dressing

"Child. Omo. Wake. Ji."

The voice is soft, a whisper followed by the pressure of a body sitting.

"Take. I found you a small dressing." You sit up from your sleepless waste. There is a soft bundle between you two. A deep scarlet gown with long sleeves. A kaftan really. The material is heavy and slippery-soft.

She takes you to the bathroom. She has returned early, the bodies remain sleeping and there is no sign of morning yet. You peel Monday off your skin and throw him into the dustbin. You wash away your sins, your father's sins and your mother's sins until you see red.

The kaftan is fine. There are tiny rococo details made in gossamer gold thread and a small, long scarf of the same fabric. You dress up quick, then, you're running out with her, your nameless savior, up a flight of stairs, down a corridor thick with wine carpet and out into the yard of Eran Riro, the strange land that you had slipped through barely a day before.

Ayamase

The breath of a new morning is rising blue in the east.

She goes up to where the okadas and rivers of bone hide in the overgrowth. In daylight, the woman is not really a grandmother anymore. She's much younger in the face.

A bell hangs, rusted and hungry. She hits it with a thick iron, in a rush of bangs and sharp tones that shatter the ear. You can feel a motion go through the surrounding spaces, even though those who the bell rings for are asleep underground. It feels like Eran Riro itself is waking up. The air purrs. An excitement tugs at you from a time ahead, when the food will bubble and scent the air, and you will eat.

You promise yourself to never speak of Monday again. He was just an excuse. You had run away from abject desolation, seeking air, newness. Fuck brothers.

You both walk across the barren half of the yard into the second kitchen. The one built directly inside Eran Riro; a room as large as the eating area, but completely separate. Like stolen twins. She turns on the light. This kitchen is all wood and utensils of steel, plains of shining granite. Everything is five times as big as in a regular kitchen. The pots and spoons and pans of giants.

"What is your name?" she asks as she saunters to the center of the kitchen, lifts a circular cover off the floor to rest at an angle on a hinge, and pulls up a sheer bag full of onions onto the table in one slick motion. You say your name. She gestures that you come to where she stands.

"Collect with me". There is a large hole in the center of the kitchen floor. A vault? Tall, oversized bodies fumble around below. They begin to hand up baskets of peppers and tomatoes, rice and pasta. There are no meats, except the large dried shrimp that makes soups into tiny treasure hunts.

They soon stop handing up ingredients. Their slow motions cease and then they recede deeper into the corners of the vault. Mama shuts the round cover gently and begins to give you preparatory instructions, and you quickly get to work. When a rowdy group of sharp uniform-wearing teenage boys and girls come in to assist, you are already scorching the base onions for the day's ayamase.

II
Roasted Black Pepper Chicken.

The first time you eat a full meal, you cry.

It is still on your first day working front end. You spend the day helping fry and boil and sizzle and scoop. You take short breaks to gasp and groan from how hungry you are. The vegetable bits you sneak into your mouth make it worse.

The kitchen fills up fast once the sun begins to really shine and melt everything away.

Mama sends all those who come late to go bring the flat, frozen cartons of various meats from the Butcher. You live under shock. You find out the old woman, is named Tutu.

Everyone calls her 'Aunty Tutu, Aunty Tutu!' Her name is the most repeated sound in the space. Aunty Tutu is white rice ready? Aunty Tutu dodo! Aunty Tutu they said the meat is not soft enough. Aunty Tutu, is there still gbegiri?

She sits in the center of the kitchen on a high stool, big pots and pans bubbling with deliciousness in a semi-circle before her, as she directs everything with her hands and her voice.

The team of seven girls and boys who join you in assisting Aunty Tutu in the kitchen all wear red button-up shirts with red shorts or pleated skirts. Their heads are all covered in the same white cotton scarf. You tip-toe around them and their eyes and whispers. You can feel them looking through you, the outsider, for bringing imbalance to their order.

They seemed to all come from the same stock; you can see that the one who collected them into this group sought certain characteristics like low body weight, long arms and sharp tongues.

When the first batch of breakfast for the buka on the front end is finished, and the Soft Girls have come to collect the bright orange grains and rivers of stew and meat in old boxy coolers, everyone grabs a plate out of thin air and runs to line up before Aunty Tutu, who hasn't gotten down from her tall stool, still perched beside the kitchen island.

You watch as they are served hot amala, moi-moi, rice, dodo, spaghetti, beans and much more, from a smaller series of coolers that stand on the Formica at Aunty Tutu's waist. They disperse and reconvene in a corner of the kitchen barely used and begin to eat and talk loudly.

The heat of the kitchen, your hunger, the aromas and gossip from the loud teenagers and the pressure in your chest that has been there since Mama's death, come together and lock you in place.

You try to move but you are riveted even as your stomach growls like lions trapped.

This is fear.

It has been with you since your father left and you began to sleep beside your dying mother. You should go. Run outside, through the buka in your blood-red dress, out into the madness of Lagos. Not stopping. Running. Not stopping until you have collided with a force greater than you. Not stopping until you break.

"October. Why are you standing all the way over there? Come here."

You snap out of it. Aunty Tutu is standing holding a steaming plate. You know it is for you. See how your mouth blooms with saliva as the lions multiply. You toddle and totter over.

Two things pull at you; the fact that you can't remember ever being this hungry when you still had parents, and the truth that with your ugly hungry motions, the Servers can now see you. They know you have come to stain their rhythms and alignment with their work with your dreadful body and your jutting bones, and mostly, your eyes, both ringed in a lunar blackness from months of sleeplessness.

Your body finally makes it to Aunty Tutu, but your mind seems to have snapped free. It is gagging, ravenous. You remember when you had barked like a dog yesterday, before the cage which had felt like home.

You stand rigid. The warm, heavy plate slides between your fingers and Aunty Tutu is saying something to you again.

"Ignore them. They're all so young. Barely out of secondary school. That's how they treat all newcomers. Sit here."

You sit on the low stool beside her high one. She hands you a bottle of cold water. You place your plate on your lap and look at it – the jollof rice is dark orange and smoky, the dodo is like cubes of smelted gold, and stuck underneath the meal is a chicken lap, exquisitely roasted. You had helped rub an oil of black pepper, thyme and yellow seasoning into about fifty of them, before Aunty Tutu had slid them into the oven. Just something extra to stimulate the customers and, of course, leftovers for Bruno, she said to herself as she shut the oven with her hip.

Now you take a bite of the jollof with some dodo perched on top. It is hot, oily, crisp and delicious. You pick up the chicken and bite, it splits beneath your teeth and juices fill your mouth, while charred white flesh moves around your tongue.

By the time the pepper ignites, you realize your cheeks are wet and you are smiling for the first time in years.

Moi-Moi of Seven Spirits.

You stick to Aunty Tutu as you settle into Eran Riro. She helps you scrape off the untamable creature that had stuck to your head and called itself your hair, and she gives you her skin and hair oils, plus a long golden-blonde wig. You still sleep apart from the rest of the Servers, but you sharply realize that they are not at all the boys and girls who work with you and Aunty Tutu.

Those are mere kitchen Hands.

These your roommates are quiet to the point of unnerving you. They don't talk behind your back, nor do they acknowledge your existence. They slink about in pairs, like some rare endangered species of cat. A young man and a young woman together, always touching, talking with eyes, the planes of their faces intersecting.

They are all very beautiful, like those beings you sometimes see in a magazine or on screen that make you know the possibility of perfection. You stare from the corner when they return from the baths, readying for the night or Banquet. They sleep all day in embrace. The women have their hair woven into thick rows, patterned styles that curl up at the nape, the ear, the eye. Their bared bodies are immaculate, hairless and even-toned.

You close your eyes when the men swing into the room, sometimes. But usually, there is a gushing from within you to see a mystery you have been forbidden from even thinking of. They can always tell when you are looking, as they turn and move their bodies in ways that made your core go slippery.

After they oil themselves, their coffee and camwood skins glistening as they slip into their stiff-ironed trousers and skin-tight red gowns, your whole body still blushes. They have not spoken to you once, even when you meet out in the melee of Banquet.

All you usually hear of their voices are the little whispers they share in bed at the witching hour. In Banquet, they sit still at the tables, gesturing to guests and moving between their tables and the kitchen to bring out food with flair.

Then they declare the delicacy, lifting their beautiful voices up to the chandeliers, as the guests watch, mouths dripping.

Night is when Banquet begins. When, as Aunty Tutu says, the rich finally feast. They always come from the shadows. You aren't sure they are all human. Most of them are cloaked in plain velvets, drifting silent towards the door guarded by the large man with the gold gun.

The cars that come by belong to dignitaries, solitary self-made paragons with full entourages to stoke the flames of megalomania. Families would often pour in, bursting out of the double doors underground without as much as a whisper of movement passing over the yard under the bodyguard's eye.

Several feet under the warehouse is a large hall, the size of a small ballroom. It is curtained and carpeted in lushest embroidered scarlet, set with circular couches and classic round tables. The silver is sterling. The bonsai is fake and the chandeliers speak of vast kingdoms, wealth beyond cash or capital. On the round ceiling is a painting of a naked man wrestling a tiger. His obsidian back glistens and blood stains the teeth of the beast. The gold of the chandeliers almost makes their eyes alive.

This is Banquet, the other side of Buka's coin.

There are reserved time slots and tables, and very specific food arrangement styles. There are impossible allergies and rival families. Separate menus for exotic pets, midnight wedding receptions, burials, séances. It is always like planning a segmented, rotating reception for some big Lagos event.

This is why Banquet doesn't happen every day or week. Its occurrence simply emerges out of the flow of days like the first smile of a new moon, along with Marrow Williamson, the brains and tongue behind all of Eran Riro.

Fishbone

The first time you see Marrow Williamson is the first time you work in the second kitchen. The place where all the exclusive meals for Banquet are prepared. The one with tall machines and an array of miraculous utensils you had never seen before. The one a corridor passes by on the way down to your room. Where your eyes always linger.

You are already used to standing alone, always a few inches away from Aunty Tutu, your wig bright against your shoulders and hot on your head. It serves as protection. The kitchen Hands are now fascinated every time you undo your silk headwrap and it falls to your shoulders. It makes you feel possible.

Late evening, the Soft Girls and the kitchen Hands are all gone. Aunty Tutu has told you that there will be work till morning. You both stand just inside the warehouse entrance, waiting. The guard who hit you avoids your gaze but you stare at him all the same, trying to burn holes in his impenetrable back.

Miss Paloma, the stern woman from when you fell into Eran Riro, appears, rushing out of the back door of the Buka like a hunted rabbit. Aunty Tutu exhales when she is within earshot.

"What took you so long?"

"Traffic. Is *she* here yet?

"No."

"Treasure nko?"

Treasure is the woman who checked your temple when you first woke up here and then laughed at you when you struggled from hunger after. Aunty Tutu shakes her head, "but I have October on hand to help just in case she can't make it."

"Thank God. Oya, oya, oya! Let's go."

Paloma doesn't look at you as she moves away, taking off her shoes and bag as she speaks. You follow them into the big steel kitchen. Aunty Tutu in her never-stained white and blue-striped iro and buba, Paloma in a sharply-cut black gown, funeral plain. The lights flicker on.

The space looks different than when you last saw it. One wall is covered in recipes, neat sheets of paper with lists scribbled on them. Almost every surface is covered in tomatoes and onions and so many strangely colored vegetables you wonder if you have stepped into a painted garden by mistake.

The Servers arrive, all three couples, dressed for the kitchen. White aprons and hats clean as their teeth.

Paloma walks to the center island. There are three kitchen islands of black marble. Aunty Tutu moves to the one on the left and you follow. The Servers split, moving to each produce-laden island to begin plucking and cutting and chopping ingredients into bowls. You are on a team of four that works fast, only whispering to say words like 'knife' and 'grater'.

No fire is started. You have been chopping spring onions, yellow peppers and a herb that makes the back of your throat sweet with its perfume when you sense the room change. Your olowosibi glows for the first time in weeks as she saunters in, atop the click-clack of low heels.

Heads lift and everyone freezes.

Marrow Williamson gazes at the affair before her with such severity that you think the next step would be for all to drop knives and bow. "Continue," she says. Her voice deep and clear.

You return to the herb, chopping with an automatic arm as she takes twenty steps across cold black marble to come stand beside Aunty Tutu. Her iro, buba and gele are made of a scaly, gleaming blue-green fabric, like the underside of some rare reptile. Neck, ears and wrists drip with pearl and entwined gold. Her scent hits you, rich, dark and bittersweet.

"Where's Marcus?"

"We haven't checked for him. We had to get the preparations ready."

"Yes. Very good, Tutu. Guests start arriving within the hour. Start with the first column of recipes. Get that girl to climb up and bring them down so you can see. You'll be preparing an appetitive platter for the Rorajes first –"

She is talking so fast, you wonder how Aunty Tutu can follow her. Her mention of you slips by and then comes back to jar you. You stop chopping and she looks to you. The Servers in your team have been at the sink rinsing cabbages serenely for eternity.

"I don't think I've seen you before." Her face turns hard again. "How did you end up in my kitchen?"

"She came looking for her brother, probably a customer. Jumped the fence. Marcus had her in Holding, but I interceded for her"

"Who gave you the right to do that? And to keep her here? Did I ever say anything about keeping strays?" Marrow's voice is a mallet questioning. You want to say something, but you find yourself speechless, instead you stagger backwards.

"I'm sorry." You hear yourself saying. "I'll go."

Marrow looks at you, eyes burning. You shut up and stop moving. She turns back to Aunty Tutu, waiting for an answer that she knows won't come.

"She has the gift."

Marrow looks to you, her face still so full of a haughty rage. "See me before I go. Now climb up and bring down those recipes." She moves across to where Paloma and her Servers are working, dropping Aunty Tutu like a hot coal. She begins asking questions and assigning names.

You walk up to the wide board hanging from the wall and climb onto the marble top. You are wearing the same long red gown you always wear and your bare head is safe under its simple scarf. The wig got too hot.

You begin to remove thumbtacks and collect the papers. Paloma suddenly whispers loud, "Please. Please, Ma!" and then breaks into a wail that nearly topples you off the marble. "Pleeeeaaaaaaaseeeeee. She doesn't have anything else. Don't do this to Treasure. Ma. Please!"

You hear a crisp "We value discretion, punctuality and order in this institution. You know how it goes. You fuck with Banquet, you're off the team. If you don't keep it down, you'll join her on

Harvest Night." Paloma dries up as Marrow slithers away from her side.

You barely blink and Marrow is standing in front of you. Her eyes are wells of gold inside a face sculpted out of dark caramel. A few strands of white-blonde hair have escaped her gele and lie stuck above her ears like free chalklines.

"Let's all hope for Treasure's sake you can put that gift of yours to good use. Aunty Tutu has never made a mistake since she...arrived here. So I trust your gift too, from Olodumare Itself, to bring forth wonders for our well paying guests later today?" She turns in a huff, her question hanging in the air as she clicks deeper into the kitchen, almost past the third island before you can exhale and shudder.

Sokoyokoto

You make it through by some rare grace. When you were a child, recipe books were like grails to you; you loved to read about ingredients that you didn't know the taste or smell of. Letting yourself imagine parmesan, breadfruit, cinnamon, parsley, rosemary, arugula, artichokes, honey mustard, umami.

Now as you shuffle the list of things you are to put together, with the help of your beautiful, nameless Servers, you can find and taste and measure. You intuit heat and duration. The olowosibi moves in a spiral.

You begin with the simplest. A Greek Salad. The woman Server hands you two saucers of olives and cheese.

Marrow Williamson returns with the Butcher, who is today wearing only a leather jacket and jeans and bloodstains. He is carrying three chunks of meat of varying size, texture, color and shape. He drops them on the tables at Marrow's directions. You toss the lettuce and olives and feta in the dressing, watching the

Butcher. He looks at you as he drops the flesh, bowing his head in a sort of reflex. A sign of respect? You lean back without lifting your own head, terrified. He had caged you not long ago.

You start to sear the meat. It is pink with char marks, like it has been pre-cooked. It is lightly muscled, almost like fish, but it smells meaty. Maybe it's one of those rare meats like camel, or, alligator.

It cooks fine for you, turning brown and peach after the kiss of the grill. You sprinkle crystals of gold and salt from a dead sea. A hibiscus soaked in wine and lime finishes the wooden platter.

The olowosibi drips, a hive of bees.

Samosa

Praise always unnerved you. They almost chant your name when they eat. Bring her to us, they say. Aunty Tutu had briefed you after she had come to where you sat eating olives and cheese cubes, staring into the black floor. Her smile was too deep. She fussed over you like the proudest mother as she told you how to find them.

The Kandinuyo Family is a quintet. Mother, daughter and three sons.

You come through, sidling past a woman leaving Banquet holding a cheetah on a leash. Chandeliers burn above, nests of luxury on fire. The hall is alive with the sparkle of light and the tang of citrus incense. The wrestling above is refracted in the hungers displayed below. Banquet sits exactly one fifty and tonight it is full and hot. Dark-faced men lap hot fiery pepper-soups like dogs from bowls. Others are being fed roast meat by nude women who cover themselves only in jewels. They eat too much meat in this place. Your arm remembers the grilling.

You're almost at the Kandinuyo table and you drift past more tables as inconspicuously as possible, your eyes widening at the ferocity of the feasting before you. They eat barehanded from deep wide pots set in the center of the their tables – iyan and egusi with more meat than sauce, Chinese fried rice and a big basket of more of that soft pre-roasted meat, sautéed with chillis and garlic and a sticky sauce sitting by the side, porridge filled with fried intestine and fat chunks of meat running red with thick palm oil, armies of kebab stand over every surface ringed in green and red and yellow chilies, still sizzling.

The air is ripe with a viscous hunger.

Biscuit

Nasco Kandinuyo rises when you come to stand before their table. Her disheveled, soup-stained blond weave doesn't move an inch. She looks so sated, a specifically fed face you haven't seen in a long time. You want to pinch her cheeks. She is smiling and saying, "That was enormously good. Munro, Mungo and Mutiu can't move. Is this your first time cooking at Banquet? I know 'cause I request from the three Agonyin in rotation and wow! What's your name?"

"October Abemise." You say, denying your father's name. You fidget and look at your knees awkwardly. The three boys are slumped in the semi-circle of the plush sofa that curls around the circular table, dressed in three-piece suits of patterned emerald. Their steamed-up monocles dangle in the crystal light.

Nasco's daughter is beside her, almost a shadow. "That's the best food I've had since we ate Folusho." She is picking her teeth and rubbing the dry back of a stained emerald lizard. Her hair is a clean waterfall of polished black. Her jeweled fingers shift over the back of the flat, hypnotized reptile.

"My daughter, Veronese. She's still hungry."

You wonder what she meant by "ate Folusho", but you don't ask. You smile at the sleeping triplets instead of looking into Nasco's eyes. She is also still hungry. Her eyes seem to have swollen in your time staring into them. You say you will prepare more food.

Veronese asks for a Bloody Mary too.

Tomati Alagolo

The Bloody Mary makes you vomit and confirms your unease. That uneasiness you have felt ever since you walked over those crushed bones to sit in that cage. You have been uneasy even hiding under Aunty Tutu's wing.

Aunty Tutu with her oblivions and absentmind. Whispering to you when you stood alone in the earliest morning before the Soft Girls and the kitchen Hands came, "You shouldn't be here." Her voice so laden with feeling that you sob, and then ask Why?

The question snapping her back here.

The Servers too. Their silent sensualities, their supple corrugated bodies fucking in the night as you tried to sleep. Their finesse in the kitchen and with the guests, almost like they were created to exist for these very reasons. They never walked up to the surface to breathe fresh air or taste sunlight.

Once you looked into a tall fair-skinned Server's eyes for too long and felt the floor of your belly shiver. Like looking into the maw of a carnivore.

The cold Bloody Mary was made of something you tasted and thought was the regular tomato juice, gin and salt. You had carried the jug of tomato juice out of the icy white gut of the freezer yourself. But then as it makes its way down your throat, you know what it is made of.

III
Bloody Mary

And like blood out of a glass, you slip away from all questions, not pressing further when Aunty Tutu responds with "Some people like cow's blood for its special proteins, and Folusho was a pig."

You seep deeper into the cloth of Eran Riro.

Your flow unquestioning, your warmth and pulse unchanging as you begin to encounter more situations and ingredients that make you want to sink underground. You stop tasting them. There are maggots, living cockroaches, perfectly spherical eggs that glow faint blue in no light, urine, tree bark, a rainbow of crushed leaves and buds, multi-colored frogs, big lizards, spices that rose out of the pot after being sprinkled in solid clouds that danced like drunken men, shredded hair, ostrich eggs, a fecund milk that thickened into butter with faces on heating, black salt, powders of turmeric, ancient crayfish the size of a forearm.

Marcus also brings strange, thoroughly cleaned flesh; fat cylinders of snake; fish blue-green within; skinned, headless dogs and cats, and more fatty chunks of that tender precooked one. The favorite extra at Banquet.

You embrace cooking for Buka as a respite, away from preparing the horrors that the people at Banquet always praise you for. You still cook in Treasure's place whenever Banquet rolls around, and you stay with Aunty Tutu, watching her meekness give way to a silent despair.

After Banquet, she takes the meat, bones and meal left over to Bruno, a black dog, tall as a ram, hidden in a rusted cage between the buka and the warehouse. Bruno makes the bones into sand and Aunty Tutu sweeps them up to pour out over the field.

You dread descending the stairs to go to sleep after every work day, because the Servers will already be there; mute, unmoving, clinging to one another like limpets, definitely cursed.

Epo Pupa, for Those Eating Here Later.

Aunty Tutu tells you to go and give the Soft Girls a set of plates, quite different from what you've seen used to serve food at Buka. They are glossy, finished red clay, etched underneath with a circular sequence of odd symbols. Inside the half-bowls, a ring of black skeletons dance, their heads hanging above the stalks of their bodies, joyous.

Your olowosibi rumbles and spits.

You drop the plates with the Soft Girls, who set them apart from the other dishes, down on the floor. Two of them kneel, make a sign of the Cross, and immediately begin to finger rub palm oil into the bowls with a hallowed reverence.

You turn to leave Buka, to go back to Aunty Tutu's kitchen where the others are at lunch, when you hear your name come from the line of hungry customers on the other side of the service station. It cannot be. You won't turn.

"It's me. Monday."

IV
Eja Dindin

You gaze at each other for such a long time. Everything seems to stop for your eyes and his eyes to meet. He looks rough. Unwashed hair overgrown all over his face and head, like your hair when you first got here, old ripped jeans, an oversized Evil Dead t-shirt and some bulldozer of a hooded leather jacket that he probably stole.

You move and push through the wooden gate that allows Soft Girls into the Buka when there's some serious matter to attend to, like spilled food or handsome men. You are standing before him in your red kaftan and a white kitchen scarf.

"Wow, Octo. I never thought I'd see you again. I went back to...to the shop, but there was no one there. So-"

"So, what?" you say.

"So I tried to find you more. I went back to our old house. Uncle Lanre has rented it out and renovated it. I was lost. Where is Mama?"

You look into his face, not as handsome as Daddy, Mr. Lanwa, but holding something of that roguish essence. His pleading eyes are stained with red and mustard splotches from his adventures with other drugs besides food. He smells of old drink and weed.

Anger rises in your chest suddenly and you want to jump and bite his ear off. You walk past him as if he is not there, making for a quieter corner of Buka trying to remain calm. The Soft Girls are already gathering and stretching their long necks and ears.

He follows, docile.

You say "Our mother is dead." before even letting him sit. He jerks too much, as if electrocuted. *What?!* You can see the false question forming in his head so you whisper it for him. *What?!*

You are livid and your clenched fists are starting to ache. The olowosibi burns like an old wound. Monday knew Mama was dead. The last time he had visited she had been unable to open her eyes or mouth to speak to him. He had come when you had gone to buy ingredients for akara. Two months after he had originally vanished. You had watched him sneak out on your return from the market, sprinting down the street like a thief.

"I saw you sneaking out the other day. Mama waited for you before she died. I buried her in the canal behind the shop." He puts a hand to his mouth in genuine surprise. "Where was I supposed to go? She never let us know her family and those Lanwa people abandoned us, they cast us out with nothing like thieves. I buried her and it's done."

Your voice is even but gets louder as you talk more. Monday is quiet, staring at you, hand on mouth with red eyes. When he keeps looking like a startled lamb, you rage at him.

"You were nowhere to be found. You wicked, wicked f-. Going away when we needed you the most. I should-" You slam a fist on the table as gently as you can. A cup rattles near the edge.

He jumps up as he always does at the slightest sound of fight or threat. "You should what? I was there as much as I could be. I am a man. I have to find my place in this world or I would have been born a mistake. Going awayaway was my way of getting space for myself."

"And did you find the space? Did you finally become a man?"

Your eyes are getting ready to spill and that pressure in your heart that comes up whenever you discuss Mama is thickening. You curse family ties in your head over and over again.

"I won't have this conversation. Eat your food and leave. Act like this never happened."

You stand up. He's talking to you as you move away. "But now I don't have to worry about money for food anymore. You got into Eran Riro! Please, sister. Forgive me."

You turn back, palm burning.

"Is this all you can think of? How to satisfy yourself. I just told you I buried our mother with my bare hands and you're worried about food. You are definitely mad."

"Don't be retarded. No one will marry you this way. Talking to your elders without respect. Now let's settle this with you getting me some grub ehn?" He smiles the older sibling smile, mocking your anger with the old tones of command that he once used, enjoying having some inherited power over you.

His presence seems to return you to where you were the day you first came to Eran Riro; that pit of despair. Fear mists your brain and you slap him.

The olowosibi had been aching to since his voice entered your ear. Buka finally stops. The Soft Girls freeze and their heads turn to you and your brother like a flock of long-necked birds. Ewedu drips off amala halfway to open mouths, soda slips into the wrong pipe and a wet cough spatters across the silence.

You turn your face back to see Monday recover from the heat of your palm. His hand caressing the spot on his cheek as his eyes find yours and fill with something you haven't seen since you were in Primary School. You stagger backwards but you're not fast enough.

His fist collides with your jaw. Everything in your eyes shakes as you collapse to the floor. You can feel him looming above you. The Soft Girls are screaming. Customers gather. You stand up and look at him, palm wet against where your jaw juts wrong against your throat. Its sharp ache drips under your words.

"You were a mistake after all, Monday."

You turn and the crowds part. The Soft Girls are looking at you. You make fast circles with your index finger and they turn and continue serving food, not missing a beat. Your entire head is pulsing with the bruise of his fist.

Aunty Tutu takes you to the clinic.

Dodo Ikire

Three weeks pass.

You continue working Buka and Banquet. Getting paid in shelter and food only. This is why you will never leave Eran Riro. Where will you go? Back to your father's venomous siblings, or off to lose yourself in Ilorin searching for your mother's family, who will not know you or respond how you wish when you find them. Or back to Monday?

Your jaw didn't break, but it was shifted out of its joint and the bone doctor had to jerk your head in a very specific way for it to snap back audibly, your cheek eaten alive by fire.

Some sympathy comes to you from the Soft Girls and the kitchen Hands. They greet you with bows of the head and bring your food to you now. Paloma remains smiling after she hears of your ordeal. Aunty Tutu asks you, in that empty way of hers, what happened.

You recite the Books of Abemise, then, October. She completely ignores the deaths and Monday and just starts telling you how she knows the name and the area in Ilorin the name comes from. They usually have the strongest olowosibis, their talents adapting quick to the culinary workings of foreign cooking, so they all just fly away.

Aunty Tutu says family is nothing without care and love, then she holds you as you cry into her shoulder.

I am lost. You tell her.

Marrow

You never went to see Marrow Williamson after your first meeting.

You entered Eran Riro in February. Met Marrow in March, and only saw her when she came through during Banquet to do her pre-dinner speeches, darting around like a drill sergeant to make sure the meals were precise and perfect. She doesn't have an office in Eran Riro, and she has basically left Buka in Aunty Tutu's hands.

Banquet is usually why she returns here.

But in October, she visits the living quarters that lie underground, beside Banquet. She comes in the middle of the night, when the Servers are cavorting. Her heels clicking like some omen. She is wearing a black iro and buba and her hair is exposed, a cloud of bleach-blonde curls. Her eyes burn with no glow, like she has just gazed into a sun. There's a loose edge to her usual airtight fuss today, but it's not calming. It feels like razors are darting off her skin.

"It's time to witness a new Harvest." She says to the Servers, in that hard voice. "You, too." She gazes at you where you lie, just snapped out of a dream of an avalanche of bones by her presence.

New Suya

You all walk with her into the night. The Servers wearing strange hooded black jackets. You slip into your trusty jalabia then walk behind them, led by Marrow. The somber air of the procession makes your heart pound. What could be happening?

You climb the stairs, drift down the corridor and surface in the compound. Aunty Tutu is there. Paloma too. Marcus and the guard. Every face shines in the burning of a tall bonfire at the exact center of the compound.

"Let's be quick. Have they returned to their bowls?" Marrow says to all within earshot as she goes to stand before the fire. She seems less sharp than usual, her hair falling across her eyes over and over again. Her legs tremble like those of a newborn colt.

"Yes. They are all waiting in Buka, for the call." Aunty Tutu responds as she moves to stand directly opposite Marrow on the other side of the fire. The six Servers flank her. The other workers at Eran Riro close the circle around the tall fire. Everyone holds hands. You seem to disappear as they close their eyes. You have no idea what the time is. Past midnight maybe. The streets outside the fence are tomblike in their stillness.

You watch it begin.

Eja Tutu

Aunty Tutu leads the call. A song sung so low, you think everyone in the circle is snarling. As they drone deeper into its chorus, Marrow breaks out of the circle, pushed by some force too vast for her body. She grabs her head and pushes at the air around her, like she is being mobbed by unseen things. Then she starts to wail. Her normally hard voice is frantic. It rises, like it is being snatched out of her throat. She falls like a woman ablaze, writhing as her screams become gibberish.

Then, an absence like death.

Utter stillness.

Isi Ewu

The call of the circle never stops but it lowers, deepens till the hairs on the back of your neck rise. Marrow remains corpselike, her hair radioactive at the edge of the ring of men and women whose eyes are still shut as they gaze up into a nothing within.

The back door of Buka clicks open and you turn your head as a stream of people begin to lurch out, slow as cattle. You scamper backwards until you are standing right beside the warehouse, about a hundred meters from where the fire burns and the circle calls.

The people walking are naked.

There are about twenty of them. They walk without will, moving puppetlike to the tune of something only they can hear. In their hands are the bowls that you delivered to Buka a few weeks ago. Marrow Williamson remains on the ground and you can swear she's glistening.

They draw closer to the circle, wavering in the heat and glow of the big fire. You see something glint inside the bowls. Knives.

The first person moves closer to the fire. He's a tall man with a generous slab of stomach. He lifts the bowl and smashes it to the ground. Bending low till his head almost catches on fire to his disinterest, he picks the knife up, stands tall, looks heavenwards and moves it quick under his throat.

Blood sprays in a gush, hissing onto the fire. He walks into the flames until he hits something solid and his body collapses into a depression under the burning. There is more sizzling as his juices spill over firewood.

You turn your face away.

You try to. But you are transfixed, as each body walks out of Buka and then lingers to cluster briefly outside the circle, waiting till the one inside finds its own point of sacrifice.

They move fast. More than fifty now. Over and over it goes. The bowl breaks, the knife is lifted, the throat opens and the fire is embraced.

Fall and sizzle.

They pile up. The call has lowered to an inaudible volume. The only loud sounds are the gurgle of blood in open throats and the hiss and crackle of the fire as the bodies roast.

Treasure appears. The woman who touched your cheek and called you a live one. She doesn't have a bowl, only a knife. The knife moves quick and she falls. Paloma continues to sing, eyes shut tight as mouths.

When you see Monday, there are three bodies left outside the circle. The smell of a familiar charred meat fills your nose. You find yourself salivating yet agitated by the shock, running for-ward against your will, something in the blood you share making you remember a distant memory of brotherly love worth fighting for. But your body is too slow, drowning. The air around you is heavy as weighted cloth. Your olowosibi is a live thing, like a rusted nail inside your palm.

Marrow Williamson sleeps. You know she has something to do with the heaviness, the heaviness which draws all these flies into fire.

You shout, "No. No. No.", but your voice is weak, then you cry, "Monday!" as he moves into the circle, naked as birth and dashes the gold of the burning blade deep into his neck.

You stumble again, as his throat spurts and he gurgles. You hear his body fall into the fire after yours hits the earth – then, you are screaming.

II: Hauntings

The Fields of Abete, Iwaya.

Down on the mainland under the simmer of Lagos, away from the market-zones of Yaba and Sabo, you can feel it pull, calling you.

You ride, sinking deeper into Onike, off in the distance glimpsing the backgates of the University of Lagos as cars and okada zoom mad around you seeking everything.

You're seated atop one now, taking you down a narrow street that reduces to a neck. The neck ends at a rusted gate behind which they play.

On the fields, they are running. The boys are circumambient around the ball. Soccer burns between their feet and they kick, rumble. Plumes of almost-white sand from a distant beach, fine enough to lie in, to want to fall in, fly off their feet and they dribble and sweat, turn dog and lion, attack defense: Goal!

The sunset catches them there. Its ochre gleam on their sweating backs. Their cries of victory echoing across the city and bouncing off the sky.

Our players go home to flat dinners, watery soup, bile.

In the absence of light, the boys who died in their sleep emerge from the sands to mirror the living, kicking chattering skulls between their toes.

Vain Knife

S *tab here with index before you tuck into foul feast.*

x

Hour at which the blind see, when night unfurls her wing and goes out, silent as shaft of moonlight. Hour of the witches' feeding; on primal pain, on corrupt love, on toothless cherub child.

Circle the table crone, with your face uncovered. Lay the boy upon the cold rock and draw a line with split tongue, from throat to belly. With your talons, pull out his entrails. Ignore his hollow screams, his squirming body.

Eat.

I

The skeletal boy is crouched on flat red earth in the middle of a brotherhood of mango trees. In their shadow, he moves a stick across the damp ground, stabbing at something unseen. Across his back, there are welts redder than the ground his feet rest on.

Beneath the tree trunk nearest, there is a mound of mangoes; some milky green, some yellow with black sores, buzzing all over with the dizzy orchestra of housefly wings. He had woken before the sun emerged soft from inside the ground, and swept every inch of the compound clean of leaves. He had then piled all the mangoes that had fallen from the trees overnight into a heap for Mma. She would pound and use them to make a spiced gruel for dinner, along with some garri, honey and pepper.

He continues to push the stick across the red earth, drawing small uneven shapes as he unfurls the intestines of the large grey rat he had found, the one he was sure had burst from eating too much bad fruit. Its innards are like a clump of thick strings and bulbs at the tip of the short stick. Once in a while, a string of dark fluid shoots from the entrails he has hypnotized himself with, into his face, the rotted gut juice touching the tip of his lip or the insides of his nostrils.

He doesn't stop stirring. The rat rolls along for the ride, the ribbed cave of its insides murmuring with every pull of the stick like a mouth speaking curses. He is in a state of deepest concentration.

Apart from the hut that he stays in with Mma, which hulks silent behind him, holding secrets in its smooth walls; there is nothing else around but busy weaverbirds flitting through fruit trees, grass that sometimes comes alive with startled duck, and wild corn. Five hundred running feet before him is the hanging curtain of the Forest. Dense mats of creeping foliage pour from the tops of the tall trees that ring the entrance, glowing and rippling in morning light as a pungent air pours out of it, air fit to turn the roughest wrestler into a slobbering animal on his knees.

Mma told him to never go within reach of the forest, but she had spoken too late. His fear of dreaming had driven him in more times than he could count; to listen to the gurgle and whistle of bottomless mudpits, and the cackling of the birdwomen who slept on their feet in the hollows of dead trees, to the chorus of a submerged hell and the wails of sacrificed babes that made his insides spin and his head fog with red, but he returned over and over, seeking out death, trying to get forever lost.

Mma had told him to never go within reach of the forest, after he had brought the devil home with him.

***

"When are you going to do it?"

"Today. When she returns from the market."

"It has been *today* for two moons now. I am tired of waiting for you to grow testicles and do what needs to be done. I must return to the Fire Below soon."

"Give me some rest. They took of me again last night, as they have for all the moons since I have been born. If testicles meant strength then I should have done it. My body can barely take care of itself, and you expect it to be strong enough to destroy another body."

"You have the knife I gave you. It has mind. Lift it against her with purpose in your heart. Do you not want to be free?"

"I am tired."

"You must do it. Or you will no longer be tired. You will be dead. You will be trapped in that pot boiling, and for as long as they are alive, they will use your soul as seasoning when they eat the flesh of coming babes."

"I want to die. After you, I am no longer afraid to die. The first time I saw you, the shock took all my fear away. You should have left me to continue suffering, maybe by now I would have died. I want to spend my afterlife in a pot boiling in the realm of the coven till my mother dies. Maybe when she is done with her wickedness in the world, I will truly be free."

"I came to you because when you breached one of the Gates with your feet, I smelt your suffering. It sustains me differently, much differently than that of the souls that wander the Fire Below. Their pain is like water, freely available, but yours, yours is like wine. The way you distill, finding beauty and dignity in such raw evil. It makes me want to never let you go."

"You've started talking like that again. It is part of why I want to die. Why will I be attracting a forest spirit with skin like blood? So is it this same pain that you drink, the pain that overwhelms me and prevents me from ever leaving the grounds of this place when I want to run into the village?"

"Yes. And again you cannot leave, because an effigy of you is stuck into the ground with a needle inside her room. Take the knife from inside the hole where you hid it and face her, even if it is the last thing you do, even if you die."

"What happens if I succeed? If the knife succeeds?"

"You will be free. You will be the greatest farmer for as far as the land feels herself to be yours. You will find a wife and many funny friends and you will stop dreaming of being eaten by witches and start dreaming of the Fire Below, where I will make you one of my many Conquerors."

"I want an end to this that is why I will try. I want to leave this body! My bones are too tired. Some part of me wants her to win. I cannot feel joy anymore, so why should I continue living? To become a great farmer? If she kills me, will you still make me a Conqueror?"

"If that happens, your soul will belong to her to do as she pleases."

"Death will break that bond. Will you still make me a Conqueror if I die?"

"First, lift the knife."

II

Mma walks in from the market, a basket of produce balanced on her head. She sees him babbling to himself again. He is now always crouched under the trees, with his mournful eyes looking up at nothing. He has his hand wrist deep in the earth when she calls his name. Her big voice rises above the trees like a clarion. The boy puts the knife into his waistband, letting its black blade line up with his spine as he walks through the trees, around to the front of the hut. His mother is seated on a rock beside the door, chewing dried fish head.

"What have you been doing since I left?"

"I sweep the yard and collect all them mango, Mma."

"What of water? Have you fetched water?"

She is beginning to rock back and forth on the rock, like she does when she is about to do the thing. If she doesn't do it once during the day, then he is sure she has done it to someone else's child. Her eyebags are heavy, black with sleepless blood and the face they hang from is wrinkled. Its left half is heavily scarred. Strands of raw pink flesh have squirmed to the surface from under deep brown skin by trauma of either fire or claw. He doesn't know how it happened.

She barely speaks to him like she bore him. "Why did you not fetch the water? It is your piss that I will use to cook the food that you will now open that your mouth to come and eat abi?" Always she fires words at him. "Fruitless child. Even the dung hill rejected you when I threw you in there after you were born." She does not love him, and does nothing hide it.

Hate lives in the corners of her mouth and turns every click and echo she speaks at him into bullets. "You are the one tying me down here. I have places in the world calling to me, but I want to see what you will do with this your half-life. That is why I am waiting. I want you to prove to me that you are not a thief like your shadow of a father."

He cannot talk properly, he never learned to communicate with anyone except her and she never spoke to him like she expected him to speak back, but when he speaks to the devil, their voices touch in a place in his head, a place beyond mouths.

As she shouts at him, spewing thoughts that only serve to feed her rage, her feet are moving towards him. He doesn't see the skinless coconut until it is an inch from his right eye.

There is a hollow *thunk!* burning through the meat of his head as it hits him, then he is falling.

The pain makes his eyes roll back; a pulsing thing with teeth deep in his cranium. The boy feels the knife slip out of his waistband as he writhes and groans on the floor, limbs too limp to touch the sore spot. This pain tugs at his brain, pulling at it with jagged white teeth and making him cry out loud in soft groans till his belly aches.

She stands and watches him. Not making any motions with her face. Just watching him with beady eyes that twinkle through that mask. It is the way a man will watch broken game die.

The boy stops groaning and twisting, blood has clotted around his temple and cheek in a shiny red flap. Mma bends down to see if there is a pulse at his neck. There is one, fighting against his throat as he sinks deeper into unconsciousness. She spits chewed fish on the ground beside his head and stands up. He will wake up and come to her for care when the night comes biting.

When she turns her back, the boy rises, black knife held over his head.

He drives its length into her back. There is a wet crack inside her body as it breaches bone. He tries to pull it back with his fist but it is lodged too tight. He staggers backwards as she staggers forward. She tries to reach for the handle but her arms can't touch it, she hits her toe on a rock and falls, first on her elbows, then on her chest, splaying against the earth graceless as spittle.

The only sound she makes is an inward whistle of air, like one who has eaten food that is too hot.

The boy watches her go quiet, waiting for freedom to bubble in him, and set him dancing about her body, but it does not come.

The devil appears on top of the hut, yellow reptile eyes smiling. His tail ebbs sinuously behind him. "You did it." He says, this time moving his mouth to reveal rows of stained needle teeth. "Now set fire to the hut."

The boy shuts his eyes to ease the ache running through his brain. He opens them. The devil is gone. His mother is dead before him, a pool of blood, dark as hate is spreading.

He is going to burn the hut.

He takes a step forward and she moves with a little jerk that sends him running backwards. He watches as the wound in her back swallows the knife.

After swallowing the knife, her body disappears, leaving behind a heap of the clothes she had tied around her body. The boy turns around in the dark. Night has fallen. His instincts get the better of him and he calls to her with the voice of a lamb surrounded by wolves. Once. Twice.

"You thought a simple demon knife would kill me?" Her voice is on the wind, taunting. "You actually believed in a thing so low. Do you really believe he followed you because of your sweet *suffering*." She laughs drily. "You are like a pawn. They'll use you to pick their teeth and throw you away after."

He falls to the floor, chest to the dust. His head still aches, and he can see nothing but fireflies. "Mma, please!"

She appears before him in a body of dripping black mud three times bigger than her old one. It is caked with slithering serpents and writhes with sheets of angry, buzzing insects and many red eyes that cluster and glow like coal. Her head is gone.

This is how the boy knows that he will die.

x

Stab here with index, try harder to resist the Devil inside you.

Sonskins

i

On a night of open flight, when healers take on the skins of their familiars to battle sickness, we stand rigid over our catatonic sons.

Our special peppersoup has barely dried off their lips.

ii

Before this night, we peer into their dreams, through crisp dense hair. They dream of palaces for us, helicopters with blades of gold spinning burning, cradling us in the noon above city heat, trips to the World's Wonders with their dead fathers kissing our cheek in the sun-decayed CANON square after, reams of overwrought handmade fabric in cool tones, spilling pearls, diamonds, sequins, stained with a drop of the weaver's blood as a gift, they dream of palaces again, of dogs splashing in fountain and barking the moon to fullness, of obedient house girls willing to suck on our split fingers and to take over the chopping of the ugwu and the onions, the frying of the chicken and the pepperfish, the cooking of a perfect pot of jollof.

Our sons dream of saving us from this desolation in which we sit like stubborn mules in mud. They wish to erase the agony that their births and their nurturing have inscribed on our faces, and yet, their dream are empty of wives.

iii

In these dreams that we gaze into upon the scalps of our sons, we find them after wading through their motherdreams, hiding in the grove. Apples surround their feet as they grasp onto each other naked except for tattered wrappers rasping beneath their low moans.

There is a beast devouring our son, under leaves fading away into gold.

Their wet skins glisten in that light of netherworlds. We have no body so he can't see our faces collapse as we behold his sin. His dream falls to tatters, corroded by our silent shout. He doesn't let go of his beast until he startles awake and in the slowness of his eyelids drifting back to sleep, taking him back to his grove of beastly desire – he wonders why the room smells of hot anointing oil.

iv

So, on this night when the very air seems to bristle with the nagual, we take off our sons' skins.

As we peel off the furred slabs of pumpkin yellow, coal black, cocoa, we watch the bark infusion in the peppersoup bind the ends of their nerves in tufts of muted lime fire. We slip off the long gloves of their arms, the trousers of their lower body, the breastplate of their torso and the mask of the heads.

Our sons are bare, glistening, squirming things. Their nerves burn in lightning paths under the exposed pink-red-cream bruise of their subdermis. We cover them with a blanket of bitter leaves and step into the heat of their fresh skin.

v

Now, we remember the names of the men that the Beast used to lure our son and we hunt. On this night of open flight, the air aids our parting of space to slip through shortcuts, to find them in their rooms asleep or eating, wrapped around other men, kissing their oblivious wives.

Our sons have been busy. The Beasts have a network spanning everywhere. They touch everything with their filth, their sticky desires, their abominations of family and love. They think we are our son when we walk out of their walls into their homes.

Some of them, the ones who live alone, soften immediately, running over to kiss us rough or soft. They palm our bodies and try to draw heat, then they look into our eyes and our fists find their throats.

Oh! The rush of breath's struggle to be free, and our insistence that it not be, that it be quiet, fuels our sonskins, causing heat to rise off us and we smother.

Others are startled. In shock, waking up at midnight beside their taboo lovers, or their wives to see the shadow of us standing bare and naked. They beg us as our son. "Why are you here now? How did you get in?". We soften a bit too naturally, pull them close into smeary kisses as their wives and lovers wake. They look into our eyes and see we are not him.

We take their skins off while they are fully awake.

vi

As this night tapers to an end, the skins loosen around our jaws and hips. Flaps start to tear up along the spine. The skins we have harvested hang over our left shoulder.

We return home, to the mat of bitter leaves under which he rests. Our son(s). We dust off the leaves, now dry and ready to crunch, and give our sons back their skins.

They will wake soon, hungry to find the Beast again. Ready to corrode the very foundations of the love that birthed them in this lust, this possession of the flesh. The heat they seek which we can never give them. The heat of the touch of the Beast with which no woman can compare. This heat better than our platters of soulfood and our washing of their clothes, our peering into their dreams, our weaving of their futures and our birthing of them.

We have birthed them so they will give us glory, show us what we could not be. Our sons stir in the thrum of the coming day. Their skins firm against their bones.

We return to our empty beds and lay the skins over the mattress before going to sleep with smiles on our faces.

vii

On some other night, not one of open flight or of the full moon, we find the girl. She walks down the street, a tray of fried shrimp balanced on her head. It is past 10pm. We steal her and execute our vision.

Our sons wake up again. We ask them of marriage and children. They fumble around as usual, unable to find the courage to tell us what we already know, then end up with "In my own time, Mom."

We smile. They are all above thirty and have lived under our skins for much longer. Their sorrows are our sorrows. Our joy is theirs. Now, we will give them happiness.

We bring in the girl, wearing the skins of our sons' kin.

Ngozi Ugegbe Nwa

I

Runs

Two bodies lie twined in afterglow. Sunlight falls across sweaty skin. The man is young and generously furred, his belly a little soft. The woman is strikingly beautiful. Her nonchalant draping of herself across the white sheets in oblivious sleep looks like something that should be filmed. This is Ngozi, fifth wife of Chief Pupo Ireke and girlfriend of Tobi, a software developer.

Tobi and Ngozi believe they are in love and sometimes talk about eloping once either one of them blow up and become stars.

Ngozi was talking to her photographer Sogo Quadri on the phone that rests in her hands just before she dozed off. Tobi runs his thumb in a lazy circle across her lower back. She can't feel it. He bites her thigh, playful.

Ngozi sits up sharply, still asleep, "I have to leave" she says. Her voice, a drone. She opens her eyes and rubs them awake. She kisses Tobi on the lips and his eyes follow her as she slides into her dress and swings out of the apartment.

Evening-time traffic in Lagos is a nightmare.

Summons

Ngozi bakes inside her car, stuck on the main road just outside Tobi's estate. She has had to turn the air-conditioning off to preserve the life of her car battery. Worse than sitting in these sweltering leather interiors with a 40' Brazilian against her back is having the car die on her in the middle of Lekki. She can already see the thugs gathering, like hyenas around a kill, ready to extort and steal from her while being rapey.

She slips down her seat, slippery with sweat and curses herself for painting the car black and not leaving Tobi's apartment earlier, but then she remembers the photo-shoot that had started the day with Sogo Quadri. Her portfolio was growing and soon, she would be able to get herself represented by an agency. The thought of becoming a jet-setting supermodel makes her stomach jump a bit. She instinctively pulls down the rearview mirror to look at her face.

She dabs gently at her skin, which is smooth as purified loam and highlighted by plenty bronzer. She looks into her eyes, co-signed as perfect by Tobi and Sogo, and sees fatigue staring back. She is uneasy, has been uneasy since she first entered Lagos in self-exile six years ago. Mama's face fills her mind and she instinctively shuts her eyes.

Something bright and gold flashes into her eyes from somewhere down in the go-slow, reflecting off the mirror.

The car seems to become hotter and the bottom of her throat begins to itch. She collects the luxurious, false length of hair from where it is soaking at her back and pulls it to the side. Her windows are half open and no whiff of air comes through, only the grumble and beep of overheated engines and the smell of ofe-nsala. Ngozi has not smelled the aroma of her favorite soup so richly in over six years. All the six years since she left Mama in that village with her archaic traditions. Ngozi closes her eyes to drown out memories of her mother that cause her stomach to knot.

The object that had flashed gold swims past her. It is a mirror. A perfectly gilded pool of oval glass. The person who carries it bends under its weight. Usually, hawkers will carry more than one item of the goods they sell in elaborate strings and belts all around their bodies, but this one is carrying just this one object. The most perfect mirror Ngozi had ever set eyes on.

Pssst!

The mirror stops instantly, soon as the air rushes out through her teeth. It turns around to reveal the oldest woman Ngozi has ever seen, bearing it on her back with a dizzy smile full of black teeth and naked gums. Ngozi swallows nervously as she approaches.

The woman's blouse and wrapper and scarf are made from different cuts of faded ankara that look older than Ngozi herself. Her skin is all melted caramel and streaked earth. It looks like it would come loose if touched.

After a couple of epochs spent creaking towards the car, she finally reaches the driver's window. She is now looking into Ngozi's car, taking in the plush seats, the iPhone charging, the colorful new clothes draped across the headrest of the passenger seat. Her eyes are milky with cataracts.

"Mama, how much?"

The old woman turns her head towards Ngozi, like she had just realized that the car was occupied. The smile never leaves her face and Ngozi can see that she is shivering.

"So you can't even greet?' She speaks igbo. It slides into Ngozi's ears sharp as a whip. Ngozi narrows her eyes and turns to look into the oblivion of the woman's eyes.

"How much is the mirror?" She repeats.

The woman stops shivering, and in the next moment, stops slouching. She rises to her full four-feet-and-a-bit height, moving the mirror to her front. Ngozi can now see it better. The gold that edges it is bursting with minute detail, a cornucopia of flowers and fish and heads.

'Ten taasan." The old woman says.

"Haba, Mamaaa! Na mirror we dey talk o, no be diamond ring. Gi me for two five."

"I am sure you're aware that even the cheapest diamond rings are priced more than all you've accumulated in your short life, Ngozi." This time, the English tears out of the old woman's mouth in bursts of acid. Her voice is low and grating and her eyes are honed in on Ngozi's face like they are firing out beams. "Even the men you sleep around with won't get you a real diamond ring, because they've already bought the only diamond they will ever buy, for their wives." Ngozi leans back in shock.

"Ah! Is it because of small mirror that you're now talking to me like this? I worked hard for everything I own, regardless of the means through which I did said work. How dare you?!"

Tiny drops of spittle fly from Ngozi's mouth. Her head jerks so much that her hair slides to cover half her face. The old woman smiles deeper than before, her eyes wide with glee.

"Like mother, like daughter. Just bring any money you have like that. I need to get out of this sun before I melt and you Lagos people come and eat me for money ritual."

The old woman attempts to slide the mirror through the half-open car window but it is too narrow. Ngozi opens her purse, confused at her outburst, discomforted by the presence of the old woman. She turns around and expects the woman to be gone, but she's still standing there holding the mirror in one hand. Her right palm is stuck out, wrinkled and darkened with dyes unknown. Money enters into it. It snaps shut. Ngozi opens the car door and collects the mirror, which is much heavier than it looks.

When she shuts the door and looks up, the woman is gone. Ngozi realizes with a shiver that she knew her name.

Entrance

Near midnight; after five hours in traffic, Ngozi finally arrives in her estate with its large pastel houses and sleeping flame-of-the-forest trees.

The small house seems to be gazing down on her, judging her as usual. She had been overjoyed when Chief Ireke had told her she could stay in one of his many real-estate assets, as long as only the two of them knew the secret, but within one week of living in the house, she started having a strong sense that the house did not want her. Her mantra concerning living in the house was ''til agency'. All she needed to do was send her new Sogo Quadri embossed portfolio to the Agency and have Chief Ireke pull some strings and soon she'd be off, gliding down the biggest runways in the world and rising above where she came from.

She slots all her new clothes onto racks deep inside her walk-in closet, which is bigger than the room she had shared with Mama in Enugu. She leans against the door and sends Sogo and Tobi brief messages to let them know she is home safe. She goes back to the car and retrieves the mirror. Ngozi enters the house and sits on her bed with the mirror. Its gilded edges are a bit dusty and the mirror itself is not as clean as it had been when she had first seen it. She finds a small blue towel and some cleansing fluid and starts wiping. The frame of the mirror seems to be richer with detail now – there are four women at the corners and between them float thin leaves, lush flowers, excited goats, sleeping dogs, fish schools and a sun and a moon. The women are depicted as busts, dressed impeccably in traditional scarves and heavy necklaces. Their eyes are judging sapphire dots, the only jewels in the entire frame.

Ngozi continues to wipe the mirror till it is clean but she is not satisfied. It still looks a bit clouded. She goes over it again and again until she has a rhythm. In the fluorescent light, she sees her perfection reflected. Her jawline and slim neck, those cheekbones and that powerful nose, the forehead fit for a diadem and eyes like some unfound jewel.

She wipes and wipes until her bicep begins to flutter in pain, but she cannot stop staring at the mirror, her reflection, the detail in the frame. At this point, she is so sure there is a river of molten gold flowing through the whole frame if she squints right.

She continues to wipe the mirror in circles.

^

Ngozi jolts out of sleep.

She has no memory of having slept. No idea of when she put the mirror down. She looks around and sees it hanging on the wall behind the bed. The old square mirror that loved to show her all her imperfections is gone. The room is different, cold. The white lights have been dimmed to a low blue, just how she likes it, and a rippling wind seems to be blowing through the entire house making a low moaning sound.

"This A/C has started again." She whispers to herself as she rolls onto her knees to stare into the mirror again. It is set at the perfect height. From where she kneels, she can see her face. If she had been mesmerized before, now she is fully in awe.

This is the perfect light. In it her physical beauty has become something else entirely. If anyone sees her face, bathed tenderly in this cold blue, it would be a bullet, a trigger to a rush of blood that would cause spontaneous combustion. She moves closer to the looking glass. Her face becomes bigger and more perfect. All those pores around the nose and the one pimple that makes her stay indoors on some days; they are completely gone.

The eyes in the heads of the four women twinkle. Ngozi's eyes twinkle. The feeling comes over her suddenly, as she stands nearly nose to nose with herself in the mirror, thighs quivering from the exertion – a full body blush of infatuation.

She does the next thing that comes to mind without thinking; kissing her reflection, glass cold against her lips, till the lights go out.

II

Pure Ada

It is silent. Unbearably so. The silence is so heavy that it wakes Ngozi from her second sleep. She opens her eyes and sees that she is not in her room. She sits up sharply and looks around.

Ngozi is in a void. Mirrors of various shapes and sizes, framed in intricately crafted gold hang from invisible threads around her, humming faintly in the air. The space around her looks boundless. The floor beneath her is so black she is sure she will fall into it when she stands up. A sound echoes through the space, of cheering human voices, magnified in the void.

Ngozi stands up and dusts off her chemise. She is barefooted as she walks through the mirrors towards the human voices. Her feet land on the void beneath her like it is made of frail glass. Most of the mirrors drift in aimless orbit above her, but some are exactly at her eye level.

She passes by one, a perfect square framed in neat gold bricks. A child smiles back at her from the glass, hair styled in clean knots. The child looks unbearably familiar and returns her gesture of cleaning her eyes. The cheers get louder and she turns away, walking faster towards the place in the distance where she can see a cluster of colored bodies moving.

Ngozi is very sure she is in a dream but she can't remember how she got here. There is a way everything feels distant yet unbearably near. She approaches the mob who all have their backs turned to her, clothed in brightly-colored robes and scarves. They all have long luxurious hair. This close to the source of the cheering sound, she can feel just how high, how endless this void is. She is about to tap the nearest person on the shoulder, to ask where she is or what is happening, when the person turns around.

Ngozi is standing face to face with a replica of herself.

She sucks in a deep breath, eyes wide, chest tight with shock. The replica looks at her and does the same. The cheering stops. The bodies all turn around to look at Ngozi. They are all replicas of Ngozi, though varying in height and weight and skin tone. It is undeniable that she is the blueprint and base material from which they are created. After staring at her with empty eyes for not more than sixty seconds, they turn back to continue cheering at what they were before. Ngozi feels goosebumps rise under her skin till it feels like ants are crawling through her.

Ngozi moves closer and looks to what lies inside the circle, what the replicas are shouting at. Her hand moves to her mouth in a silent gasp:

She and Sogo Quadri stand, side profiles washed in the deep red light of a darkroom. Ngozi sees herself snap her fingers and watches a gasp of fire erupt out of her palm. Sogo Quadri shivers and steps backwards. The crowd cheers. They don't murmur or speak any words, just a loud chorus, yeeeeeeeeeaa!

The Ngozi in the circle, bathed in red light is saying something very quietly, but her body language is all threat. She wears a long skintight black dress that tapers at the ankles. Her hair is a slippery flow of braids instead of fine Brazilian silk.

Ngozi watching, who believes that she is the original Ngozi, has never made fire with her fingers before. She watches as Sogo hands over a thick brown envelope to her replica. Somehow, she knows she's looking through a living window into the real world. Sogo is handing over the portraits from their last shoot, including negatives. She can see her name written on it with black ink in his handwriting. *Ngozi N.* As the envelope touches Ngozi in the circle's hand, she puts her palm to Sogo's chest. He spasms as if electrocuted and sinks to the floor, his long dada spread out.

Ngozi in the Circle turns and looks straight at Ngozi Watching. She crosses out of the darkroom into the void and heads straight towards her, heels clicking and echoing through the emptiness. All the Ngozis part for her to pass.

She stops in from of Ngozi Watching. "Burn your idols." She hears herself say softly.

The envelope in Ngozi in the Circle's hand catches fire and disintegrates slowly, so Ngozi can see the film rolls and the large pictures of her face turn to ash.

"It's a dream. It's a dream. This is a dream!" She squeezes her eyes shut and shakes her head from left to right.

The other Ngozis begin to float. Their bodies turn soft as silk, billowing and folding and twisting in the air as they are pulled back into the orbiting mirrors by some unseen force. Only the two Ngozis are left.

Ngozi that Burned smiles at Ngozi who thinks she is dreaming. A diamond glints in her nose. She puts a hand on Ngozi Dreaming's shoulder. They both rise, folding and billowing into the oval mirror.

The four mothers who circle its frame are smiling.

Shatter

The two Ngozis pour out of the mirror to stand in the master bedroom in Chief Ireke's white house. The Ngozi with the Braids who Burned the Pictures whispers in singsong, looking into her eyes. "Row, row, row your boat, gently down the stream...mmm..mmmn...mnn..mmm...life is but a dream."

At the end of the song, she breaks into powdered glass. The glittering mass of her body flows back, dissolving into the pure plane of the mirror. Ngozi sits on the bed. Her head feels a hundred times bigger and her body is wound tight as a doll's.

She sits there till morning comes.

Nkiru

When the sun breaks her out of her fixation, she picks up the phone and calls Nkiru. She can't call Tobi. He is always busy building new software, to make enough money to get her away from Chief Ireke. If she told him what was happening, he'd say she was doing 'the dreaming awake thing' again and would tell her to go do research on the internet or read a book.

She and Nkiru became friends the day she came to see Chief Ireke for the first time. Nkiru had been the last on a line of prospective new brides until Ngozi arrived. The moment they exchanged greetings and a few words, it felt like they had known each other forever. They had both been chosen to move to the next stage, where they both got to see the Chief face to face. Ngozi had been chosen by Ireke. Nkiru had been chosen too, as a gift for Ireke's best friend, Okoro.

"Hello." Ngozi croaks into the phone.

"Ngo-ngo! My friend. See how you just forgot us. How are you now? Hope the Chief is treating you right?"

"Nkiru, I think I'm in trouble."

"Ehn! What happened? Did you and Chief fight?" Ngozi can hear the rustle of cloth as Nkiru shifts her body.

"I bought a mirror in traffic."

Nkiru knocks in threes on the gate many times before Ngozi stands up from her bed. There was no gateman, for safety purposes. It only made the house seem more like a tomb. Ngozi pulls open the heavy black metal and Nkiru is standing holding her belly. Short gold curls rest around her head. She is wearing a long floral dress, white and streaked with green leaves and thorns. Nkiru is at least six months pregnant.

"Baby'm!" She exclaims as soon as she is inside the compound and Ngozi has locked the gate behind her. She pulls Ngozi into a hug. Ngozi feels like she hasn't blinked her eyes in twenty-four hours, but in the warmth of Nkiru's embrace, her eyelids shut and the bliss of closing her eyes, of having someone around who cares for her, makes tears fall. Nkiru pulls back to look into her face.

"You look like you've seen a..no...several ghosts. Let's go inside."

They walk straight to the bedroom. Ngozi's feet feel heavy. The room is bright. Sunlight flows over the overgrown garden behind the house and through the wall window. It reveals the smoothness of the unused bed and the dent where Ngozi sat all night, mind whirling at the brink of breaking. The mirror sparkles brightest. It catches the sun and seems to pulse with a life of its own. Nkiru stops moving the moment she sees it.

"Blood of Jesus. Blood. Of. Jesus! Ngozi, you cannot tell me that you saw this thing and brought it into this house with your own two hands?"

"I didn't know. It was just so out-of-this-world, so beautiful." Ngozi is on the verge of tears. "Please just help me get rid of it." Nkiru, though the third wife of a Chief, is a devout Christian, complete with holy water and anointing oil. She also happens to believe in at least one hundred and one superstitions from various parts of Nigeria. She holds her stomach and sighs. "This will be very stressful for Eze. He's practically pulling on my placenta to get me to run out of here."

Nkiru sits on the sofa opposite the bed, beneath a yellow and blue painting of a Lagos that seems to be melting into its own heat. "Go and bath first. Pray while you are at it too 'cause that's what I'll be doing here."

Ngozi turns and walks into the bathroom. A full-length mirror stands just inside. Her skin is dry and her eyes seem to now be permanently wide in shock. Her weave remains lustrous. She walks into the bathroom just as Nkiru's prayers begin to fill the house, sacred whispers.

Ngozi has forgotten how to pray.

When she returns, head and body wrapped in soft white towels, Nkiru is standing at the edge of the bed, looking into the mirror.

"This is no ordinary mirror o." She rubs her stomach again. "It's a gate, a window to somewhere else. There is...it might even be more than that. There are presences held within it, banished things."

Ngozi moisturizes while Nkiru wonders aloud.

"Now, I would say we should involve a pastor or at least someone with basic spiritual knowledge, but I wouldn't be surprised if they try to harm us and steal it. This sh-," She points at the mirror as Ngozi slides into a knee-length black dress, "is pulsing so wildly that I want to steal it too. God, I look more beautiful than I have ever looked and somehow the more I look, the finer I get and the closer I want to move towards it. Are you ready?"

"Yes." Ngozi pulls the flow of her hair into a ponytail and winds it around the rubberband till it becomes a bun. Her voice is devoid of life.

"You can't destroy or drown these things, they only come back stronger. We must bury it deep, as far away from here as we can. Bring that towel." Ngozi hands over a wet white towel.

Nkiru climbs the bed and walks on her knees to the mirror. She begins to pray hard under her breath as she throws the wet towel over the mirror and lifts it off the wall. She hands it to Ngozi, whose eyes go even wider as she collects it, like it's a hissing snake.

"Let's go."

***

They drive to Sango, Ota in the neighboring state. On their way there, Ngozi calls Sogo Quadri and gets a friend sounding somber on the phone. Sogo is in a coma and not likely to come out anytime soon. Doctors suspect some ill-mixed chemicals from his work in the darkroom. Ngozi closes her eyes, she sees the Ngozi from the Void touch Sogo Quadri. Sees him fall. She switches off her phone.

In Sango, they drive onto one of those stretches of wild land at the side of the Lagos-Ibadan Expressway that no one owns. The cars rush deeper into the West behind them, trying to be one with the wind.

Nkiru and Ngozi carry the mirror between them, down a path, until they find a patch where fresh grass grows beneath some trees. The earth is soft as butter and Ngozi's heels sink in and cause her to stumble and fall. She lies on the ground helpless and limp. Nkiru tries to help her up, her swollen belly making it an impossible task. Ngozi slips off her heels and stands up. She throws them into the deeper bush with a long rough scream that she seems to have been holding in since she returned to her room from the void. Nkiru jumps and holds her unborn.

They use thick branches to burrow into the sticky clay, getting stains on their dresses. They set the mirror, still wrapped in the towel into the shallow grave and with their bare hands they push large clods of soil onto the glass and gold, stomping the mound flat with their feet in a near-dance.

Ngozi drives them back to Lagos. Her eyes stare into nothing as she speeds down the Expressway too fast.

III
Boys Named Tobi Have Delicious Hearts

Ngozi walks barefooted and mud-stained into the house, alone. She can still hear Nkiru's car driving off. It is night. The compound is completely dark and she can barely see her way over to the front door. She enters the house and shuts the door behind her, turning on her phone torch. A ray of blue-white light falls before her. She stumbles to her room and falls on the bed. Every joint and muscle in her body sighs. She means to stand up, to walk out back to the switch that turns on the generator. It would have taken less than thirty seconds, but she is too tired to move a muscle. Instead, she falls into a dreamless sleep.

She wakes up cold again. The electricity hasn't come back on and the air-conditioning is off, but the room is bathed in a familiar deep blue light and a chill blows over Ngozi in waves. She sits up from the bed.

The mirror is back. It hangs up in the air at the foot of her bed like a faithful pet, waiting to be stroked. Ngozi still dizzy from her sleep doesn't register its presence at first. She shifts forward till her legs are hanging off the edge of the bed. She rubs her forearms, wipes her face, and hangs her head low. She looks up. The gold frame gleams like silver in the strange blue light. Ngozi stands up and her face fills the glass of the mirror.

Dread runs through her as she beholds the perfection of her face again. She knows she is not looking at herself but something that has taken her form. Something whose home is within the void of the mirror. The thing that has turned her perfect in its image beckons. Her stomach is one big knot but she doesn't grimace, that would ruin the beauty. She turns her face left and right, trying to get the best angle, posing in the dim light that turns her dark skin into sapphire dust.

Her nose hits the glass. She can't remember moving towards it. She looks into her eyes in the mirror. They are twin pools of nothing. She kisses herself again. Her tongues slide over one another like cold tentacles.

***

Ngozi is flat on her back in the void. The mirrors hang static as stars. The gang of Ngozis remain on the near-horizon. This time, there is no out-of-rhythm cheering. She stands and walks across the fragile nothing again, her black dress fluttering in the stillness. The selves stand in a neat circle, silent as air, watching the center.

Her mirror is hanging in the center of the circle. She watches herself emerge, like a newborn, from the mirror hanging in her room, clad in breathtaking red satin cut to the middle of her thigh. Her hair is short and in neat waves. Large rubies drip from her ears. She walks out of the house, moving through doors and walls. She is not incorporeal, the air just seems to part for her.

She walks through the car and onto the street. On the street, she stands still and the earth carries her in a blur to a house in Lekki Phase One, past a flurry of streetlights and car headlights. Ngozi shudders. She knows who the replica is going to look for. She enters the gate and walks up the stairs to Tobi's door.

Tobi opens the door and smiles with mischief when he looks her up and down. She doesn't smile back. Instead, she rubs her hand down his rough stubbly cheek. He moves to kiss her. She turns her cheek, then walks deeper into the apartment to sit on the couch.

"What's wrong?" he asks, voice raspy and face soft.

"Nothing." She says. "Come lay in my lap."

He comes around and does as she says. She begins to rub his chest and belly, sliding her hand further down with every breath. He falls into the sensations. She stops rubbing and places a hand on his chest, then she begins to push down, building pressure until Tobi jerks awake and puts a hand up to her wrist.

"What are you doing?" he asks.

"A late dinner." She responds. Her fingers sink into his body. Blood spreads across his singlet and his eyes widen, then fill with tears as she grasps his beating heart and pulls it out, ending his life in a gasp.

Ngozi in Red stands up and Tobi falls heavy to the rug. She turns and looks straight at where Ngozi is standing in the circle of the void watching, her face wet with tears. Ngozi watching feels completely numb.

Ngozi in Red walks out of the apartment, the heart in her fist like a heathen ruby. In one breath, Ngozi in Red crosses out of Lagos into the void.

She walks up to Ngozi and takes a bite of the heart. She offers the second bite to Ngozi. Ngozi clamps her teeth shut and begins to shake her head vigorously, as if to dispel the nightmare she stands in. Tears flow down her face.

"You must consume your beloved's heart, or your emergence will be incomplete." Ngozi in Red tells Ngozi Crying.

The Ngozis in the Circle turn soft and light as silk again. They begin to flow and billow into their respective mirrors till only the two Ngozis are left. Ngozi looks up, like there is a god in the sky of the void. She sees nothing but mirrors glinting. She falls to her knees, body vibrating with a sudden rush of hunger. She roars and begins to sob raggedly. Ngozi in Red takes another bite of the heart and looks bored.

"You must hurry. The sun rises and the portal will close with you hanging in this middle place."

Ngozi Crying looks up at Ngozi in Red. She can't seem to understand or accept this fate. She rises to her feet. Something is coming, walking slowly out of the darkness behind Ngozi in Red. A giantess with eyes of blue light.

"They must not meet us here. Eat!" Ngozi in Red is suddenly frantic. Ngozi Crying pulls the fist of the replica to her lips and takes a slimy bite.

It is delicious.

Following

Ngozi wakes up when the sun is high in the sky and the mirror is back on the wall behind the bed. She calls Tobi and the phone rings and rings till she collapses back into bed. She doesn't bother to tell Nkiru any of the new developments. The aftertaste of Tobi's heart burns her tongue. Chief Ireke had also told her to never call him when he is out of the country. The only person left to call is Mama. She throws the phone at the glass wall that leads to the garden and a long crack smiles back.

She walks out of the house without bathing. Her long hair slithers behind her. Ngozi drives back to where she bought the mirror. She parks her car in the middle of the road and stands, barefooted, waiting. The sun causes her to sweat but she does not move. The old woman with the melted skin does not return.

She enters her car and drives back home, back to the mirror.

When she gets home, it is evening and she is tired. She walks into the bathroom and showers. When she exits, her mother is standing in the center of the room, at the foot of her bed, looking into the mirror. "Mama!" Ngozi shouts, hand on a heart ready to jump out of her throat.

Her mother vanishes. Ngozi sinks to the floor.

Nkiru comes by before it is night. She is not surprised to see the mirror has returned. She is cold and sober in a way Ngozi has never seen her. Ngozi tells her about seeing Mama in the room but not about eating Tobi's heart. Nkiru says it is time for her to return to the village and ask for her mother's forgiveness.

IV

Sever

Ngozi wakes up for the last time. The room is cold and blue. The mirror is hanging in front of her face when she sits up. Her face stares back hard as a jewel. The tumbling of her gut that started when she first slipped into the void is gone, replaced by shards of ice. She kisses her looking glass and is pulled into the void.

Ngozi who burnt her idols and Ngozi who ate Tobi's heart are waiting for her, flanking the mirror. There is a fire burning in a floating calabash in the center of the circle. All the other Ngozis watch, their long hair turning their faces into shadow. Ngozi stands up.

"I want to see Mama." She says to no one in particular.

The Ngozis flanking her; one with braids and one with rubies in her ears walk up to the fire in the calabash and bring it to her, both of them holding it at chest level with poise. They speak to her with her voice doubled.

"We thought you'd never ask. We might have eaten your friend's baby next to get you to know that Anwulika desired to see you."

Anwulika is her mother's name.

"Hold the fire" They say. Ngozi who bought the mirror places a hand under the calabash. The other two leave it for her. It is hotter than a furnace but she cannot take her hand away from it. It seems to be eating her fingers raw. She shudders in pain as her other hand rises up to stick beneath the calabash holding the fire. She feels a strong force inside the mirror pull her into its mouth, dragging her legs across the empty floor of the void, even as she begins to cry, "Mama, please. I can't do this! Please"

Her body is bent over in agony. She doesn't want to belong to her mother. The fire in the calabash that is eating her hands is moving, dragging her forward without any care for her legs.

Nne

Back in the void, the Sisterhood departs. They are now themselves, no longer reflections and replicas of Ngozi. Some of them are men. They are all beautiful enough to crack glass. They hang her mirror on high, adding it to the constellation of Ugegbe Nwa.

Anwulika

Ngozi falls out of a mirror, empty-handed. Her palm is covered in burns. Sobbing, she holds her hand to her chest and kneels up.

It is morning wherever they are. Mama's eyes are shut and she sits on a large rock in the center of a cold, round room. Ngozi stands up and looks around. A mirror of the mirror she bought hangs right at Mama's eye level. Inside it she sees a black void.

She turns to her mother who is dressed in all her finery like she is going for a great party. Her neck gleams with gold and sapphires.

"Mama?" Her voice sounds too loud in her ears after she has spoken. There is a heavy silence in the hut. Her mother doesn't respond. She remains still and her eyes remain shut.

Ngozi looks around. From the corner of the room, someone stares back – the woman who sold her the mirror, smiling with dripping black teeth.

The Visions of Atanda Ekun

Ariyike

The man did not remember when time dissolved into nothing.

He remembered coming into the heavy black house that seemed to have been carved from the heart of an evil god, long dead. He remembered his wife coming in to see him. She had worn ruby aso-oke shot through with gold. Her wrists and neck were caked in milky gems and the petals of her gele reached far into the darkness above.

Her mouth was shiny red fruit, splitting when she spoke to him.

Atanda, she said, *pull yourself together and come home*. She tilted her slim regal neck in a gesture he recognized. *The children need you, there is only so much comfort I can offer. Your mother cries daily for you, she won't leave our home, she believes you have become just like your father.*

The man couldn't talk, his tongue betrayed him and he wanted to be away from her as much as possible. Ariyike, his serpent wife clothed in false compassion. *Give me a few days*, he had whispered, *I might finally do it today. The words have told me of their coming, I just have to be there when they arrive.*

She hissed, full of poison and barely masked contempt. Her eyes had hardened. *You had better be there, I will leave if you don't come home in seven days, it's only fair, and you have been here for close to seven years.*

I'm trying, he had tried to say, tried to convey the viscous heaviness in words. They had failed him.

You are weak! She spat and shot up from the stool, a scarlet explosion in the room's dreary air. *A simpleton! A slave to your mind!*

Be quiet, Ariyike! The man had whispered harshly, as if to prevent his wife from stirring things forth from the blackened walls. *Leave if you wish, but do not come here to gloat.*

She left, trailing her fingers down the black and white teeth of the large shiny piano. Her final impression, a sour D minor.

He retreated back into the shadows. They comforted him, hid him, erased him.

Ori

The man was always still.

His shoulders sloped in distress, his hair crusted with flecks of white. He was still before he came to the house, and he remained still within the house. His stillness was one borne of a belief in existential futility. His thin bones sloped in a ragged sketch of inner solitude.

He was still while he ate and still while he worked. He was still in the streets even as humanity fireworked around him in an eruption of boisterous voices and bending bodies.

In this stillness, his mind would flee to places no one else could ever dream to glimpse. Sky castles and flying leviathans and dark maidens and dreamt wars. He was alone as he beheld these wonders, and he believed that this was why he was trapped in the house; he had gotten some dream out and they had seen.

He was still as he sat alone in a room at a table carved from the same heavy blackness as the walls. Light was a dim afterthought and the blank sheet before him stared back relentlessly, its emptiness a white judgement.

His fingers would pinch a dripping quill between thumb and forefinger for brief moments, waiting on something to come lancing electric through the air.

When nothing happened they returned, sweaty and nervous, to his thighs.

Give them one and they let you go. How long have you been here? His mind was berating him again, whispering confusion. Dread began to pool in his spine. *You like it here, don't you? Lost in nothing but this fever of a house, dwelling in the hot stink of your own sweat and cowardice.*

She came out of the shadows, an antithesis to his rigidity. The red smokesilk that was always wrapped around her, billowed across the floor and walls, rasped over the table, pooled around the typewriter. Ori, muse with skin dark as beaten bronze cut through the air like a scarlet feather, whispering words and murmuring thoughts in singsong. The air was ripe with the smell of charged metals and dark joy.

Atanda, beloved sorrowful one. Wild tiger of the pages, ferocious hunter of words, grasper of the slick and slippery, loosener of the unknown, proclaimer of the unseen, revealer of the seen. Your mind falters.

The man struck senseless by the nymph who vibrated with vitality before him lowered his eyes, sinking even deeper into sadness, unable to speak.

Come alive, Ekun! She trilled as she hopped in a dance of grace to sit before him, she drank deeply from the goblet she held, tossing her head back to drain it for what seemed like an eternity. Her arms were girded in curls of beaten gold and her eyes when she looked back at him, burned black. *You do not know what you find solace with in here, Atanda. Those intoxicating darknesses. Dangerous little fuckers. You do not even know where you are, or what you are. Take a walk.*

The Fathers put me here, they know me, where I am, who I am. He had tried to say, to explain their coming, their ownership of his soul. *I cannot dare to deviate, Ori. Do you want to put me in trouble?*

She giggled drunkenly, and turned her shorn head skywards. *You foolish men. Slaves to minor thought and unnecessary worry. I believe my job is done here, for this current cycle of madness anyway. If you fail to do as I say, I may never return. I fear your head erodes.* Then, she swam up into the dark of the ceiling, trailing volumes of silk like a bird of paradise and echoing beatitudes in that sweet voice of honey and smoke.

Iku

The man's head was an animal.

It roared and writhed and spat. He heard the muse and the Fathers. He spoke to himself in voices he didn't know he had, as he roamed the house lost. There were cathedrals within the house, with idols and symbols he had never seen, corridors that stretched into nothing like rivers of blood, rooms filled with screams and rooms leaking fear.

The quill fallen from his fingers to stain the red carpet like a weapon lost in battle. He kicked walls that breathed and screamed. He ripped at his hair as madness coursed through him.

He broke chandeliers of black glass and upended tables piled with strange food.

Then he stepped outside.

He was in a forest.

One so still, he could feel the blood coursing through his veins, feel his pulses beat to ancient rhythm, feel his heart dance in air that was neither night nor day. A light, deep blue and cold, bathed everything in watery relief.

The man moved forward, his feet crunching in fallen leaves, the trees rose sleek and branchless to his right and left and disappeared into the sky beyond his craned neck. The earth of the path he followed was smooth and white as a picked bone. He walked, marveling at the silence that rang in his ears like an eternal gong and at the strange white motes that danced on the air.

The forest watched him with many eyes.

If it isn't the scribe, Atanda. The man turned around and beheld a skeleton, tall as two men. Death had a cheerful voice. He wore an abeti aja of obsidian silk upon his finely cracked cranium. His eyes were pits of foul darkness and from his mouth came the rot of a thousand bodies. The man's soul shook, making his limbs tremble. *Be still, I am not here to harm.* Death's marionette-ing bones shone with the slime of sweltering sickness. *You called me, friend. Of all the souls, wriggling in the pit like maggots in fear of my wake, you shone like a bulb.* He flickered, hanging from tree branches, and melting away into shadows and whispering from one place and all spaces. The man didn't attempt to look up at all, he was as he had always been, afraid.

I can show it to you, you're safe as long as the Fathers will. Your Chariot awaits. A warship foul with termites and black worms and gold trim hung atop a shuddering black cloud, amongst the trees behind him.

He lifted a heavy arm to be taken

and the words came.

A swirling cloud of dusky white and black moths, flowing against each other in litanies. They crashed through the ribs of Death and through the dead cabins of the armada. Soft wings chuckling, they moved on heading straight for the house, for his blank pages.

He ran like he had never done in his life
and Death watched him leave.

Awon Baba Wa

They came on snow lions, decked in heavy red agbadas with lines of gold coiled around necks and ankles like fed serpents. The Fathers. One, thin and limby as a starving tree, the other, round like a tomato ripe to burst. They walked somber like funeral walkers, and swarmed around the man in his chair. Tossing cowries upon the man and reading truths in the constellations they made upon his prone form. Elere, the thinner, drew his brittle neck back with a snap! *You ventured into the night,* he said. *Broke a hundred rules and shattered a hundred laws.* Itage, the rotund, screeched. *You spoke to Him. You shouldn't speak to Him, he will cause you to rot!*

Show the words to us. Elere presented spidery hands to receive. His oblong skull tilted curiously. The man jumped off the chair. *I have nothing for you. I will give you nothing. You are ticks upon my mind. Slowly draining my soul of fire.*

He very slowly flipped the bird, and then vanished into nothing.

Aye

The man and the darknesses— now twin bears that seemed

sculpted from furry dark, walked the wilderness of his mind endlessly. Through eternal valleys that stank of death and windy woods that whispered harsh songs.

Over indigo seas that thrashed with phosphorescent whales and into deserts dry and hot and festering with horrors and scarlet eyes.

They came to a village and they were now his shadow. The people in the village were still as statues under the sparkly light of a forest sun. He moved between them, feeling their emptiness and his emptiness. Their bodies served as fleshy cocoons for the replenishing minds they held.

This was the place of the Clear Sleep and the man moved to join them, to wait, and become suspended in effigy.

Kikelomo Ultrasheen

I: Crown
birthmark

When you are born, your mother, Aduke, cries when she sees your full head of hair because it means you will be abundant. It also means you will grow up to be like her, with soft hair to your shoulders that you will weave, braid, and twist into new forms as inspiration strikes and you learn what beauty means to you.

She sees herself teaching you all the secrets of adimole, hair-weaving; the way to work the warp and weft of a cornrow from hairline to nape, the oils and butters and dyes to blend into the styles to make the finished crown shine. She sees herself seated between your thighs, and your fingers, which are barely longer than her fingernails now, grown long, strong, and pliant, weaving her long locks into gorgeous ridges.

She names you Kikelomo — caring is for the child.

She kisses your tender, crumpled face and rubs her palm across your scalp. Your baby hair feels like silk. Beneath your scalp, right in the center of your head, against the pale pink of newborn flesh, is a perfect circle of coal-black skin. When Aduke sees this, her gentle tears stop flowing and her mouth dries up. She lifts you and looks into your eyes, her joy turned sour.

A black moon against your skull means you will not belong to her long enough. She holds you to her breast, shuts her eyes, and prays, prays that they never see you.

puff-puff

You are two years old. Your scalp is still very tender and Aduke fears it will split like overripe fruit if she pulls too hard. The black moon remains against your scalp, unchanging. Your hair is too slippery to be woven, so she uses a coconut-and-mango paste to massage your head, then she splits your hair into rows and cuts these rows into small squares out of which puffs, bound in rubber thread, rise.

Baba says when he sees you, "My daughter is now a big girl, she can carry puff-puff!" He carries you and throws you into the air. His back aches from long hours of continuous farmwork and weekly travel between the village of Iludun and Lagos.

Your squeals of joy keep him going.

koroba

Your hair grows faster than normal but your scalp remains soft. The first time Aduke tried to weave your hair, you cried for hours and spots around the baby cornrow had swollen with tiny boils. She waits two more years before she tries again.

Koroba is her first choice because it won't pull on your hairline and stress your edges like shuku. Your hair is plaited, out in a radial pattern from the center of your head, then down, to fall off the rim of your hairline like the legs of a spider.

By now, you are beginning to pay attention as your mother makes hair in Arewa, her beauty shop. Your brittle blonde dolls suffer from your repetitive attempts to mimic her. Baba is still busy farming in Iludun and then traveling to Lagos to sell his produce. When you finally get an image of him fixed in your mind, it is of a white-haired man, thin, tired, and tall, who fondly calls you Kiki through tobacco-stained teeth.

adiseyin

You can now plait your mother's hair just as she imagined when you were born, but it is still rough, the work of novice fingers. You try to weave her hair into adiseyin, "all back." Aduke carries your handiwork around like that and proudly shows it off to her customers. In adiseyin, the even rows go across the head from the front hairline all the way to the nape of the neck, but your splitting of the rows is uneven and some are bigger than others.

Aduke does the same adiseyin for you but her version is mathematical and clean. Your hair gleams and all your friends want to touch your all back to feel the firmness and texture of the plait against their fingers.

You girls are at that age where you now watch out for hairstyles to tell your mothers and sisters to replicate, even more than you care about the English and math books you are being taught from in the primary school on the outskirts of Iludun. You are discovering beauty atop the heads of the women you see every day. Their crowns rise and pour down their backs; some simple, some intricate, all gloss.

Your mother gets more customers by using your head to show off her skill, and you keep your eyes open for what grows out of the tops of the heads of the women of Iludun, to know what other hairdressers, from far and near, are capable of. You telegraph what you see to your mother with charcoal sketches on the wall at the back of the house.

ipako elede

Adiseyin in reverse. The plaits start from the nape and ride up to finish in curls across the forehead. Above your direct gaze, eyes black and clear. The back of your head is revealed, fragile, smooth, and ready to be palmed by those you allow.

You are sixteen and no longer going to primary school. You have your own room in the house, a cement bungalow built by someone who studied Urban Planning at a Lagos polytechnic. After the low verandah, a door leads straight into a long corridor that opens onto four rooms. One for you, one for Aduke, one for Baba, and one empty.

There is one boy who works for your father. He is brave and always sweaty and funny. His name is Ade. He rubs the back of your ipako elede, down to your neck when you join him under the mango tree you have marked as a meeting spot. This makes you feel warm down to your toes. He promises you a sweet life in the future.

You both like to listen to the rush of the highway that lies on the outskirts of the village, alive in the distance, loud like plenty falling water. He dreams of Lagos for the both of you, but he's too much a son of Iludun to really want it.

You only meet on nights when the moon is full and can cast its chalky light on Iludun's overgrown paths. Fireflies settle on his forehead and the wide arm of his buba as crickets' night music erupts around you both. Ade's mother has been sick for many seasons and all her hair has fallen out. His father had left when he was barely a boy, leaving him to become her sole caretaker.

You hold him in your arms and sing to him. You promise to always be with him and to never let him go. This is your first love. As you sing this song, the black moon tingles against your scalp, squirming in cold spirals.

After you kiss his nose and his neck good-bye, you are on your way back to the village square which is where your mother's beauty shop is located. You can always be sure that once you break out onto the path that leads to the square, you'll be guided toward the shop by the flickering glow of lanterns that light up the low cuboid Baba built with his hands, the space that you know as a second home, always humming with a chorus of women talking.

The moon is full and your heart wells for Ade's predicament. You are halfway between your mother's shop and the tree where you have just left him with his head in his hands. Sauntering through sparse bush flush with whispering knee-high grass that you pluck and crush between your fingers, you feel a frisson across your neck and lift your head to see it gleaming in the air.

Your heart stops and you begin to blink rapidly.

A gleaming black moon eats up the space before you, bathed in the light of the pale one far above. It is hanging perfectly in midair, a few feet above the dry grass beside the path you stand on. The deep hum it emits sends out waves that cause the grass under it to ripple in reverse.

You stand and watch, heart beating, eyes riveted by the sight before you. The black moon doesn't seem to spin or move, nor does it make any other sound besides the *omomomommmomomo* that it steadily emits. You take a few steps closer to it, stepping off the path, letting the grass scratch your calves.

Closer. You can see that it is not a solid black like charcoal but blue-black like a dye pit. As you stand riveted, cold water fills the follicles of your hair, pouring out of the moon in the center of your head.

patewo

You wait for a few weeks, till it is night and you and your mother are alone—cooking egusi, eran-igbe, and iyan for Baba, who has just returned from a farming trip to Lagos. You try many times until it slips out of your mouth in an unsure whisper.

"Ma'ami, I saw a black moon."

You have dreamt about it every night since the day you first set eyes on it. It sometimes speaks to you in the rough voice of a beast, asking that you kneel and offer your hair. Mostly it is quiet, big and high in the sky, emitting a low blue light that turns everything it touches into indigo monochrome, like the world has suddenly been flooded with aro kiun from the dye pits of the sorceresses who make adire. Once, it breaks open and a mass of darkly glowing women fall out of it onto the dry grass of the field where you first saw it.

Aduke freezes where she is stirring egusi into the palm oil and pepper sauce. She turns her head slowly. Her patewo is old. Its once-neat lines are fuzzy with white and gray overgrowth.

"What did you just say, Kikelomo?" She looks straight into your eyes, still stirring the pot.

The soup fills the air with a fecund beefy aroma. Palm oil smoke stings your eyes.

"I saw a black moon . . . I was out in the field, just off the forest . . . and it was late, but it was there, Ma'ami. It stayed in the air and was humming. I felt something like cold water flow *inside* my hair as I looked at it. It was the strangest thing. Like a dream. But it was real, I know."

Your mother covers the pot of thick yellow soup. She sits on a low block of wood close to you. She looks into your eyes again.

"What were you doing out in those bushes so late? Are you sure you didn't drink something from that boy you have been following up and down? Did you hear any voices? Did you see anybody inside it?" You say no to all her questions.

She continues talking in the low tone of secrets. Her breath touches your ear as the firewood beneath the soup occasionally crackles, sending up showers of sparks. She sighs. A *hmmmn* that comes from a place deeper than her belly.

"You have been seen, omo mi." Her voice trembles.

You exhale and try to prevent your stomach from knotting. Tales of those "seen" by irunmole or orisha never end well. Their aftermaths always reek of misfortune, sacrifice, unspeakable labors.

"I told you no one said anything to me. It was quiet. I even left it there, after my ears started paining me. I came to Arewa and helped you with some work before we went home that night."

"And you didn't tell me. Have you started dreaming of it yet?" she asks. She shifts her attention to the black pot bubbling.

You freeze at her question. She stands up from beside you. You can hear the gurgle of the soup and the hiss of water on coals as she uncovers the pot again. "Yes. Many times." Another *hmmmn*. She tastes the soup and smacks her lips.

"They will be back in time." Her tone is no longer hushed. You wonder who *they* are. The host of bodies, slimy as newborn snakes that poured out of the egg of the moon? Or something else entirely, something larger than the black moon, larger than the endless night sky?

"Your grandmother was chosen by Onidiri, too." You do not know your grandmother well. She died before you were born but she managed to hand all the secrets of adimole, the art of woven hair, to Aduke, your mother. "It was wonderful at first, her . . . gifts, but in the end, Onidiri took more than they gave."

"What is Onidiri? Isn't that just the ordinary name for people like us who weave hair?" Aduke adds chopped pumpkin leaves to the thick yellow soup in the pot and she gestures for you to help her hold it so she can stir.

You stand, dizzy from sitting for so long. Your mother has never sounded more honest as when she speaks about this Onidiri.

"They started out that way. Asake, your grandmother, says that their core is made up of some of the very first people to touch, understand, and weave hair on this our land. They discovered true power in their craft and could soon shape the workings of the mind by simply touching the head. Onidiri and the people attached to it became a mystery that brought healing and destruction as they moved across the world.

"Eventually, their founding mothers went to be with Olodumare, but not before they had birthed successors by passing on this gift. In time, as the ranks of these founding mothers grew in the Realms Above where our Ancestors Slumber, they began to help their children defy death. They collected them in that nest." Her voice sharpens around *nest*.

You respond to her wealth of information. "You know so much about this thing o." You continue listening intently but she doesn't speak yet, she is still waiting for you to help her with the soup which she is half-leaning toward. When you look at her, she whispers, "They took my mother. She never died or got buried. One day, she said she was going to pluck herbs for a hair soap and she never returned. When I went searching for her, I saw this moon you speak of."

Your hair is loosened and waiting between styles to be shaped into new paths around your head. A cool breeze blows through the kitchen. It slips through your hair till it feels as if cold water is running across your scalp, like on the night of the black moon. You sigh and run your hands through it.

"Please. Hurry. The soup is burning." You look and catch your mother staring at you. Her gaze is hard, like a dog staring at an intruder. It makes you feel like you had been doing something bad.

The soup is stirred; thick with pieces of meat, dried caterpillar, and crayfish. The pounded yam which is wrapped in leaves is unwrapped onto a plate. A big bowl is filled with the delicacy.

You move to go and see if your father is awake but your mother intercepts you.

"Wait. I'll go alone. You might upset him with your . . . Look, Kikelomo, you are my child and I will be honest with you again, you have been . . . seen . . . looked at by them . . . it means you might have been chosen. I should have told you once you were old enough to understand. You are marked. In the center of your head, there is a black moon. Onidiri *will* come for you. Open your eyes and stay awake. There is very little I can do to help you. No babalawo will attempt to sever one who has seen osupa dudu, black moon, nest of Onidiri."

She turns and walks into the house, carrying no firelight. You are perplexed. You want to continue to talk to her, to ask about the mark on your head, ask more questions about your fate now that you have been seen or chosen by this strangeness that feels less real as the days pass, but you can see that she is done talking for the night.

The way her back is stiff and her head held up, ready to face an always-tired husband and the possibility of a child cursed. Her patewo seems to glow white in the night as she goes.

Patewo is when two currents of weaving flow equally from both sides of the head. Their curling tips unite in a ridge at the center of the head, like clapping hands.

shuku

You dream of the black moon. This time small as a sour cherry, floating before your face. You open your mouth. It slips in and you wake up coughing indigo light.

***

Three moons have passed since you first saw Onidiri. The black moon constantly haunts your dreams and the periphery of your vision.

You are at Ade's house. His mother is dead. He rests his head on your shoulder as his body shakes and he holds on to you tighter than he ever has. She died in her sleep, completely hairless, down to her eyelashes. Your heart hurts for him. You do not go inside to see her, but you wait outside his small mud hut every morning for five days, until she is carried out to be buried. The body is wrapped in a mat and your scalp flashes with heat when it passes beside you and Ade on its way to the grave.

***

Your father becomes bedridden. Many moons and seasons after the conversation you and your mother didn't finish, his bones become too brittle to assist with farmwork or travel to Lagos. A delirious fever follows.

Aduke is glued to his side, responding to his every need and mopping his head every other moment. She stops going to Arewa, so managing it is now your responsibility. You and the new apprentice, Bose. Your mother's patewo is still in, now completely buried beneath an overgrowth of white fuzz.

Two babalawo come in shifts, morning and night, dressed in dust-coated dashikis and carrying satchels filled with bark, root, leaf, and tincture. Your father refuses to go to the new hospital.

Ade comes to comfort you. After his mother's death, he has stepped into a bigger role on the farm. It should be perfect as there is more time for you two to spend together, but every time you stand too close to him and he mentions feeling his mother's spirit while gazing into nothing, you take it as an omen. The death he carries on his shoulders seems to be spilling onto you. You can barely look him in the eye, but you share the naked warmth of your bodies.

***

Bose is doing shuku aladimole for you. This style of weaving is thick and broad like a flat, long leaf. The thin central plait is the spine of the leaf and the broad swath of hair on either side of it is the soft, crushable body of the leaf. You are both seated on low stools inside Arewa, alone. It is evening and the air is cool and a bit misty. Under trees and around bushes, children run, chasing the wind and playing tinko.

Bose finishes your hair and oils it. You look in the large hand mirror that she holds up for you. You turn your head this way and that, eyeing the shuku as it pulls your face up, lifting your cheekbones and eyebrows. You rub your hand across the velvet of your smooth neck and press the edges of the plait to test for firmness. Perfect.

You stand up and Bose puts the mirror away. You excuse yourself. It is time to go home and cook for your father and mother. You tuck the day's earnings in the waist of your wrapper and walk home in the dark, slowly thinking about how your mother appears to be fading away along with your father. Your parents who seem to always find a way to love one another even with great distances between them, who always choose a shared silence over words.

You walk into the house and the corridor is filled with the leaning bodies of the two babalawo and your mother's friends. They crowd around the still figure of Aduke, seated on a low stool. Everybody turns toward you as you enter the house and your heart stops.

In the light of the lanterns, you can see death standing to the left, mute in the shadows of their faces.

II: Rectify
afaridan

Your hair is gone, shaved with a sharp, flat razor that nicked you in three places. All that is left is smooth scalp. When your run your fingers over it, it feels like an object apart from you. A large, sweaty egg placed just above your real head. Your long hair has been cut off as part of a rite for Baba's burial. Your mother Aduke's hair is also gone. She cut yours and you cut hers.

It is the third day after Baba's passing.

Every day since Baba died, a lot of people have come by to pay their respects. They bring soup, honey, and warm assurances that you and your mother will survive this. Aduke has been quiet, uttering strangled sounds at the most unfortunate moments and looking only at the door guarding where Baba lays and nowhere else. Her eyes carry all of her hurt and longing. You cannot look her in the face for too long.

You wait for Ade but he doesn't come. Your mind chases memories of him around in circles. You two stopped talking after he became too cold and full of gloom. After his mother's absence finally settled under his skin, inside his head. He was talking a lot about leaving Iludun, just before all he was able to do when you both sat together was stare at you with accusing eyes.

Baba's body is in his room, flat on a mat on his bed, treated with oils and wrapped in pungent leaves and a length of white cloth, waiting to be buried. The house smells bitter from the special bark that the babalawo tell Aduke to not stop burning, and sweet from the rot that is leaking out from inside the wrapped body.

This night, you and your mother retire into the empty room where your mourning has been taking place for two sleepless nights. Aduke's eyes are bloodshot and rimmed with heavy shadows. She has not slept since the first day. The real reason she cannot talk is because her throat is raw from her guttural lamentations. You and she wear nothing but wrappers of black cotton around your chests and eat nothing but eko, corn jelly.

You both sit on the cold floor, ready for another night of weeping and cold winds that whisper. Aduke begins the vigil by letting out a string of stomach-burning wails, calling on Bolaji to return from the land of the dead if he didn't want her to come and meet him shortly. You realize then that you can't feel your own sadness fully because your mother is using up enough air and sorrow for ten people.

You turn to the side and curl up on the cold floor, trying to understand why you still can't feel anything about Baba's death; maybe because you have learned to expect it since the time Ade's mother died, when it took a while for the teeth of loss to sink into his head. Maybe the weight of grief is on hold till you are ready to mourn in your own way.

You doze off, dreaming of the black moon of Onidiri again. It hangs and watches you as you swim in orbit around it in a dance with the iridescent fish of your father's ghost, until a large black bird dives to grab your ear in its beak.

The pain is so sharp and real that you wake up screaming, to find your left ear in your mother's teeth. She growls and shakes her head left and right like a dog with stubborn prey. You shout and saliva fills your mouth as she rips the ear away from your head and spits it out, onto your chest.

The pain erupts in one hot wave, blotting out your mind and making you shut your eyes. You can still hear her in your other ear. She is cursing you, a string of venom burning out of her bloody mouth. She grabs your shoulders and shakes you violently as she spits at you.

"You think I don't know that you killed my husband. Witch! Eater of heads and destinies! You will die and I will be the one to kill you. The two of us will be going to see Bolaji wherever he is today, so you can confess. I don't want to live anymore. Somebody help me. My daughter is a murderer!"

She stands up from where she has knelt on your thighs and screams the end of her tirade at the top of her lungs. There is no light inside the house, excepting the candles in Baba's room, where no darkness must fall until he is buried.

You stand up, blind with pain, and stagger toward her.

You see that she has forgotten you. Now she is hitting her head on the wall beside the door. Hard. The *thuk-thuk-thuk-thuk* of her skull hitting cement makes you feel sick in a way your torn-off ear does not.

You try to stop her. You do. You beg her.

"Ma'ami, please stop, you will injure yourself."

When she stops hitting her head and turns toward you in the empty, lightless room, you can tell that she is gone and something else gleams from inside her eyes. Your mother grips your throat in her hands and begins to squeeze without even looking down at your face. You struggle until you kick her in the knee and she falls hard, back onto the floor, laughing thin and high.

A new panic blooms beneath the numb ache that is burrowing into the side of your head. Onidiri is behind your laughing mother, burning with indigo fire in the dark. A ray of violet light shoots into your chest from the center of the black moon.

After the ray hits you, cold water seems to gush inside, from the top of your head and down your throat to fill your heart. You rise up, listening for the distant rush of the expressway. Your blood is pumping so hard you can almost smell it burning through your veins. Your heart is drumming a thousand beats a minute.

You start to run. You are going to Lagos.

small afro

You run up the slope of the hill and out onto the expressway. Cars stream by bleeding white, amber, and red light over the asphalt. They make a sound like big water. The road snakes down and up ahead, flanked by tall forest. You turn toward where the cars are going and continue to run. With the cold water gushing through you, from head to heart to limbs, you feel like you are flying.

As you run, your hair grows back till it is a small curly afro. You run wild for more than one hour, through the brush and grass on the side of the expressway, refusing to stop even when cars make that loud, piercing noise.

The cold water stops rushing through you and you feel your strength ebb. The black moon that you follow, the one that has floated before you, pulling you with an unseen force, fades into nothing. You collapse onto the ground and your muscles catch on fire.

mohawk

You come to when a man is carrying you into his car. The sides of his head are shaved, and a large comb of blue hair rises down the center. He slides you onto the passenger seat. He smells strong and sweet. His neck is covered in heavy gold chains with sparkling pendants of $ and the word "CUTS" and fists pumping.

When he speaks, his voice is soft: "Just lie back and relax. You ran too far too fast." He gives you a bottle full of a bright orange liquid that fizzes on your tongue, and as you drink it, you can feel the acid in your limbs stop burning.

You sleep.

When you wake up again, you are in Lagos. Every surface is covered with people walking, hosts of okada zooming past, and many danfo belching black smoke. The man, whose beard and moustache are also dyed blue, gives you a black satin dress and tells you to put it on fast. You slip into it, using your mourning cloth as a cover.

"Wait on the bridge. Bisi will come and get you, okay?" he says quietly, with his hand on your back. "Now hurry up and get out. I have several appointments scheduled for the day." Before you slip out of his car, you see that his fingers are stained a royal blue.

jheri curls

You walk up to the pedestrian bridge. Your head feels naked even though your hair is growing fuller. It feels like someone is drawing something on top of your head very slowly. The new hair is all wet. You wrap it up in your mourning cloth and walk into the crowd flowing onto the stairs of the bridge. They push and rush. You don't know where they are going. Every movement your limbs make, makes you want to lie down and cry.

You reach the top of the bridge and walk to the middle to wait. Some people stumble and slam into you. They hiss and give you bad eyes but continue to walk on, rushing nowhere. From up here, you can watch the city stream by beneath the vast hand of the sun.

A woman touches your shoulder after you have been standing long enough to watch the stream of people become small and big and small again. She is wearing yellow lace and gold hoops in her ears. Her face is almost white with pancake and her eyebrows look like weaponry. Her hair is brown and curly.

"Are you the new girl?" She speaks Yoruba. You nod. "Come with me."

You follow her down the bridge, the other way. A long, black car waits at the foot of the bridge. You both enter the back of the car. Another woman is seated there. She is tall and her eyes are full of sorrow, like she could cry if the car jolted to a sudden stop. She is wearing a white lace gown with a red turban around her head. The car moves once the door shuts. The woman in the yellow lace shifts to the other side of the car and you are left sitting beside the woman in white.

"Do you know why you are here?" she asks, gentle as a dove.

You exhale. "No, ma."

"You are here because Onidiri has chosen you."

"Hmmmn." You sigh. "I know. My mother told me about them. But why now? On the night she tries to kill me. Look at my ear."

The woman doesn't look, instead she laughs. "The ways of the worlds are an eternal mystery. You will know why in due time."

The car turns onto a beautiful street with huge houses, paved with clean roads and lined with trees blooming. It stops at one house with tall pillars around it and golden statues on the roof and a circular fountain inside an overgrown garden. It looks like it fell from heaven.

When you get inside the house and you are waiting in the parlor, Bisi, the woman in yellow lace with brown hair, washes her face and removes her wig. She ties a white wrapper around her chest, and the tall woman in the white lace changes into a black wrapper. She tells you to follow her and you three walk through many parlors with velvet chairs, silk flowers, and dripping chandeliers to reach a small room at the back of the house with one single yellow bulb and one low stool. The room has no window.

The woman who wore the red turban with the pearls has not removed the turban. She sits down on the stool, and gestures for you to come stand behind her. You are still wearing the satin dress and your black cloth is tied around your head.

Bisi comes to stand beside you with a bowl of steaming water as the tall woman, who is the owner of the house and the car, removes her turban and says, looking into your eyes, "Onidiri, cleanse our heads."

You think it is jheri curls at first, but as you continue to look, the woman's hair begins to do slow slow coili coili like snake. Your body starts to itch and you turn away.

The moon is waiting behind you, small enough to fill the back of the tiny room. It spits indigo fire at your chest. That familiar coolness falls upon your heart.

You close your eyes and clear your throat. You hold your body together even though you still want to run away and scratch your head and bathe for a very long time. You put your hands in the hot water and it becomes very, very cold. You stick your cold fingers inside the rich woman's head and begin to pull her writhing hair loose, out of the shape that the turban has formed it into.

Small headless snakes the size of big earthworms come off in your palm. You really want to scream and run, but you just retch and throw them into the water Bisi is holding. You remove twenty snakes from the woman's head and she shivers and shakes as you do it.

Her real hair grows around the snakes' bodies, tough and full. The snakes have bitten her scalp and grown directly into it. The cold of your fingers causes them to stiffen before you pull them out.

When you are done, the woman in white puts down the basin of water where the snakes now swim slowly and brings out an empty calabash that fits into her palm. It is covered in carvings of heads and snakes. She hands it to you. You don't know what to do with it.

"Pull the honey from the wounds," she whispers.

You turn back to the older woman's head and there is clear fluid coming out of the deep holes that the snakes left behind. You press the sides of a wound and a mess of the thick, clear, sweet-smelling goo rushes out onto the scalp. You scoop it up with your fingers and fill the small calabash. The wounds close once the honey has been extracted. The woman you have just helped is sobbing with relief.

"My name is Taiwo. I will make you very happy, just as you have made me happy today. The last time I had those curses removed, I was thirty years old, but they grow back faster the more I find success. I am now forty-five years old. It is a miracle that I have not gone mad."

"I am grateful to have helped you, ma." You whisper.

Your hands are now on fire as if the skin is being stripped and dusted with black pepper. You begin to hiss and moan, shaking the hand in the air. "Bisi! Bring ori and ice water," Taiwo says as she rubs her scalp in sheer relief.

Bisi rubs your hands with shea butter and places ice on them and they cool down. You begin to shiver and sweat hard from every single pore, till rivulets flow down your back. Taiwo calls her bank and opens an account in your name. She puts in one million naira for Kikelomo Ojo.

You don't understand why.

heavenly king

Ms. Taiwo asks you for Heavenly King. She says that the person who does the extraction of curses must also complete a hairstyle to seal the healing. For Heavenly King, the scalp is divided into three tiers; the back is made into adiseyin, the middle is patewo, and the front hair is woven into a fringe that falls over the eyes.

As you work, she tells stories of people cursed with bad ori, incomplete ori, and poisoned ori. Some from birth, by their witch mothers, their wizard fathers, and some later in life by angry babalawo or upset orisha.

The only ones who can help save these people with deformed ori are those seen and gifted by Onidiri. It is Onidiri's mission to repair all the ori they can, through humans like you. Onidiri cannot walk the Earth in their true form, and even when they assume human forms, these do not last.

Ms. Taiwo prays to Olodumare for you as Onidiri has not seen anyone new in a very long time. The older people who were seen and gifted all disappeared at once, more than a decade ago.

When she leaves you on the soft couch in the parlor, you sleep and your hair grows fuller.

In the morning, Bisi takes you to a bungalow at the back of the big mansion. She calls it a boys-quarters even though you will be the only one staying there. She says this is where you will be living and working until you are ready to go. Ms. Taiwo has given you the space to use for as long as you want.

Bisi says she will call all her people who know people who have cursed ori and they will come here and you will help them. She tells you to pray to Onidiri to come to you and give you the wisdom to face the work you have been chosen to do. You have never prayed to Onidiri before.

When Bisi removes her wig and shows you the lumps under her low-cut hair, you pray to Onidiri before you put your hands on her head, massaging till cold flows out of your fingers to smoothe the woman's ori.

Onidiri rolls around your head. You can see the black moon in the mirror.

one nation

One Nation is when all your hair is plaited to one side, from right ear to left ear, but just above the left ear, where the hair from the right side comes to rest, a small shuku is planted like a blossom.

This is the hairstyle you carry as you work for up to eleven moons at the back of Ms. Taiwo's mansion with Bisi and Onidiri hanging around, helping you.

Bisi brings the people with the bad ori and you remove their ills. Some of them will have been half-mad for many years, but then you will remove large red cockroaches from inside their scalp and they will become normal. You mostly remove snakes, centipedes, houseflies, bees, wasps, and stones.

One red-eyed man came crying, saying he hadn't slept in two years. His hair looked white when he removed his cap, but it was maggots that were dancing on his head. You almost vomited, but then you felt Onidiri minister cool breath to you and you just scraped everything off with a comb like you were removing soap.

That man paid you five million naira when he woke up three days later. You now have many millions in your account and many people call you every day, praying for you and telling you that you should continue to let Olodumare work through you.

You feel good and grateful when they tell you these things, but your stomach is always heavy like a stone. You cannot forget Baba and your mother. Your hand is always burning after you do the surgeries and sometimes it will turn red and all the veins under the skin will come to the surface, but Bisi always has shea butter, ice water, and bandages ready to go.

irun

After all the many months working for Onidiri, you have one dream. In the dream, you are back at Iludun where you first saw the black moon. It opens up from the core like a flower and three identical women and a god step out of it.

The women's hair is vast and full of tiny curls. It melts together into one mass and shines around their long bodies like a thunderstorm. Their skin is soft and brown. It glistens in the darkness of the dream. A tiny sun hovers in front of the forehead of the woman in the center. They are naked under the cover of the cloud of their hair.

Around the god's waist is a tiny wrapper that gleams like your satin dress. His torso is matted with dense black hair that looks like a breastplate. In the center of his chest, the hair turns into a bright golden burst that burns with fire. His hair is plaited in big shuku adimole that make his face look like a beautiful skull. At the tip of the shuku, the part that juts up from the scalp, a small black moon spirals. He is holding a thin staff of gold that ends in fine teeth like a comb.

They speak together, one entity split in four. Their request is sparse, repeated over and over till the stone in your stomach rises to your chest.

"Kikelomo, return to your home, to your blood. Atone."

sade adu

Your hair is long to your waist and the moon is full when you return to Iludun. Sade Adu is when, from the hairline to the middle of the head, hair is plaited adiseyin, then the remaining hair on the other half of the head is braided into Bob Marley, long black braids that swing with every movement.

You asked Bisi to put cowries and beads at the tips and they click loudly as you walk quiet and slow as a returning ghost toward the house where you last saw your mother. You have come in the late evening, but it is still bright enough to see you, a young woman in black satin walking with her head down. People are staring.

Your father Bolaji's grave greets you at the entrance to your house. They used bricks and tiles to make it look clean, but the tiles have turned orange because of dust. On a small bronze plaque, they wrote, "Ibi La Gbe Sin Ogbeni Bolaji Ojo Si. Suun Re O!"

You stand with your chest heavy, head bowed in front of it, till the sun has gone down, and when you touch your face, it is wet with tears.

A stone flies past your ear.

"Who is there?" A familiar voice, trembling with fear. Another stone flies when you don't respond fast enough.

"Ta lo wa'n be se?"

"Ma'ami. It's me o! Your daughter, Kikelomo. I have come back."

The hardness of your stomach turns cold. You will not run away or cry, yet. You can feel Onidiri above you, inside you, all around you.

A shadow walks out of the house toward you. In the light of the moon, you see her. Aduke's hair is wild, tattered, and white around her deeply wrinkled face. She is still wearing the black of mourning. Her body shivers from stress as she reaches you.

"Kikelomo Adunni Wuraola mi?"

"Ma'ami?"

"I thought you had died in the bush. I know you ran away after that time when we were waiting for Bolaji to wake up and you got tired."

"I went to Lagos, Ma'ami. Do you not remember when you lost your mind and tried to kill me?"

There is a silence as she finally stands before you, close enough to touch your face. Her eyes are dirty, and she seems to have aged twenty years in one.

"I remember when we were playing and I pulled your ear and you fell me down." She says, "Why are you here?"

"To make your hair. It will soon start to fall out again. I'm happy to see that it has grown back since the last time."

"You remain so sweet, omo mi. Come inside. We don't want to keep your father waiting."

Your mother lights a lantern and sits on a low stool in her mourning room, waiting for you to begin. The entire house is spotlessly clean. You go to her old room, once familiar but now strange and unknown to you. You find a cutting comb and the special shea butter with orange peels and other herbs that she once loved to make.

You return to the empty room. You mother is talking about you to the darkness in the corner. She is not sure if you are really you or an impostor, a skin-taking witch. Her hair smells. You say you want to wash it and she responds with lethal silence.

You comb it and flakes of dead skin and hair float around. You begin to part and oil it. The collected perfumes in the hair butter are stronger than the smell of her hair, which has grown longer than you have ever seen it. You begin to cut the strips and plait. Two flat currents of cornrows flowing to unite in the center of the skull, one each from the front and the back.

They call it Shut Up.

to braid yourself into fullness

As soon as you finish plaiting your mother Aduke's hair, two things happen.

First, she falls into a deep sleep and slides down to curl on the cold cement floor.

And then, your hair begins to loosen itself in a flurry of quick undoing motions, cowries and wooden beads first clattering to the cement floor, followed by the kanekalon attachments that made your hair long to your waist.

The cold currents that come when Onidiri is around flow into the center of your head as your natural hair loosens itself from its woven path into a large untangled cloud.

You tease it with your fingers and hear the hum of the black moon calling you, telling you where it rests. *Omomomomm-momomo.* You leave your sleeping mother with a kiss on the ear, touching your own half-ear in reflex. You gaze at her and wonder where her sudden wickedness had come from, her ignorance and fear of something she barely understood causing her to scar you forever. Or maybe grief had possessed her like it did Ade, turning her into what she was not, letting loose pent-up things seeking destruction.

You touch her shoulder with knots in your belly and walk out of the house like you are running away a second time, past your father's grave with your back held straight. You run your hands over the tiles till your palms are stained with orange dust.

You do not look back.

You walk down to the village square and cut off onto the path leading to the richer untamed forest, where you and Ade used to meet under the mango tree, where you first saw Onidiri.

When you walk off the path into the field, Onidiri hovers and hums in the center of the overgrown bush, exactly where it had a year ago.

Under clear moonlight, knee-deep in night, two lines of people stand, in gleaming blue-black cloaks. The Seen. They create a path that leads to the black moon which is also the essence of Onidiri itself. They are all singing a song so hushed, you think it is wind rushing through grass.

You walk down the aisle they have created, buoyed by the silence inside the song. Their hair is an array of miracles—thick, looping twigs in which moths play; combed-out afros crackling like small storms; one shuku ending in piled disks that defy gravity; twins with braids of silk flowing down their backs to wet the moonlit earth like pure water; gray hair woven into an overturned basket housing birds of night; dreadlocks around blind faces; low-cut gold hair trimmed in patterns so true that your eyes question themselves.

You notice that all their heads are connected by thin braids of red at the nape of the neck.

After passing this procession, you reach the women and the god from your dream. They stand here as they did there; the women beautiful enough to cause blindness, with the small sun on the forehead of she who is chief, and the moon above the god who grasps the thin gold staff, his eyes pale with unseen glories.

One of the three women bound by their hair hands you a cloak that is softer than the satin you have been wearing for months. The satin Onidiri told you to wash daily but never discard.

"We are Irun," they say, one voice echoing three. "Go on in, your time is now."

"Find a crown that suits you," the god echoes, still nameless. Onidiri is open. There is gold and indigo fire far inside its black heart, like something at the bottom of a deep, deep well.

You look back at Iludun and memories surface; of you in your father's arms, "My daughter is now a big girl, she can carry puff-puff!" He throws you up and you squeal with joy. Of Aduke letting you carry Baba's food to him, when you ended up eating with him and talking to him till you both fell asleep long after midnight. Of Ade holding you to warm you in utter silence as the night swirled around you.

You turn your attention back to where you stand, eyes wet with lost joy, and gaze at all the parts of Onidiri you can see, the queens and the god, the subjects, once seen like you, standing in rows, now lifting their hands in calm farewell to you.

Somehow, you know that other parts of Onidiri lie hidden under the scalps of people in distant lands. A braided language spoken in excess and cut and texture, in gloss and sheen, in times before and ahead.

You walk up the tongue of the moon, into the spherical nest made of the finest hair in all the living worlds. When you are inside it, the heart of Onidiri pulls at you, an intricate flower of gold, shrouded in mists of burning indigo.

As you walk toward it, you see, growing against the inside of the nest, a multitude of hard ebony heads, small as walnuts, in forever rows, around and around from nothing to nothing.

They all wear forbidden crowns.

III
Opon Onidiri

We watch the new child walk toward our heart, slow and afraid to let go of the broken world she had been born into. Deep inside, she burns with a fire the same color as us; a fire tainted indigo by our collision with her, but still shot through with that incorruptible clarity that made us want to see her.

She will be good for us. A grand instrument in coming battles. She walks deeper, and we watch from where our hearts rest immortal in the walls of our nest like fruit. We pull her deeper toward our heart, toward union with we who have lived and we who are yet to be born. She slows down, shuts her eyes, and lifts her arms to embrace all.

Knowing floods her mind in a rush of cold ase from the center of her being and she falls to her knees, sobbing as her heart opens into the Harmony. She slides down boneless and sinks into larval slumber. Our unseen hands pour down and slither toward her head and her loose hair. We begin to weave her a new crown, one unlike any other.

In us, one is all and all is one.

We are the voices of Onidiri. We are the voices of osupa dudu, the black moon.

III: Heralds

LSD-1842

I

Mary Had A Little Lamb *(July 6, 2019: 12:08am.)*

Hello! This is Osi.

I hope you can hear me.

Mary is dead.

She died less than twelve hours ago. She was standing under the shelf.

Baba Sumbo had warned me about that shelf more than twenty times. About ten times after he started warning me, Mary and I shared our first kiss. It tasted like gbegiri but it was all soft and Mary smelled like Hair Wonder. Under the shelf. She died under the shelf. I did not mean to get anyone killed talk less of Mary. The whole shelf fell. Please help. How do I untangle time? Whom do I ask for help? I need to see Mary again. I must undo this or I die, by my own hand or by letting another man be my savior.

I beg. Please.

I love her too much to let her go without me.

(i.a)

Osi's First Glide *(July 25, 2019.)*

Fadugba gives Osi the keys to the car. Plate No: LSD-1842. It is an old Volkswagen Beetle. Bright cyan skin scarred with atlases of rust. It must have been dead in the sun forever. The car is in Fadugba's backyard under a mango tree. It is parked, small, inside a rising splash of green weeds, old tools and long dead leaves. No tree. The earth is a soaked ochre under its tires. The key to the car has three cowries attached to it. Every time, Osi glides through time, a cowrie goes.

One cowrie costs $1000. Fadugba says he got the car from betting right on an eagleflight race, seventy years ago.

Fadugba explains why they must buy more than one contract in sand.

First, sand expires with the rising of the sun, so no saving for tomorrow. Once the sand is in the engine, it must be used.

Second, Fadugba has things to also correct in time, for his Brotherhood and its constant war with rival Brotherhoods in their Endless War, and

last, no one ever corrects, or realigns with Igba, the Temporal Circle, in one try.

They walk to Fadugba's backyard. The backyard of the neat brick house that he and his Brothers built. Fadugba says Osi came to the right place. Fadugba is an original. He did the big exam for babalawohood.

Fadugba opens the door of the Volkswagen Beetle. Nothing pours out. They sit and the seats are buttersoft. Inside the car, it's all black leather, chrome accents and swarovski buttons, all suffused in the clinical glow and blink of the more overt technology on the side Fadugba sits in.

Fadugba is reading future possibilities on the touchscreen under his nose, smiling. Fadugba makes him nervous. The man has such a chewy element to him, asides his aromatic chewing stick that smells like fire, his skin looks all tough, like an alligator's and his eyes go milky then clear then milky again. His silver hair is cut too trim and he looks 25 going on 150. To find Fadugba, he had had to ride in a basket on the back of an omiran to get to Amunudun, the forest village in Osun State where he was hid.

There is no steering wheel in front of Osi, only a spiraling of water in a white marble bowl etched with the names of the five Oosha Igba, Madiens of Time (Iseju, Bai Bai Bai, Nsinsin, Titilai and Igbakiigba).

Another unknown language, curls inside the bowl, like worms desperate to be seen, a language written in breath and blood and thinnest gold.

"Say when you want."

Osi whispers, "July 4, 2019. Baba Sumbo Mechanic Shop. At around six in the evening."

The water swirling in the scrying bowl purrs, gurgles and with a splash, a bust forms. The woman wearing heavy grey aso-oke from head to sternum, the grey so heavy it could be iron, rises to face Osi. Diamond strips hang from her ears. She has three tigerscars on either side of her face and her eyes are so shrewd, almost avian. Osi starts to blubber, to confess to her after looking into them for five seconds.

She shuts him up and speaks politely. "I am Igba'naa. Off-spring of Igbakiigba. How much time do you need?"

"Just ten seconds! To fix the shelf."

Fadugba slaps his arm like a child who has spoken out of turn. "Ehn, Eye, an hour of sand is what we desire."

"And what will you pay for it? I'm still waiting for the school of rare rock fish whose ancestors were confidantes of Mother Osun that you promised me. I better talk to the boy, you're too slippery, Fadugba."

She turns to Osi, her ears blazing white fire. "He charges in that dollars. We charge in things that time has swallowed." She says.

"Do you have any such objects? Old clothes, books, cutlery, china, or even better *jewelry*?" Her voice rises a pitch on jewelry but it had seemed very hungry from old clothes.

Fadugba holds Osi's arm to keep him quiet and turns to Igba'naa. He says, "I have such an object. A statue from the time you walked as woman."

The maidenspirit's avian eyes turn human, wide with need. "*What?*" She says. "You can have a day." Then she slips back into the water like a thing that wasn't.

Osi wonders why Fadugba would give something so valuable away for him, then he remembers the money that he is going to have to go to another babalawo to get. Before the glide, as Fadugba called it, the sky got so black that Osi thought he was going blind, until lightning struck the engine

and then they were flying with a swarm of titanic babies burning blue with sorrow.

(<o>)

Square One: July 4, 2019. 6:00pm : *Baba Sumbo warns Osi about the shelf and Osi-1842 knowing Fadugba is waiting for him in the Beetle outside, waits for Osi Original to close shop, then he sneaks in and hammers the shelf back into place a bit too hastily, in this process, he dislodges a paint bucket full of heavy screws and bolts. He makes it back to the car within an hour and he and Fadugba spend the remainder of their day of sand driving around as helpers in worlds full of men and women fighting battles against night.*

Square One, Part Two: July 5, 2019. 11:01am : *Mary enters Baba Sumbo Mechanic in her sunflower yellow dress. Baba Sumbo is at home, eating eba and egusi and watching action films. She knows Osi loves her, is ready to leap onto a train track to save her from herself. She also knows she is going to die, but she doesn't tell anyone. Osi (back in native timestream) is under the car, his shirt torn to reveal his fine earthtone torso. Mary looks and looks. She leans against the wall. The paint bucket lurks.*

Osi slides out with a smile. "How far?"

Mary pushes herself off the wall forcefully, so she can meet him before he meets her, so that the kiss will have a stolen quality. A rushedness. The wood of the wall shudders.

The paint bucket drops and Osi tastes blood.

(i.b)

Osi's Second Glide *(July 25, 2019.)*

Fadugba is reading future possibilities on the touchscreen under his nose, smiling. Osi is watching the water swirl, the strange serpentine language etched and colored inside the bowl seems to say many things, but it says nothing Osi can understand.

The water is mindless. Swirling and sparkling with its own amber light. It purrs, gurgles and with a freezing splash, another bust emerges.

The second cowrie begins to melt.

This time-maiden is young and wide-eyed, shaven head fuzzed with blonde, looking directly at the air in front of her and so still Osi thinks she's a statue wrapped in aso-oke with moons hanging from her ears. She feels deaf to him. Then, she blinks three times and out pours a torrent of talk.

"Bai Bai Bai is my name and immediately is the game. When, where, what, who? Do you need to seek the exact moment that your iPhone slipped into the gutter? Or do you want to take it back to the time you told your mother she was a liar? The now of then is alive in my breast. Tell me what you have for me so I can go now, now, now!"

Osi just stares. Fadugba looks sick, like the embodiment of cyclical moments that feel forever present talking up the scrying bowl isn't giving him good memories. He runs out of the car like a shot. Osi watches him jump and catch something. Fadugba runs back inside the car. He opens his hand. A moth, alive.

Bai Bai Bai eats it, says "30-deg of sun!" and goes back into the bowl.

A girl with sand in a fluted calabash comes and fills the car with it. Osi sees the golden sparkle of it as it pours into the engine. He didn't see her the last time. The hood shuts and the sky turns blind. Lightning again and the car is riding through Regret, a land where a century of men bash their heads against boulders, senile from eating their own children.

Osi doesn't come out of the car this time, he just slips into the moment, aware of the rerouting of time (sand).

One body, two senses of time.

(<<o>>)

Square Two: July 5, 2019. 11:08am : Mary pushes herself off the wall forcefully, so she can meet him before he meets her, so that the kiss will have a stolen quality. A rushedness. The wood of the wall shudders. The shelf collapses. Osi pushes Mary to the side. The paint bucket gouges the earth.

Square Two, Part Two: Immediately After: Baba Sumbo once put some jagged metal rods in the corner, lying horizontal on their side to produce a perfect weapon. He believed there was nowhere else to stack them. They were hidden, but out of the way, slipped between a crack in the wall. They used to joke about falling on it drunk. Osi looks to Mary. She is impaled on them, the raw iron rods, stacked carelessly in the corner by her own father.

(i.c)

Osi's Third and Final Glide *(July 25, 2019.)*

Fadugba is reading future possibilities on the touchscreen under his nose, smiling. The bowl swirls. Osi can't believe Mary died even worse when he was trying to save her. Nsin Nsin shows up. Maiden of the moment just lost, with the permanent face of the surprised bride. Her ears are bare but her aluminium gele is like a satellite.

"Just now?" She asks as a form of greeting.

"We are on our third and final cowrie for this session, Eye. Take us to the moment just missed in my friend's native stream."

"It cannot happen. The thing that you want. You die or she dies. You're just wasting sand and cowrie. You can go to the moment a million times, death has marked her. And she knows." Nsin Nsin has tigerscars too. Three, neat as light rays in shadow. Her response is brusque as her voice.

"What?"

"Yes. She has clarity."

"What?"

"A gift from Olodumare. Sight and knowing beyond time."

"So she knew and still came to see me. To die beside me, so terribly...?" Osi feels the ache that had chased him into a forest village to ride in a piece of arcane technology with a babalawo come to a point so sharp that he sobs.

"I'll die." Osi says.

Nsin Nsin sighs and shakes her head.

Fadugba asks Osi how he is going to pay for the cowries.

(<<<o>>>)***

***Square Three: You Didn't Even Say Goodbye: July 5, 2019.
11:07am*** *: Osi slides out from under the car, a minute early.
"How far?" he says and leaps faster than Mary Sumbo can catch.
He swings her around and kisses her before pushing her away.*

*The shelf falls, slices through his neck, severing spine, killing
instantly.*

II
His Fleece Was White As Snow

Square Four: Mary, You Lied: *Mary Sumbo is standing very,
very still over the body of the man she loves. She cannot look into his
face, all she has to look at is the open gash and the flopped neck held
by mere tendons. Baba Sumbo Mechanic Shop is empty because it
is Thursday and the assistants don't come till hot afternoon, after
they are done from public school. She cannot cry. He took her place.*

*She had peed a little in her pants this morning before she stepped
into the shop knowing what the clarity had told her. He had stepped
in her place because he knew somehow. Mary Sumbo is still. Her
entire being a question, as it always is whenever the clarity double
crosses her like this. Usually it is with smaller things – where she'll
find soursop, maybe it will rain, a song heard by only her.*

How did Osi know to move into the oath of death for her?

*Fadugba walks in and sees. He turns away, lights tobacco and
doesn't cry. He speaks to Mary from this position. She jumps because she didn't see him come in and turn away.*

Fadugba says, "Come with me."

Afterburner: July 26, 2019. 7:47am

Mary Sumbo is carrying Osi on her shoulder.

Not his body. Fadugba had reprimanded her for looking at that for so long, her shock hitting so solid it felt like peace. The body mangled, torn apart or dismembered should not be looked at for so long.

Osi's bodyless soul takes the form of a man the size of a bottle of wine, hooded and cloaked in white, so densely that the shadow of the head only suggests his face.

Mary Sumbo knows it is him. Fadugba said he saw him clinging, formless and heavy as phlegm on Mary Sumbo the moment he had stepped into the shop. The babalawo says his soul is so visible because he died while spilt between two time streams.

First, Fadugba drove Mary to the future in a small ugly car with insides of chrome and leather, then he had scraped Osi together, off her shoulder and sides, with a golden spoon and brought him to boil in a lined ball of gold.

When the ball had opened and steam tall as a man rose to fog the room, Mary Sumbo took a step back, because she saw Osi for a split second behind the white.

Then suddenly, Fadugba had started calling praise to Osi's soul and she had looked down into the golden bowl and really seen him. It was like seeing a viper. The soul, stripped and boneless, riveted to a spot, unable to move yet.

After a while he moved, walking (sliding forward) at a tilt like a thing going against the wind. He reached Mary and she lifted him in her hands. It was like holding a rushing icy wind. She kissed him without knowing. Their reflex.

"Osi?" There was no response. The soul just stared at her from that shadowed hood. Mary Sumbo moved him to her shoulder and said, "When you are ready, you will talk."

Fadugba stands wrapped in white cotton from waist to toe. His body is marked with white lines of chalkwater. He looks at the crowd of ancestors gathered on the altar of his divinatory;

all no taller than his arm, carved from white, black, red and blue chalk. He asks for help as he confesses he loves them. He hears them, feels them toe across the room like tiny hurricanes.

Mary Sumbo just keeps on doing the clarity exercise Fadugba has given her. Looking into a bowl full of blackwater, trying to see tomorrow. She sees herself cradling a lamb.

Fadugba stands up at the same moment and says, "We need to get a lamb, white as snow, to serve as host for the soul of Osi until his time of upper migration comes."

III
He Followed Her to School One Day

What is Osi?

Dissolved man with only love.

He fell the moment he asked the question not often asked (how do I untangle time?) and also when the lamb ate him like a frozen yogurt to his utter dismay.

If you wish to edit time, prepare to die, or something. And who is it who knots us so? Seeding little bombs between the ribs of our loving, so that we never see each other more than once in a hundred lives, until memory is all that keeps us breathing.

In Mary's arms, warm cotton cradle. No death till I am of horn. This spilling of blood must be done by the hand of the one I love upon a rock in desert sun. But first, we leave the city for Ogun – me and her on a farm, eating corn forever.

The Waterwidower

The Waterwidower

Sade Taiwo's brother, a lanky rebel seven years her junior, called her phone one Friday night and proceeded to nearly drive her mad. She had just lay in bed after a healthy meal of eba and egusi, topped with goat meat, seven hours of torrid Nollywood drama and lots of cold Fanta. Her thoughts were wild as usual, running from why Jim Iyke would bother to chase after that garishly colored Tonto Dikeh girl for three movies, to why she hadn't just gone out to the bar nearby and gotten sloshed, to the fact that her mother had called earlier to ask how work was doing, to how that conversation had quickly devolved into a near-shouting match over her age and her lack of a potential husband. The call had ended when her mother had dropped a caustic retort in her usual cloyingly sweet voice;

"Maybe if you stopped chain-smoking, tattooing yourself and talking back at your suitors, maybe then you'd get married."

Sade didn't waste any breath telling her mother anything else. She simply depressed the red button. The glorious freedom she felt after having lived with her mother for more than twenty-five years of her life was indescribable. Far away from home and hee mother's disarming brand of vitriol-infused love, she had found herself a nice self-contained apartment on the mainland and a job as a secretary to a man so young, she was convinced she could have birthed him.

The spastic juju of Wizkid brought her out of stewing thought, Aaron was calling. He never called. The original black sheep of the family, he had escaped Mumsi's grip three years ago. Dropping out of school, choosing rap as a career and vanishing into the underbelly of the Lagos upcoming artist scene.

She braced herself and picked the phone.

"Hey Double A, longest time, what's up?"

"Sister?"

"Yep, it's me. In the flesh, or is it the voice?"

He chuckled. It sounded like the clucking of a wet chicken cornered by a dog.

"I'm in big trouble. Really big trouble."

Sade sat up, her heart leaping.

"Jesus Christ! What is it? What did you do? Does Ekene have anything to do with this?! "

Aaron's band of upcoming artist friends were unstable, veering off the keyboards and drums to deal drugs on the black market just so they could survive long enough to get *that* hit.

"Uncle Sunday. He sent me to go collect something from his friend at Berger. It was a trunk. One of those apoti fedecos. He said I should hold it, that someone was coming for it by midnight. So I -"

She groaned. Uncle Sunday was the black sheep of her mother's family, unlike Aaron, he dealt heavily in something Sade could only describe as magic. She knew very little about the actual process, but her mother had warned her to stay away from Sunday too many times.

"Ugh. Why would you go on a Sunday errand?"

"He promised me enough money to 'get me through life for now' – you know how he's always talking weird now, and I'm broker than an egg in an epileptic--"

"Yeah yeah." Aaron had a habit of sneaking 'punch-lines' into daily conversation. They were occasionally cute but now was not one of those moments.

"What was in the box?"

"You wouldn't believe me."

"Just say it. You came to me first, remember?"

"There was something moving in it through the okada ride back home. I- "

"You biked that far?" Berger was at the end of Lagos, almost entering into the next state. Sade couldn't imagine driving there with her precious Mazda, riding a motorcycle for that long was a death sentence.

"Please now let me finish, it's almost eleven thirty"

Sade sighed. "Go on"

"When I got home, I put it under the bed and went to urinate, when I came back, there was...fuck....something was on the bed."

"A dog?"

Aaron laughed manically, his voice hitching oddly. A chicken warbling from fear.

"I'm twenty one fucking years old. I can handle a dog."

"So why do you need me?"

When he finally spoke it was in one high pitched garbled breath.

"There's a dragon in my room"

Sade threw back her head and laughed.

Aaron stood outside his room clutching onto his elbows hard. The night was cold and the silence bit down like a blunt knife. He leaned against the low cement wall that stood opposite the door of the apartment and stared into nothing. Spilling to his left and right, crude wooden doors edged in chicken wire and mosquito netting protected the occupants of two unpainted bungalows barely seven feet high and built so close to each other, doors on either side had to be opened in turns. A roar jerked him out of his existential lull. He had been staring into the gutter that ran between the 'face-me-I-face-you', the spirogyra-green muck that lived there was glistening oddly in moonlight that had managed to sneak in through slivers between the nearly overlapping rooftops, and reminded him of scaly skin he couldn't get out of his mind.

The roar that vibrated through his body wasn't loud, it sounded more like the rumble of a small Hauwei generator starved of petrol. Unlike the generator's cry, this one trembled with the growl of vibrating tonsils. The grey door of his room suddenly turned dark and wet with condensing water molecules. It was freezing. He could see the veins of ice spread their tentacles across the rotting wood. His heart leapt into his throat again, any second and Mama Sumbo, his neighbor would come out and ask him to turn down his non-existent air-conditioning. Sade or Uncle Sunday needed to get here fast.

He couldn't begin to imagine the havoc that the creature was causing in his room. The skittering noise that had emitted from the metal of the trunk while he rode home filled the air. It was an unsettling sound - parts rattlesnake, parts murderous cyborg. It chilled him cold to the bone, like his heart had gone after he had exited the bathroom and re-entered the room to see something pale slithering across the naked foam of his bed. The air had gone cold after the creature had spread thin skeletal wings and let a football-sized ball of bluish flame fly before his eyes. It had all happened so fast, less than thirty seconds.

He had run. He had never run from anything in his life -- except his caustic mother -- but this time he had run, nearly breaking the door with his body

He had waited outside, his skin crawling every time he saw it in his head again. The blood red eyes, and a long spear-ended tail that whipped around like a flame. When his panic attack stopped he had called his sister, she was tough and sharp. She also smoked enough cigarettes daily to create small clouds. If no one came, he was running away at midnight. Vanishing into the city like his father.

"Psst! Psst!"

Sade was shrouded in the darkness a few feet from him. She was wearing sunglasses and a large patterned kaftan. He waved her over. She snuck slowly along the wall he leaned on into his vision. Her face was blank and the giant knot of braids above her head looked odd in his current state.

"I'm not sneaking because I'm afraid of your *dragon*. I don't want to wake that your mouthy neighbor."

Aaron smiled. Mama Sumbo was mouthy. She had an oddly deep knowledge of pop culture and always attempted to make conversation with Sade the two times she had come visiting.

"It's in there. Can you hear it?" Aaron's whispering was beginning to border on comical, even to himself.

"No"

Another roar filled the still darkness, followed by the sound of something else freezing to within an inch of its life.

"What was that?"

"The dragon. Can you see the door? It spits blue flame that makes shit really cold."

Tendrils of white 'fog' were beginning to curl up from under the door.

"Fascinating. What happened to your lights?"

"But..but..there's..... NEPA rolled away our wires and Mama Sumbo, Fly and the rest are all *broke.*"

"So? Didn't Mom warn you about Uncle Sunday? He will never send you to go get rice or wine like his peers. Remember when he brought that parrot? Or the blanket? the *tea?*"

When their uncle was still allowed to visit by their mother, he had always brought special gifts.

The parrot had been able to have speak in a coy French accent and hold conversation. No one thought it was weird, till it had escaped from its padlocked cage, leaving behind a golden egg.

The blanket had been weirder; a deep hypnotic midnight blue, it was always the right temperature and gave Sade the most terribly realistic dreams (complete with tiny healed scars when she awoke). He had brought it for their mother when she became pregnant with Aaron and was having nightmares.

Most unforgettably, she had begged for a sip of his sweet-smelling red tea on one of his visits. It had tasted like honey. Later that day, she had seen a desperate looking man soaked in blood, with a gut full of knife and spilling innards, smiling at her from the corner of the dining room and had fainted and broken a finger.

"Also it's Monday, you'll survive."

She pulled him down to the dry cement floor, where she pulled out a cigarette and lit it. It glowed like an evil eye in the murky darkness. There was no doubt there was something at least vaguely dragon-shaped turning Aaron's room into Antartica at that moment, but Sade didn't want to get too involved. She had learnt from Uncle Sunday.

"It's 11:40. If no one comes for this thing by midnight, I'm coming to live with you"

"Whatever you want. Now sit down" Sade said more firmly. Aaron slid down to plant himself beside her. She folded her legs into lotus gracefully, ignoring the dust that streaked across her boubou. He sat like a stick insect, with long legs that had refused to meet up with the length of his torso since puberty.

"How's music?"

"It's cool."

The skittering filled the air again. Aaron rubbed his goosebumps away. Sade sucked in a big lungful of tobacco smoke, and said nothing for a moment. When Aaron's face let go of his unease, she continued;

"No, really, how is it? Is it working for you the way you expected?"

Her brother's brow crumpled and he started to draw absent-mindedly on cement he couldn't see.

"I haven't booked a studio in ages. I've been living on your not so anonymous deposits into my account. And my debts keep piling up."

"I warned you to be careful before you left home. Stay alone. Come ask me for money if you need. Call me regularly. Living alone in Lagos, especially for someone like you, is not healthy."

"I know. I'm young, and stupid. I guess that's why I don't call. I want to become my own man myself, or at least do so with the help of strangers who wouldn't judge"

Sade sighed and rubbed her brother's shoulder.

"I'm the last person you should worry will judge you. I'll probably sing you ethereal hooks for free".

Aaron smiled and his brow smoothed out for a few seconds, before something crashed loudly in his room again.

"Mama Sumbo must be really tired."

Another half-laugh from the boy tangled up in his own worry.

"Do you want to stop? I could help. You'd stay in and think stuff out while I work extra nights with my boss."

Aaron remained mute, still absently rubbing the floor.

"Say something."

"I'm afraid, Sade. I left home to become better than Mom thought I would be, through means that would make her, rollers melt."

The image of her mother, who after her father left never wore her hair out of rollers flickered through her mind.

"Now I'm here, babysitting our uncle's *thing* and having a meltdown. I guess I always knew I would end up here, just getting tangled up tighter with all those boys. I'm so lost..."

His voice has cracked. It is so unexpected and heart-breaking. Her half-tough, life-loving brother brought down to silence and tears by a dragon in a box. Sade wondered if Uncle Sunday making him hold the box is a coincidence, or if the old dog thinks it's a necessity. She is still for a few seconds before she pulls him to her chest. He cries silently, and she smokes. The red-hot tip of her cigarette is an entity of its own. Shining and dimming. The soft and sharp hug of nicotine comfort her in return. This was not where she saw herself at the end of today. Another muffled roar echoed out of the room.

He simmered into slow breathing. The green glow of Sade's wristwatch tell her it is 11:57pm.

"I should call Uncle Sunday"

Aaron whipped out his Blackberry, kept in shape by invisible tape and rubber bands, and began pressing buttons. Soft beeps filled the air. The door shivered again. Whatever was in there needed to get out. Fast.

"Get up. We need to get out of here."

She unfurled herself from the floor, lithe like a panther.

There was a man in standing in the narrow space Aaron had stood in since sunset. His form, shaded by the darkness and shown by dim moonlight was almost seven feet tall. An ear was arrayed in a shower of gold hoops from crest to lobe. He smiled and walked closer, Sade and Aaron shrank back.

"You are the boy housing the water widower." His voice was rich and crackly, like brand new cloth, and he spoke with a *knowing*. No hesitation colored his voice, just a grave solid intelligence. His skin was a velvety black. His three piece suit even darker.

Water widower. She had heard those words before somewhere. Probably when Uncle Sunday was spinning her tales about the mythical spaces he said rested beneath, within and above Lagos.

"Yes, he is. May I help you?"

She stepped in front of her little brother, blocking him from the view of the man.

"I am Balogun. Resident cryptid handler. I need to retrieve the widower and pay the messenger before the night turns. I mean no harm"

Aaron nodded and pointed to the door of his room. The man bent steeply and went in, a large draft of cold air and freezing vapor poured out after him. He swiftly held his sister's hand.

"Should we run?"

"No, I need to see this."

She sipped the last of her cigarette and tossed it into the still muck of the gutter.

Odd cooings and low growls began to filter through the darkness of the room, then silence. After a moment, the man walked out and Sade gasped.

Draped across his large shoulders was a pale silver dragon. Dog sized, its scales glimmered with youth, health and perspiration from the change in temperature. From behind its triangular reptilian head, a frill of white flesh was spread in defiance. Its eyes were slanted red ovals, smooth as fruit with no pupil. Its short, sharp clawed legs hung useless on either side of Balogun's shoulders and its very prehensile tail swung lazily. When it passed by them, it lowered its pale graceful neck and gave a half roar that released a cloud of thick cold steam that made Sade's skin *retract.*

Without turning Balogun spoke, "Thank you for your services, Aaron. Give my regards to Sunday", then he walked out, down the narrow corridor, cooing softly to the snarling creature around his neck.

Sade looked at Aaron as the strange man vanished into the darkness. His face was dour, and staring at the floor. All he had said to her was beginning to haunt him now that his dragon was gone. Sade snapped her fingers in his face.

"Get your shit, we need to leave"

He moved then, swallowing hard and sneaking fast into the dark rectangle that held the room.

"Fuck." It was a loud whisper. Sade crept to the door and peeped in. The place was a mess. The lone chair, table, mattress and curtain looked like they had been attacked by an angry bulldog. There was rapidly melting ice on almost every surface, and five inches of water on the floor already. Cold stale air wafted out carrying the stink of old sweat with it.

Aaron was still, staring at something on his bed. Sade crept closer taking off her slippers and stepping into the icy water. On Aaron's bed, amidst torn pieces of foam, chunks of ice and wet clothing, a pile of bright gold coins glowed.

"Jesus Christ." Sade couldn't help herself from calling to a man she hardly believed in anymore. She had no idea what to do now. Aaron's eyes were going to spill from their sockets like broken eggs as he stared at the shining coins scattered across the bed. They shone gently, like they knew their worth.

"Are you going to touch that?"

Aaron looked at her as if she had just spoken ancient Hebrew. Then he started laughing. Deep chuckles escaped his lips, they tapered off till he could get out what was tickling him,

"Uncle Sunday is mad."

Then he moved faster than she had ever seen him move in his life and her life. He grabbed a ghana-must-go and emptied it contents --garish t-shirts, faded jeans, a pair of rat-eaten shoes -- onto the floor.

Then Sade Taiwo watched, standing ankle-deep in dragon vomit, as her brother shoveled the heavy coins, clinking, into the bag. She thought of her uncle, his grey-white beard always unshaven yet trimmed, his eyes bright with oddness and wisdom, whispering an "*I told you so*" into her ear.

& she smiled.

We Are Born

I

Once before, in a moment before this final birth, Wura molded me to life.

After ten years of being the most prolific sculptor in the village of Àlá; bending stone, clay, wood and metal to the kinesis of her hands, the woman who was to become my mother, Wura, was still without child.

The joy that all of the village took in her craft, the smile on her husband's face as he filled hemp bags with cowries and the thrill Wura felt when she worked, all paled when she realized that her womb was cursed never to bring forth a child that would stay to be soaked in her care and love. She had an abundance of it; Ojo, her husband had glowing skin and the healthiest of bellies. He even lorded over a farm that she had acquired; five-hundred arm lengths wide. There, an abundance of beast and crop thrived – goats and tomatoes, sheep and corn, turkeys and yams, chickens and peppers.

Everything, but a living child.

Three times after her marriage to Ojo, Wura had given birth to daughters, and all three times, her babies had died before they could walk or speak. They said that her children were afraid of her. Ojo would disappear into a new farm project after each mourning was over, and Wura would feel her feet sink into mud from the weight of the gloom that settled over her. She would pray; angry and distraught, to Olodumare to reveal why he had given her offspring at all, if He was going to take them away before they could even speak her name. There would be no answer and she would return to work, giving sorrow form.

On the night she made me, a mighty storm came ravaging.

It brought wind that howled like night spirits cracking the heavens open and lightning so bright it briefly turned everything it touched to white stone with every flash of its teeth. By a clap of thunder, Wura woke up and knew what she had to do. She walked quietly out of her hut with a single-mindedness that caused her bones to thrum, dropped to her knees in the center of her compound and began to dig, parting the ground with her palms.

The earth, softened by battering raindrops fell away beneath her fingertips as she pulled the entrails of the land to the surface. Red mud; soft and thick, brown mud; dour and fragile, no better than a leaf sucked dry by harmattan, pink mud; heavy like raw meat. These formed a discolored hill around her, and as she dug deeper and deeper; rain fell harder.

With a lunge that caused her to stick her shoulder into the hole she had dug, she hit it with aching fingers – clay, off-white and exuding a warmth like it had been waiting for centuries, holding sunlight in itself. She had never seen it in all her time sculpting in the medium, but she knew it would be there and she knew it would give her what she needed as it pulsed in her fist with life.

She scooped it up and began to work.

The rain fell harder but the mud did not run.

From the shapeless mound she made by slapping together the clay, which remained sunwarm under the rain, she began to use her fingers to press, bend and shape the white, sculpting out a body – gentle arms to care and a waist to balance baskets, eyes to spot the faces of liars and legs to run fast through the night.

She pulled structures, a slender back; smooth like the bottoms of rivers, the knobs of a strong spine with which to carry babies, sad dogs and lost cats. Teeth white and sharp enough to eat roast goat, prepubescent breasts like shut flora and hair plaited in rows that ran across the cranium, curling at the nape.

The clay tensed the longer she worked on it and so she could turn her child over and work on making her going as lovely as her coming. The clay acted like white hot steel, yielding yet staying firm.

It was her purest work, one that had come from a place she often sensed within while working on taller, wilder forms. This time that place had burst forth, taking her over just as much as she took the clay in her palms to task. Wura's skin felt like silk on fire and wherever she worked on the body before her, with fingers pinching and smoothing, that part on *her* body also squirmed in response to some unknown hand.

She completed her work and it lay nude and face up, staring empty into the depths of the storm above. At the sight of what she had made in her frenzy, Wura felt the place she had been in fold away from her, the heat on her skin cooling like coals under water. She could see steam rising off her own shoulders in the downpour. She stared back at the clay girl before her, and felt herself overwhelmed. She crumpled to the ground, sobs wracking her body as the air began to crackle.

With a burning from above, a ball of white lightning fell into the clay figure and moments after the light vanished, I came to be.

II

I remember the moments of becoming conscious in my new skin vaguely. The rain fading as wet clay fell off my body in patches. Skin the color of just-split wood. I remember the cold that chilled me beyond my bones, a cold that radiated out from inside me. I could hear the storm that had brought me as it rode away, grumbling like God's angry belly.

I tried to make a sound with my mouth, but nothing resonated. My throat felt devoid of whatever organ produced sound. Wura had been able to create a perfect girl but was not allowed to give her a voice. How strange the ways of those beyond.

I was terrified and shivered even more as I looked in the darkness around and saw only blurs of color, like a newborn. All I could feel was the warmth of Wura's body, her cheeks and jaw resting against my head as I held onto her waist and rested in her bosom.

She was looking above. A final sigh escaping her, not one that was an overflow of old familiar aches, but one that poured out of her mouth, the sound of a heart stunned, the undulating language of the fire that had made her a miracle.

Still exuding joy, Wura carried me indoors.

***

The next day, she brought Ojo to witness her handmade marvel. He looked in disbelief at the perfection of my body, my skin, the way I held myself. He did not believe that she had molded me out of white clay and lightning. Only a witch could attempt something so defiant of Olodumare.

He chose to believe that I had wandered into the compound, a likely refugee of the same War that had brought about the founding of the village we were in. He smiled as he saw me cowering over a bowl of hot ogi and akara, crouching on the floor instead of sitting on the stool Wura had given me.

My body was not used to the way the stool instructed my spine to line up straight, or the strain it placed on how I carried my head. When I first walked in the light of morning, my knees wobbled and my eyes would not stop leaking water. I felt askew within. But with Ma'ami's gentle urging, and the love that filled her eyes every time she looked into mine, with the heat of the sun that seemed to dry me inside and out the higher it rose into the up-place, I was able to stand and walk the way she taught me to. Gently, like the whole earth was anchored to the swing of my hips.

When she rubbed a lotion of shea butter and perfumed herbs across the length of my back and neck, I nearly called out her name to ask her why it made me feel so held, why the sense of being askew within could be averted by this simple application of softness by her palms, but no words would sound outside of my mouth.

All of my understanding stayed inside; trickling, rushing, and tidal, in the ark of my skull. I found that in the eyes of those who looked at me and in the many tones of their voices, I could read faintly, the ways that they thought and felt.

I was cared for greatly, though never allowed past the walls of the compound. Ma'ami did not want to have to deal with the questions that would arise once my age-group found out I was not like them, nor did she want me to attract any men, young or old.

She would brush my hair nightly and tell me stories, real and imagined that sprung from the fertile place that gave her art. My silent laughter, motions of the neck and varying levels of rapt silence, let her know that I understood what she was saying. She never spoke of the daughters before me.

I could not let myself get close to Ojo, who I knew as Ba'ami. He cared for me regardless, sneaking me roasted corn rubbed in honey and even bringing me a wild kitten once. The kitten was named Ere. She told me when I looked into her eyes. She loved to play and be tickled on her soft white underside, and we were united in our peculiar silences in hiding places for two moons, before she disappeared into the village to look for a mate.

No one was allowed to see me. Not any of the one hundred workers who worked with Ojo, nor those who came to purchase Ma'ami's work. I stayed in Ma'ami's hut, quiet among her adire curtains and the first four carving posts she had ever made.

The only one who saw me aside from Ma'ami and Ojo was Falemidebiire, who swooped down on the compound one evening, not long after Ere ran away, and found me asleep at Ma'ami's feet. He had recoiled in shock at the sight of my body, like he could see something more. I had scampered away at the sight of this robust sharp man swaddled in white, going to hide behind the hut to eavesdrop on his talk with Ma'ami.

"She is an abiku, spirit children who always die prematurely and return to do the same again and again. They relish in the cycle of agony that their mourning parents carry, but this one is not like the one that has come to you three times before. She is older. You must have caught her on a trip back to Olodumare. My old teacher told me they fly in storms, the thunder and lightning is the sound of their *ere* – play,"

Falemidebiire crunched on fried goat bone and slurped the vital juices out.

"Your vessel is very beautiful, you were truly struck within. But your knowing, of how to dig in the earth to find sunsoil, only the Osoro'nga, only they know how to taste its hiding sediments with their feet."

Ma'ami recoiled at the hidden accusation.

When she spoke again, it was a half-whisper.

"Haa! Baba 'Debiire, how can you say of me, such a thing? I am not of the Iya Mi Osoro'nga o. I simply woke up during the last big storm and felt an urge beyond me to do what I did. I did not tell you because that was what Ojo said when he first saw her. I am too full of joy, her being here makes me too happy, to question her existence. And still Baba, there are certain things that make it impossible for me to be one of them; first, I am too young and I already have a craft of my own that I would never give up to tread that path."

"I meant no alarm, Wura. It is just that when I first saw the child, I knew that she was made with that sacred soil, and those black women are the only ones capable of finding it and using it in the way you did. I thought you had gotten weary of waiting and took matters into your own hands, but now I see that you are as much a vessel as your vessel is, in this matter." He had grown quieter and his voice more serious. "A word of warning, Wuraola; do not grow too attached to her, she could be gone anytime. They who gave her to you might be testing you."

After he left, Ma'ami had come into my hut as I pretended to sleep. She lay beside me and sang that she would never let me go.

Her lullaby was a dirge.

III

I stayed with myself in a void, enjoying nothing but the thrill of my mind, the way it leapt and shaped itself in the new situations that Ma'ami gave me – introducing me to an iroko, a tree so tall that I fell over backwards trying to see its crown leaves; learning to sculpt red mud into a cat that looked like Ere, eating new soups and gruels and feeling a party of spices and textures on my tongue. All this was enough to keep me going nowhere.

And even more, I craved my ever-new mother's attention and care. Every bathing and feeding held the weight of the world in it. Her showers of praise after I got clean and dressed to sit indoors, made my insides erupt with so much......that I cried out of not being able to echo the things she made bubble inside me back to her. The joy of her love kept my sense of being askew away.

I wanted to believe Falemidebiire was wrong about me being an abiku, since I held no thoughts of hurting my mother by ending my life, but one thought that hung around me was so powerful that I was willing to forsake Ma'ami's love to under-stand it.

This thought was a dream that I began to have nine months before birth.

In this dream, we will be laughing and flying in darkness. There will be a constant rumbling, of far-away thunder in conver-sation with an eye. We will be flying and laughing so fast in this nothing, empty above and below, that my core will begin to swirl hurricane blind.

Then the lightning will flash gold, once, twice, thrice, stutter. Each time burning out slower like a flare and it will illuminate ahead of us. We will see a vast pocket of sky filled with swirls and planes and chunks of night cloud. We are inside the gut of a storm and it is taking us back to Orun. We are playing. Many thousands of us, swooping through frothing mountains and valleys, tiny as sparrows in migration.

We flow silent as a river moving towards the eye, one moment – see our naked backs and arms flow in unison as we round a bend – the next moment, scattering across the seemingly endless space inside the storm like dust motes triggered with a broom, gently whirling, drunk on the freedom of being bodyless.

We will be singing for the storm, whenever we separate to dance alone, clapping and singing and spinning. The song always the same but viewed from different angles through our throats. A song that ripple like a constellation of choirs mimicking birdsong at dawn. A song that tell of all our tears and laughs, our deaths and loves. Singing with our body as much as our heart, all the melody leaving our mouths in ribbons and sparks of light. All the melody flowing to the eye of our storm.

We will not have faces or names. When the river of our souls about to start flowing towards the eye again, where some of us become lightning to go touch the earth below, one of the body will tell me that the thunder is sweet to dance to, that we should leave river for this turn to go dance, but then as they pull my palm to fly away, we will fall out of the storm, down to the earth, into a shell of old sunsoil with a jolt...

I would wake up with my heart in my mouth, confused and even more scared, remembering Falemidebiire's words about abiku travelling in storms and shut my eyes tight till sleep washed over me.

I kept my dream to myself. I knew it was true.

Three months after the dream started, Ma'ami showed me her belly. It looked different, gently swollen, with a glow that seemed to come from within. Inside it was a growing baby that she would birth in six months. Of all the things that Ma'ami had brought to me that caused me stimulation, this one nearly made the tides of my mind run out of my nose in confusion.

I could not believe that a living being rested in watery slumber within the sphere of Ma'ami's belly, waiting to come forth and walk around and see trees and eat soup like me, her, Ojo and the hundreds of men and women that I watched daily, as they worked on the farm. She made me put my ear to the taut skin of her middle and I could pick out the faintest heartbeat.

I sighed, shut my eyes and fell into her arms, still in disbelief. She smiled and told me that she hoped it would be a girl like me, so we that could become sisters.

IV

On the day of birth, Ma'ami Wura is inside one of the spare huts with a midwife. The noon sky is a clear blue and her groans and screams color the air as she labors. I am scared. I know that carrying another being inside your body is unkind.

I imagine it must feel like how it feels to be askew in this body. She has been in the hut with the midwife since dawn. Ojo paces around the center of the compound, where a mound of earth barely rises. The air is calm. In the distance, the farm's workforce can be heard; hoes and cutlasses chorusing against the earth as they sow. Falemidebiire said that by creating me, Ma'ami had healed and opened the doors to her womb for one last child. All he would do today was pray from dawn till dusk, prayers of safe birth, prayers that this one would stay.

-swim

I hear the voice right beside me. It is clear as a bell, ringing through me to the core where I felt cold when I first landed. I remember who it comes from and see her in my mind. She is the voice in the eye of the storm that our songs flow to. Mother of our migration from death home.

-sswwiimm

It comes again, this time ringing from all around my head. A chorus of the ones who play beyond space.

-swim

An itch begins to spread across my skin. Ma'ami screams again, like she is being ripped open by the other being that has lived inside her the past nine months. They haven't seen a head or leg since.

-swim

Rashes begin to spread across my body. They race across my back, searing skin with tiny pins from within. I leap up from where I have listened to Ma'ami cry in pain and watched Ojo's legs strike the earth as he paces anxious.

-swim

I run.

My legs fly beneath me as my skin ripples with the spreading rash. I run down the path behind the compound, I run through the farm and past the brown bodies of the men and women farming. They pay me no attention, probably because they have not seen me before. I run a final lap through a small patch of forest, itching at my back and cheeks and hair. I wonder what will happen when Ojo or Ma'ami cannot find me.

I burst out of the patch of forest and stand before the still lake from where another mother calls. The bright green water is mirror still. A streak of burning rashes flashes down my back and I cannot hold myself anymore. As I twist, trying to peel open my skin to remove it, I fall. The splash I make is quiet and the water is warm as it closes over my head and I begin to sink.

I open my eyes beneath the water and see them, the faceless children from my dream. They are moving with the gentle heave of the lake, a mass of arms and feet and smooth bulbs of skull.

Go. They say. *You are free.*

Little arms and legs barely waving in the water. *She took you, and now you are hers and not one of us no more.* They sound like thunder itself. The water is beginning to churn, I realize I can breathe here, beneath this green lake.

Leave us! The scream lashes out from their lips and hits me across the cheek like a whip, snapping my face sideways.

When I turn my face back up, I find that I am alone. The faceless children have vanished fast as fish and beneath the lake, it is still again.

I am alone.

I feel nothing at their rejection of me. It feels customary, like something I have been through many times before. I am just glad the rash is gone and has been replaced by a sweet chill. I relax into the ebb and flow of the lake which Ma'ami once told me lured young boys to the sea to become mermen.

Questions begin to flit.

Who?

What?

What am I?

Girl or child of sky? This body of sunsoil that sometimes looks like polished gold in daylight, this body sinking in this lake, *why does it feel like a home built nowhere?*

Why does it carry me so kind and gentle and then turn around to push me out of its pores to gaze upwards, hungry for a freedom that I know beyond bone and breath but cannot have?

Until this body is destroyed...until I dig myself out of its organs and red lining, I will never be...until this body is destroyed

....I put my fingers on the sides of my belly in rigid claws.

As I continue to sink to lake's bottom, I hold myself by the waist and push all my fingers into the soft flesh of my stomach with all the strength I can muster. The sunsoil gives. My fingers are knuckle deep inside my stomach. There is pain, but it is muted, like hot irons wrapped in cloth.

Unaware of what is really happening, I wonder what will happen when I completely destroy my body? How will I find my way back to Wura? They said I was hers now, but I cannot stay in this body any longer.

I pull my belly open and all the water around me turns red.

Something changes.

The water is moving differently, I am no longer sinking but drifting along with a wide circular current. The water is becoming redder and thicker and warmer. I move to swim to the surface but the water is too heavy.

Blood pours into my lungs. The lake has become a whirlpool and I fall into its center, fall through the eye, back sliding against blood flowing so fast it is nearly solid, fall out of this whirling, shoot like a comet into nothing.

Weightless, I open my eyes and see a host of tiny lights drift past me. They pepper an infinite that I want to reach out to but cannot. I am being returned to the one who wanted me so much she made me a body outside of natural birth. A body just destroyed.

I feel myself start to swim in the emptiness, towards one light, but it is far.

A hand, big as an iroko reaches out of the light I am moving towards and pinches my head between thumb and forefinger. It pulls me away from the diamond mist, the swirl of universes, out into tight round warmth.

I know the lining of her womb as home, feel my body suspended in amber fluid, feel her heart tremble mad with stress as her walls contract and expand, hear her scream force me awake, as she splits herself in two to bring me to life. Two hands, now small and wrinkled, pull me again, gently, through slick gate into evening air.

I am born. Screaming my lungs raw. The sound coming from my throat shocks me so hard that I inadvertently produce louder quantities.

Everything is new again. I feel fat and one with this tender body.

I stare into Ojo's proud and kind face. I am placed in the wide arms that once made me. I look into her eyes. Her immense love shines through though her body is weak.

Wura smiles through phlegm and tears at her newborn. The midwife lifts me up triumphantly by my left leg;

"It's a boy!"

Take Wing

The girl and Bear lumbered ahead. The lovers walked behind. A path of dark loam snaked through tall grass, away from the hostels, into the unknown. The diary said it would go all the way to the beach. The grass parted gently with our passing, bending back with a rustle like we were the wind, or ghosts. The forest stood dark and tall. The night ahead of us stayed silent. Soon we were close to the fecund warmth of the forest, I could smell the air suddenly, feel the cold shift of wind in the grass and feel curling fingers of fruity rot beckoning.

"Stop." The girl whispered. We could see why; a fence glistened ominously, looking ready to burn with silver fire in the moonlight. "Give me your hands as we practiced" Bear walked through the fence and stood at the edge of the forest. *Oh Bear, so fearless, so brave, so strong, not actually real.* He was being projected ever so dutifully by Salome, who until today had been something of a myth at the Aviary.

I held her outstretched hand. Her ebony flesh was striped with licorice scars from cuticle to where they disappeared into the short arms of her uniform. Her palm was cool and soft and smooth, strong bones gloved in silk.

"Jegede, focus. You'll probably be holding my hands a lot more than you think in there." I had to look into her eyes, I was the first and most important link in the ghost and therefore I had to look into her eyes.

She had these feline ovals, large and dark as the strongest liquor. They were intense to look into. Her hair was wild and cotton-thick and her ears were studded with gold drops. Oversized on her shoulders was a cracked leather jacket that was beginning to turn color. I called to John and K; Move your asses over here. I held on to John's rough digger fingers and watched him hold K's palm in a tight and strong grip. We moved forward. I took her hand and the wind blew through me.

The diary was pieces of paper slipped under a stone. It was a diseased yellow when I found it, sparkling with termite bites. It was in the Knot, the gnarled cave of looping branches and roots that looked like a giant cancerous ribcage from within. Most of the Facility knew the Knot, it always had cigarette butts, sweet wrappers, chewed-up pencils (from the ones slowly going insane no doubt), condoms and many more tiny sheddings lying around like confetti.

I wondered if the Bird knew and didn't mind since it was still within the fence. I found it, not by sneaking through the tunnel behind the run-down Department of Luck, like every other inmate at this place, but the first time I had tried to run away.

Stumbling through the dark, sweating, muscles going limp, breath leaking out of my tight chest too fast. The Hounds were behind me, tall as thoroughbreds with raw metal plates laid in jointed stripes, flying over the moist earth with a limber grace that bellied their mass and ferocity. The manic squeal of unoiled joints haunted me days afterwards. I caught my ankle in a fallen branch and rolled down into a ditch, where I fell against one of the looping roots of the Knot and slid in seconds before those snapping teeth (also very haunting) were snarling, unable to tear down the thick diseased branches. I had passed out and woken up in Solitary. Was down in that hell for three days.

I returned to the Knot and was crouching over the upturned stone that had acted as concealer and paperweight, trying to make sense of the water-stained yellow sheets I held.

"What are you doing, going through property that isn't yours?" I practically left my skin and she enjoyed every moment of it.

"You new kids have no manners." She was just there, walking across the floor with a feline grace, almost on her toes. There was an air of manic coyness in the way she pulled a handrolled cigarette from behind her ear and lit it with her slender index. My eyes widened.

"Don't worry, that's all I can do flamewise." Her eyes narrowed.

"I don't say this often, but today is your lucky day, Jegede."

"How do you know my name?"

"I do."

"You're the crazy girl that made all those dopes at Testing go through therapy."

"He's also smart. Get him off my precious paper, Bear." I had just been sitting there, watching split beams of moon pour cold and liquid across her slender shoulders. Wondering how she got here and why she was here, no one came to the Knot at night anymore, not since the Hounds. Then realizing she was the Thunderbird, I felt caterpillars of cold race down my spine. When she called to Bear, I leapt to my feet but he was already there; large and soft with that dull lumpy grace with which he existed, he put his paw (well, large hand) on my chest and pushed me backwards gently. Bear did not deal in pain.

The papers fluttered to her hands, all five of them.

"I need to get out of this place soon. Or it'll be bad news for everyone." Her eyes grew strangely sad when she said that. "Now come over here, and look, don't touch. If you can read it, I'll let you out with me. If you can't, you can sweetly go back to your room atop the Aviary. Great view, I hear."

I moved closer, watching the pages hang in the bright moonlight. "We'll be reported to the authorities once we step within ten feet of any city."

"You, probably." She said, as I began to make sense of the dainty scribbling. "I'm going to the beach."

They shot my spine yesterday and while I cried and fled to the knot, I fell in hidden well and found a path in the most unbelievable place. To the most unbelievable place. A patch of forest, so strange and so beautiful. Can you imagine? I could not. I believed it was not real for so long, but it is. It's what I needed. I do not want to go back to those people. I will marvel at this place and myself. Even if I don't go beyond the stone. I must run to there was a lake, so quiet. Its peace stilled my heart and numbed my sore soul. There is so much current they run through spine for tests. I cannot stop these minute vibrations when they jump and attack me like ghosts.

It is tiring and dangerous to go into this forest but it feeds my soul so. New girl Eagle is definitely Thunderbird. She is why I write now, because I will not let her fall to Testing. The horrible stories I have heard and read. The one I live. Those large cold rooms, with all the steel and sharp light. And the injections. I need the forest more than ever, but I do not want to run away. I do not know what lies beyond. I can only play and stare and be soothed. I saw a large crying bird yesterday. So strange, with shiny feathers bluer than Dr Ikpako's overalls. It made me go to sleep and wake up without my scars.

"I like the man who sits in lotus."

"Tutor Moshood? Of course. He's the purest thing in that filthy place. Supposed to be our spiritual center."

"I don't know the names of anyone. I got here barely two months ago—"

"And you want to leave so soon. 'Patience is a virtue.'"

"I haven't stood in the sun for so long, that's all I want. The Hounds will probably get us before we find the end."

"Hounds? We have Bear and two Eagles and *me*. The Hounds know not to bother the wrong people. Artificial animal intelligence and whatnot."

Her eyes burned in the fire John held in the air. It revealed how dwarfed we were by the giant trees. I imagined we looked like a tiny crawling glow from any respectable distance.

There is a sea! I smelt the salt and heard the roar and sigh of the waves! I walked far because Biodun, fellow Thunderbird and friend, died in War. I do not want to go to War but that is all they believe we are for. I wonder why they bother to tell us about the deaths. To rabbit us into holes where we can be smoked and eaten? I haven't eaten in so long. Rabbit meat sounds like gourmet right now. Hearing the sea was the most beautiful sound in the world since I came here, then a roar that sounded like the earth tearing split the sky and made me run back to that cold damp bed. The Bird gave me the talk yesterday. Said to be 'unafraid'. Unafraid. Unafraid. Unafraid. Unafraid. I rolled that word around my tongue so much it lost me.

"How far till the beach?"

"I have no idea."

"It cannot be more than a day right?"

"I hope not."

That night we slept in a huddle under the fallen pillar of a rotting tree. The moss was better than any bed back at the Facility. John and K were curled around each other like twin commas,

Salome and I were brackets holding conversation. She told me of home.

Rich parents, big payoff from post-apocalypse investments, replaced themselves with bright shiny toys and one maid, whom she loves more than anything in the world. They sent her here as soon as she turned sixteen, because she wouldn't stop killing the gravity while she slept. She said learning to play the piano young unleashed her kinesis early. She spoke all this with so much life and energy in her voice, with her forest ravaged face smiling softly. My breath caught whenever she smiled at me in the nights, because she never did during the day. She was like a flower, closed up for survival in the day as we twisted and wandered across the curls of faded paths beneath the eternal shade of forest canopy, but at night she revealed herself, the softer sweeter colors within.

She never talked to Bear about her problems (*"That's slightly masturbatory. And he's only here for a while anyway."*), had been at the Facility for four years, had more needle scars down her back. She always provided dry bread and tender oranges whenever someone cried "Food!" John was her half-brother and K, his burning desire whom he met cleaning floors in Testing.

We once burst into a wide clearing (one of about three in so many square yards) filled with a column of fluttering white moths and had all gone still. They danced on the light, tiny living things that made the breath catch with their purity. K laughed and ran through them, he burst out on the other side with several clinging to his bald head and wide shoulders. I had never seen him smile so wide.

"I have to see the beach, or I will know I belong on that cold slab." Salome whispered into my ears, then ran to join Bear and K in the flying snow.

The Hounds came in the night while we slept. I woke up to great skin-raising howls. From where I lay I could see Bear throw himself again a leaping Hound, grabbing its middle and squeezing till gears and bolts popped.

Salome had two of them in kinetic fists, squeezing and breaking them slowly, as another writhed in the dark soil at her feet. John and K were back to back a little further away, sweating and sending invisible javelins and bombs at the four Hounds that had them boxed in.

I rose to my feet and immediately saw a silver mass leap at me, out the corner of my eyes. I swatted it like a fly, cracking its shiny flesh, sending it sprawling struggling for balance. The Hounds had John and K shrinking into a smaller space. Salome was still killing the writhing ones in the air. I sent a fist into a canine skull and watched the body fall over.

Metal teeth sank into my arm and began to shake.

The pain was acid and I screamed, even as I watched the two Hounds left reverse for killer lunges.

Salome saved us, with her wild dirty hair and leather jacket. Screaming blue fire from her throat, as she ripped the Hounds into the night. I fell to the ground, clutching my broken arm and convulsing. The last thing I saw before unconsciousness drowned me was John holding K like he was a cracked vase of diamond glass, and the last I heard was Salome's voice alongside a great bird, singing.

We find the sea. Her hushed blue discussions wake us in the morning. My arm is whole and everyone has no scars, not even old ones. When we burst out of the forest onto the pearl sand of the beach, we behold a sight we never expected.

The dragon is dead.

It is a great albino sprawl across the strip of the beach, white armor scales sparkle and its tail dances with the tugging waves. The sky is the blue of pure happiness, the sun, a smile on the skin. The sea sighs and in the distance we see the spires of network aerials and a hint of urban blocks at the lip of the horizon. Lagos. Home.

The Facility will send a helicopter to search for us soon, we have to hide but first, Salome spins and laughs as the azure water laps her feet. John and K dance to no music.

I sit in the sand and smile.

What Not To Do When Spelunking In Anambra

Moaning heads fill a sky the color of bad water.

In their mouths; black disease and rotting teeth. Their mourning lances our ears, causing clotted blood to trickle down, past chests already sticky with sweat, to clump at groins.

People are on their knees, in the gutters, on their backs, convulsing and squirming like large dying worms. Abandoned cars and burning danfos litter the streets, and there is a horrible sound, constant beneath everything.

The keen sound of screaming.

The heads fall almost weightlessly, in large dripping swarms. Their song is inhuman, its pitch boils brains and rolls across the air like sharp teeth. I hold Link to my chest and keep staring up, waiting for it to abate. He wants to speak but only gurgles. The phlegm and blood that slides out of his lips is blacker than hate. I know he is about to make a pun about heads. I shush him.

A few feet away, a fat man is clawing at his face. His fingers fly across his head and cheeks as if to catch and stop something from swimming beneath his skull. His head implodes quietly as I watch.

Link strokes my cheek one last time, his fingers smear the blood that leaks from my eyes and ears and nostrils into streaks of sorrow.

"Please stay with me." My head hurts, but not bad enough that I want to stop it from imploding. Tears pour from my eyes, clear and wet and heavy. "They're coming...please, just look at me -"

I pull his drifting lids open with my fingers "Don't take your eyes off me. I love you, please. Remember when you were documenting? The Glossary says the heads will stop soon, they're not even real. Just......stay"

He smiles, a curve of flesh almost too pure for this moment, then his words come fast, final, between puffs of poisoned breath.

"Go...hide...they lied
...eat....our...minds.
There is no...ultimate
...knowledge, only...death."

He dies with the word on his lips, his eyes cloud and his tongue bursts.

Nothing could have prepared us for this, no herbs or prayers. The etchings on the walls of the cave back at Ogbunike foretold an outpouring of knowledge from the sky; there are kneeling figures, headless, their bodies bowed to receive the necks of other heads falling from a large object above. All this was carved into the slippery bluewhite phosphorescence that the cave walls seemed to bleed.

I still remember the sense of dread and awe that filled me with every click of the shutter. I remember Link coming to meet me nearly bursting with a fizzy joy, joy only a rogue speleologist in

Nigeria could feel at discovering a new cave system complete with terrifying etchings that glowed as if alive.

"It's a glossary of future possibilities and events!" he had whisper-shouted. "They're bringing knowledge to save us all! Can you imagine what this means for the fate of the entire planet? And for me, a young Nigerian man, not only finding ancient impressions of alien life but also deciphering their impact on our futures?"

Link had rubbed my ears the way I liked that sent warmth straight to my teeth as he said this. His eyes were glittering so wild that day. Afterwards, our entire shared universe had changed forever.

Now, I rub his ear and it is cold. I rise and his vacant head falls to the road with an immodest thunk.

The heads remain swirling, never hitting the ground. They dance across the air like blackflies over a corpse, crying with rotted throats. I am the only one standing on the bridge. The water below is bloated with bodies.

Above their deathly song, a greater heaving wail tears across the firmament, and through clouds far away, I see a shadow pale, grey and vast as a city.

The Librarians are here.

Biscuit and Milk

I

Oat

1. In the Summer of Milk, a crew of fifty Africans ascended into deep space on the oriship, *Biscuit* (also known as the Pan-African Bi-Solar Circuit Expedition). They carried precious cargo: a self-sustaining biodome of flora and fauna from Earth, as well as one thousand almost-born human babies in incubators, suspended in warm saline sacs, held in eternal sleep, to be watched over by the nurses and Midwife. These babies were gestated in hope, to save something of us if the world burned from the overheating of the sun.

2. The crew of fifty consisted of a nursing unit across genders, made up of fifteen pairs of homosexual mates and the disembodiment known as Midwife, four biodome nurturers, a Captain and her Senses, a Matron, six god-bits and other miscellaneous artificial forms of life.

3. *Biscuit* had a Mind of its own. That's why it was called an oriship. It was called *Biscuit* because its hull was made of a living nanospheric mud which "dried up" to become lighter and tougher than the hulls of any

of the older ships that had made genesis voyages into our galaxy. It was the size of a regular village, about thirty soccer fields wide, and had three main quarters: the Nursery, the Biodome and the Living Station where rooms bent and curved, warm with citrus oil, filled with cots, docks and cradles plus paraphernalia from the lives that the nurses had lived on Earth.

4. The Captain, ceremonial head of the oriship, was often psychic. A trait sought-after by the CSE above physical strength, love of solitude or the ability to fast for months; the selected sensate would leave their institutional work on Earth to take charge of the oriship for the duration of its expedition. *Biscuit,* and all the other oriships on Earth, are built capable of self-sufficient circumnavigations of the galaxy, but the Captain comes aboard to telemesh their mind with the true ori, the living Mind of the ship, to bring about consciousness. This ori was said to exist as a perfect sphere of radiant plasmium hidden somewhere in the crunch of *Biscuit*'s mass.

5. Other free space in *Biscuit* was taken up by the roaming radial cockpit where the Captain and her Senses were usually stationed, each organ (Oju, Imu, Ahon, Eti, Ifunra) had been grafted into her nervous system, no less than the size of a nail's flat top. The Senses were born when the Captain meshed her mind with *Biscuit*'s ori.

6. The Senses tuned into the Captain from the body of the 'ship, routing its senses to her. When *Biscuit* was in full manned flight, they stood around her as techni-

color avatars, like the advisors of some ancient queen. They never strayed from the Captain's perimeter, so the tubular corridors that ran between all the segments of the ship were fun to go and stand in because you could look really hard between your toes and see the universe zip by, on fire.

7. The mates, generally known as the nurses, were chosen over the duration of a decade. They had to let each couple decide thoroughly. The eyes and ears of the Council for Starward Expedition had requested data w/r/t crew for the voyage of *Biscuit*, and found that MTHR kept bringing up names in twos. It only later made sense that an Incubatory Mission should not be manned by solitary soldiers and artists but by soldiers and artists in love.

8. In the midst of this choosing of the team that would help ferry these unborn would-be survivors of the race into the uncertain black of deep space, the air on Earth had increased in toxicity, until elaborate face-gear became functional fashion. Asides a gauze mask, everyone had a fishbowl of oxygen necessary to walk around the outside world, which remained clear and ordinary looking, while free inhalation of it accelerated a cancer in vulnerable cells. All CO_2 emissions had to cease completely, and this left cars and industries asleep, near dead, with a multitude of men and women across the globe stranded with themselves in tension islands of home. The Council for Starward Expedition had no specific haven or valid second Earth they wanted their yet-to-be-born offspring to survive on. They held on to

them as hopes headed nowhere, tentative sacrifices for some unseen tomorrow.

9. The discovery of the hyper-oxygenated planet Milk, eleven light-years away from the Earth's solar system, orbiting around a binary-star system buried in a small bright diamondblue cluster, changed Earth's relationship to its climate forever.

10. While industries for the manufacture of artificial oxygen and the acceleration of forest growth rose in number, *Biscuit* was telling its crew that it was time to leave Earth. For Milk. The selected had almost forgotten about their binding agreements and they sat in silences after the videocalls ended, dumbstruck by the thought of being out in space for over a decade, alone together.

11. The Summer of Milk was a plunge into deep ecology. Every possible surface in the global cityscape was overrun with the rush of new plant life. This shift to mass horticultural splendor was organized by the artificial quintessence, MTHR, and several non-governmental organizations. Botanical rarities and their uses became a general interest. Tree worship was commonplace, with people laying orchid garlands and giving hugs to their favorites in the mornings and evenings. *Biscuit* was going to fly soon. Earth was breathing again.

12. The oriship, *Biscuit*, ascended at noon, midyear. There was a gathering of many hundred thousands of newly healed and breathlessly fresh Africans from across the continent, assembled in the clear air of the Ghanaian spaceport, the Aloft, taking pictures and gisting be-

tween the trunks of young trees, as the nurses emerged from the central pyramid in the local interstellar station, moving languorously towards the body of their ship, skin suits tucked into moonboots, shoulders covered by free lengths of bold patterned cloth.

13. They held hands as they walked up to the ship. The people were behind a fence that curved around the Aloft but their cheering rose high as a crashing wave as the miniature nurses they saw reintroduced themselves to the Captain. She stood before the ship in white plate armor, a pale ant before an enormity, a blue hooded cape around her dark pointed beauty. The arched headband that protected her temples and connected her to *Biscuit* was shaped from gleaming plasmium. She was quiet as she handed each one of her passengers a handwrought badge of office and an air helmet in response to their gentle heys and air kisses.

14. The Matron came last. She walked slowly, a bit too imperious, air-trailed by the cores of the hibernating godbits that she had co-programmed with MTHR for use in home ecosystems. They looked like spools of fine silver floating in a line above her. She wore a black cowl and dress, black sunglasses like she was hiding, mourning something.

15. Fifty-nine Presidents out of the Earth's 5000 visited to meet the crew and watch the launch of *Biscuit*. They walked across the vast white marble field of the Aloft in their black robes, staves tipped with gold, national emblems in their hands. The crew had to come back out again. This time without the bright splashes of col-

or that had followed them in. They now wore puffy yellow-blue & green-black space jackets and had black shorts above hide-thick socks and moonboots. They stood, air helmets under their arms or already in place around their necks. Some were adjusting their scarves and tiaras as the Presidents touched their shoulders with their staves, and said the Statute of Starward Expedition together as one voice. Photo drones flashed like an army of knives in the sun. The Matron was not present.

16. Everyone cleared the lightly forested area when it was time for the lightjump, driven backwards in large buses over twelve kilometers to watch *Biscuit* from a concrete shelter through mono- and binoculars. It was a medium-sized engineless ship, unorthodox in its flying capacities and capabilities. *Biscuit* was sourced from MTHR but it wasn't tethered into the central Mind of the MTHRSHIP, which was why it had no Son or Daughter or Offspring in its name.

17. Each immense pyramid of the trio that formed the Aloft was made up of tinier crystalline pyramids. *Biscuit* sat at their center, at an equal distance from each one. A crusty magnitude of these pure pointed crystals came together to form the pyramids which were each waiting to pour out a dense beam. That pure energy filled the pyramids now and the dense beams, blue as the beloved oceans below, trained their rays towards the fathomless ocean above. The triple-beam method would create a wormhole above our stratosphere, spinning the oriship quick into the depths of space, to emerge directly on a path that led to Milk.

18. As the dense beams filled a point above with kinetic energy, the Aloft filled with a dense white mist, thick like chewy morning clouds. This mist growled as it rose and tumbled slow out of the ring of the space-station, towards where the crowd watched. Lightning filled the air as the pure-white-carrier beam formed at the point where the triple-dense beams kissed high in the ionosphere, fell back down onto the oriship, like a hand onto an object.

19. The hand of the carrier beam flung *Biscuit* away from its home planet at many times the speed of sound. The noise it made as it disappeared into the sky like a white-hot bullet sounded like a deep voice saying, "Go!" across the skies of all the Earth.

II
Cabin

1. The sphere of comfort that sat in the center of *Biscuit* was coated with a shell of indestructible parts of itself. All openings, orifices and doorways of the main ship were sealed blind. The rough tough skin of the sphere ran fluid as *Biscuit* shot away from its small blue-green home, gathering speed, soon past Jupiter, riding inside a ray of live light. The crew were nestled in a soft black goo that didn't stick to their skin. It had protected them from the initial shock and vibration of the lightjump. They climbed out of where they had curled up inside the goo like they were moving through melting cushions.

2. The spin of the rim of the shell of the oriship, tense

against the spin of its central body propelled it through the void. It rolled white-hot down a street with no form and no name, leaving a trail of bright fire in its wake.

3. Captain Sade Seyitan was the first to stand tall, floating down from the opened impact sphere to place her feet on the bare floor. She tuned into the Senses and quickly groaned in agony as her mind caught flame and she fell to the floor. Above her, the nurses and the Matron unraveled themselves from the black, tumbling in no gravity without a care, their weightless daze too strong.

4. Captain Seyitan stood back up, put her hand on her temples, then went unusually still. *Biscuit* came alive inside.

5. Soft glows ran across the ice-creamy whorls of the walls, pillars and nooks that filled the middle point of the ship. Finer white lasers covered segments of the walls with active vital information: life-charts and a map of the ship that would change as it did, temperatures and gravity (several hovering bodies fell like feathers to the floor), humidity, important facts about Milk and other random glowing symbols that would only be understood by those who knew them. "And we're on our way. May starlight guide us to our new home." Captain Seyitan's deep relaxer of a voice thrummed through *Biscuit* as its cabins continued to fill with light and information. The crew clustered around themselves, air helmets snug as anxiety crawled around their earlier excitement. They looked around like stunned deer.

6. While her voice ran through the oriship, Sade stood

unmoving, eyes closed. She lifted her hands off her temples and moved them slow in the air before her body as she continued to talk. "Please make your way to your respective living stations and settle in. Biodome nurturers are expected to sleep within the Biodome section of the ship. Nurses will be allocated Nursery sectors after we reunite here in one Earth day. This will be your home for the next decade and more, so relax and forget what came before. Pay attention to what is around you now." In response to her hand movements, the "flour" that made up *Biscuit* in body rose around her into a hip-height-control-center. No buttons, knobs or screens covered it. It was just a pale arc of orange sandglass that rippled when it was touched.

7. The Senses materialized around their Captain, who watched as the Matron knelt down beneath the impact sphere and released the godbits from her side bag. She tilted her hat and closed her eyes as they began to spin in a lazy circle above her. "godbits will be awakened shortly," the Captain said.

8. At the first meeting, the unhoused godbits towered above the humans, their heads almost reaching the ceiling of the cavernous interior of *Biscuit*. They gathered in the Biodome around the Matron and shifted with every motion that she made.

9. The godbits were very specific manufacturers of energy and matter: {stars} provided lights and music and held a million Earth films in its memory. {fire} gave heat and warmth. {cook} dressed in white, looked like a tall mirage of the tight-lipped man you would find at some

corner eatery on the streets of Lagos, and could provide an endless variety of cuisine from a base of wheat flour. {moon} was a security system that also synchronized internal rhythms. {water} was a self-sustaining water body. {soapstone} was the hygiene and cleanliness system for both human and ship.

10. The crew watched the godbits swirl and twinkle from where they stood in the Biodome, on the other side of the Matron, who was wearing her sunglasses again and sitting on a mossy rock. Most of the crew were still latched tight to one another, merely glancing at their co-habitants, while others were already letting pranks loose as others held conversations about shared interests that would last for many years.

11. "How are you feeling, my people?" Captain Seyitan spoke in her normal voice as she walked barefoot out of the grove of many trees into a mossy clearing. Her plate armor and cape were gone, replaced by a too-simple gown of white silk. She wore large amber-tinted bottle glasses to hide her raw eyes. "Late, I know. Had to get the Senses into autopilot and still remain in link with them." Her hair was a tender falling of soft black curls and she rubbed her scalp through it as she looked round at the small crew. "How are you feeling?"

12. "Hungry." "Cold." "Unwashed." "Afraid." "Numb." She heard them but they didn't move their lips. "Why are you people acting as if this ship wasn't built to sustain human life? There are bathrooms and a huge kitchen somewhere. And we got godbits!"

13. The Captain tried to make {cook} prepare a picnic to be spread across the moss they sat on, but the ten-foot-tall form in white continued to gaze into nothing, until the Matron turned to it and said, "Kitchen!" Then {cook} glided out of the Biodome to find its natural habitat, the kitchen.

14. Captain Seyitan made the Matron house all the other godbits before she said anything else. {fire} went to warm the Nursery. {water} would flow through the Biodome. {soapstone} stood in the bath orifice in the Living Station, while {stars} and {moon} remained roaming. Even though they were housed, the godbits could still replicate themselves (in minor form) to be of use wherever they were needed across the 'ship.

15. The nurses and the biodome workers ate the food that half-a-dozen small robots had brought from {cook}. It was spread out on sheets in the moss. They fed themselves coyly and laughed at dumb jokes to find a sense of togetherness. The biodome workers spoke of how big the Biodome was, probably the biggest segment of the ship. The Captain and the Matron stood unusually close at the fringe of the picnic.

16. Captain Seyitan stood over the Matron on her rock seat. She didn't move to look towards the steaming plates of different rices, or the salads, the roast seitan, or the dumplings in broth. "I know you're watching me for the Council. Watching us. I will be in correspondence with Earthbase about our progress through *Biscuit*'s Mind, but I know they won't trust us, or maybe they don't even care anymore since they found their salva-

tion, ironically, in Milk. Why did they have to continue with this expedition if the greenhouse effect has become all but history? Feels like they just want to be rid of the offspring they made. They can probably hear all I am saying right now. Or maybe not." She leaned down to whisper. "Just stay out of the way. Don't bother me, my crew or my ship and you won't be bothered."

17. She almost turned away to go join the rest, but then she held back and looked into the Matron's glasses: ". . . droid."

18. Captain Sade listened to the crew members share stories of how they fell in love. She sipped on cool water and ate an apple, watching them laid out on the soft moss by the fullness of their bellies. She could see unease ricochet between them as it dissolved into familiarity. The static of their uncertainty and some little pearls of hope washed over her open mind. There was freeness, lust, hunger and desire for solitude. She didn't say much. Told them to pay attention to the offspring once the 'ship handed over most of their care to the nurses, and to always anchor themselves in the Biosphere, if they felt anxious or overwhelmed. {water} flowed around them like an enormous gurgling snake, playing under the light of the sunlike ceiling of the Biosphere.

19. Time lost meaning fast, even though the light in *Biscuit* mimicked sunrise and sunset. Its only true notations were the slow gong for meetings or meals in the bright warmth of the Biodome's fields and the steady hum of the 'ship's spin that became second nature quick. The nurturers had woken three young creatures from the

cryogenic zoo that rested at the center of the Biodome like a flat silo. So mealtimes were punctuated by long cuddle sessions with lamb, pup and bunny.

20. The nurses watched over their segments of the Nursery, spending time flitting between it and the Living Station. Each cryogenic incubator was shaped like an egg with shells lit from within with a white glow. {fire} sat at the center of the vast Nursery, burning low enough to warm the offspring when they were thawed for checks. The instructions were to birth them halfway through the voyage to Milk.

21. It started a short while after the third light-year had been breached. Midwife wailed her alarm like a living banshee, during rest hours. The nurses woke to find several incubators dead (neither the blue light of cryogenic sleep, or the pearl-white of the thaw came on) and the offspring within them discarded. The Captain was furious and nearly ate the Matron up asking, "I want access to your visual databases now! So, *this* is why your councilors were so adamant that I take an archaic machine onto my ship, not to run godbits, who run themselves just fine, but to murder precious cargo." Her mild fury caused the lights to flicker, the gravity to double and the ship to seemingly tilt, and for the first time the crew could feel the floorless gut of the Universe that they fell through yawn forever everywhere around them and they held on to themselves in fear, until she turned away from the Matron in a huff to seal herself in the Living Station.

22. The Matron who barely spoke, and who some of the

nurses believed to actually be a reanimated woman with deep cyborg grafts, began to scream. Her voice trembled just like said old woman's. "These abominations must find no life. Not on Earth, not on this ship and certainly not on the new world that we approach. They were not made to be natural. Their very being is against God's law. They have no fathers or mothers and were made too quickly in moments of fear. Man is not supposed to triumph over his nature by the help of science. We can't let them live."

23. One of the aghast nurses, a man they called Sweet Mam, said, "Excuse me, Matron, but you seem to forget that your augmentations were once contested in courts of law across the Earth, as being unnatural. Remember the decades of 'Man not Machine.' I was a child then and you sound like a living irony right about now. Anyway, what is it about these kids anyway? They were artificially conceived for the specific purposes of interplanetary seeding. Their futures have nothing to do with your pre-recorded rants that sound like they're coming from really far back in some dusty forgotten Archive. They will not be citizens of Earth but of Milk."

24. Sweet Mam looked around from where the others watched his speech in mild shock, and saw the back of the Matron running in a limp towards the godbit at the center of the Nursery. The battle she had fought in silence behind sunglasses was lost. She had strained as they spun through empty space, questioning the rage that filled her as she walked through the Nursery, un-aware of the urges that came from code-knots and key-

pads beyond her as she asked herself to destroy innocent life, and then nearly cracked open her iron-skull for entertaining such deadly thoughts. In this moment, her human heart had given up. Its fight against the neurocode put into her plasmium brain by her creators too one-sided to be fair. The Council sent one last request. As she reached the center of the Nursery, she shouted, "{fire}: inferno." and the column of the godbit's body went from blue to bright orangeyellow in a blink. Heat flowed in sudden waves away from the phoenix-like form, razing over the resting offspring around it as the incubators began to crack and steam up. The crew scattered in panic when all they could see and feel was {fire}.

25. A gunshot pewed across *Biscuit*. The Matron dropped into a black heap among the scalded eggs, and {fire} rested once the heart of the Matron which was the center of its orders shut down. Captain Seyitan stood among the heavily steaming unborn in the Nursery holding a stun gun. She lowered her arm. "Get her out of here. And someone go get us {water}."

26. While they waited for {water}, the crew member that they called Doctor Love came over to her, stroking their mustache as a river crashed through the entrance into the Nursery. They looked amused and their face didn't carry the weight of their words: "Midwife says we have to birth them all now. Or they die."

27. The river of {water} ran around their ankles and washed over the heated incubators. Emergency numbers made of red light scurried up the walls of the Nursery. Midwife switched from sonic to visual appearance and

stood beside the meditative {fire} which was completely unaware of the impacts of its automatic actions. She was almost tall as the Captain as she stood flickering with real static. She wore a red habit and cowl and her fingers were sheathed in red latex. Her high voice ran across the Nursery, startling the confounded nurses where they stood around. "I need blankets! And towels! And heated water bottles! Give me scissors! And cradles! Everyone looking at me get some gloves and begin to open the incubators as fast as you can."

28. Captain Seyitan called {soapstone} from where it rested inside the Living Station. She snapped on the egg-yolk gloves it provided and moved to begin birthing the offspring from grave and womb.

III
Digestives

1. Did they think they would ever see the smooth blue-white pearl of Milk? Only *Biscuit* seemed to care about their voyage and destination at some point in the loose time that followed the All Birthing. The unusually large babies grew slow and were rarely awake, preferring to sleep in cradles over trying out newborn feet.

2. The Nursery was transformed into a Care Zone with {fire} still maintaining its place at the center, burning low through the sleep of the nurse and the child.

3. They began to babble and walk one year to their arrival on Milk. The nurses followed their every move, chasing them with bottles of warm milk and folding

their sleeping forms into heated blankets. They were relieved when they found out that suspending the gravity made them stop fussing and try swimming. They had no names but numbers and less than half of their original number had survived the All Birthing. When *Biscuit* made a clear window and opened up the cosmos rushing by for them to see, they quieted and fell to sleep quicker.

4. The nurses and the biodome workers had grown comfortable in their loosened bones and gone grey at the temples. There was less romantic experimentation after the All Birthing brought them closer together as pairs. They became so absorbed in being parents to hundreds of fragile beings that their senses grew more acute than *Biscuit*'s in detecting shifts in the biological states of the offspring. They sensed that these babies were much different from any others they had known in their time on Earth, preparing for this voyage. They did not know how they differed, only feeling a tug that could have been fear in their chests, as they drew them closer to their breast, and their eyes became winged with care, dove's feet.

5. **Three days to Milk**: The Captain reappeared in the Biodome as if from a dim memory of the past. *Biscuit*'s flight was slowing down. She seemed less overwhelmed, and strong enough to wear her plate armor and blue cloak again. The Senses had run a majority of the voyage on their own, even if they would not exist without the roots of her nervous system. The offspring tottered on the moss around her knees. In the corner, a

mass of toddlers watched mesmerized as {stars} broadcast a universe of cartoons from the world left behind, hand-drawn-and-colored stories of love, play and home from times that changed quicker than a chameleon on fruit. {moon} seemed most affected by the cinema of {stars} from where it floated above the gathered offspring; spinning with glee, shuddering in grief.

6. *Biscuit* entered Milk, three years and nine months after the All Birthing, nine years and eight months after lightjump from Earth. Both homes were about the same size. From the windows that *Biscuit* opened like so many eyes as they neared Milk, the crew (turned into jungle gyms by their offspring) watched a new world draw closer. It was mostly white, but cloud cover ripped in neat shreds to reveal a hypnotic cobalt terrain beneath. "No one said anything about water," the crew member that they called Vulture's Song said to their partner, Nyakinyua, who responded, "Water comes in rivers and streams on the planet Milk, and that looks very much like an ocean if memory serves me well."

7. The crew gathered the offspring into their cradles when it was time for descent. It was as smooth as the low gravity and gentle winds of Milk's atmosphere willed. They sank through curtains and curtains of thin clouds washed in a sharp light that was blue where the Earth's was yellow. *Biscuit* landed on its edge in a perpetual morning.

8. The doves, the ram and the dog breathed Milk's air first. Captain Sade Seyitan followed. She took a deep breath and exhaled cool mist, then fell to her knees and cried

till she lost all sense.

9. When the Captain came to her senses, they were surrounded. *Biscuit* rose behind them, an obscene am-
phitheater on its side. The things that walked, swirled
and drifted around them could be likened to seaweed,
octopi, jellyfish. Their mass was larger though, about
the size of a bus on Earth, and they moved about in
the double sunshine, blowing cold and warm. The offspring were yet to climb out of their locked cradles and
their terrified cries seeped out of *Biscuit* and filled the
air of Milk. Captain Sade looked over at the nurses and
the biodome workers who were also crouched as unknown life swam around them, exhaling fast waves of
air. "I think they're harmless," the zoologist they called
Ewe Egbo said to his partner, Mr. Alcove. "Me too. I'm
going to the kids." He ran into the dancing mist and
immediately collided with what felt like a strong moving
current. He fell back, stood up, and began to dance with
the oxygen masses, seeking gaps and paths with his hips
and feet, while making his way back to *Biscuit*.

10. *Biscuit* fell in slow motion just as Mr. Alcove got near
enough, as the beings swimming pushed soft against it
where it blocked their paths of silken motion, to land
on its side. The Captain danced, the nurses danced and
the biodome workers collected samples.

11. Watching from where they sat and rested on the cool
glade of their new home, the almost-mothers watched
in tender trepidation as the unmothered children of
Earth communed with the oxygen masses (who mimicked their growing human bodies in giant simulacra,

made from meldings of their thin filaments) and learned to use the air of Milk. They grew strong, very very fast. Stronger than human, or neomachine. Their nurturers couldn't gasp loud enough as each one of them became capable of flight at great speeds, while gradually becoming imbued with a mythic superstrength. Some of them grew power in (and over) All-Mind and shared their imaginings of the world that they wanted to live in with their siblings. Their nurturers watched them place their foreheads against one another unaware of what was occurring beneath their skulls. This melding triggered a unification as their minds fell into a lattice and they became one macro-organism capable of future memory.

12. When the Biodome fell out of *Biscuit* to land on the soil of Milk, {water} became an ocean of freshness. The ship segment rooted fast around the heave of {water} as the cryogenic zoo thawed out and a thousand species of Earth creature rushed across the surface of Milk. {the stars} became co-architect with the Offspring who worked to build with what matter they found on the planet; towering rocks of a chalk hard as ice, a variety of harder crystals and strange fibrous roots that led to no tree.

13. First, they took apart the Matron and buried their siblings who did not survive the All Birthing. They planted a flag of the motherworld, Earth, and then built a replica of *Biscuit* to temporarily house those they had come to love as parent. {fire} split into many tongues and went roaming, falling in gang with a school of oxygen.

14. {moon} gave itself to {water}.

IV
Shortbreads

1. "{cook} will be the Core. You'll be the Undercore. No need for head, ceremonial or otherwise," the Offspring said to their guardians, fathers and mothers when they had finished building their own new worlds, apart from what the Council for Starward Expedition had envisioned for them when they were nothing but incubating foetuses. They placed them, all grey and holding on to each other as the only way to remember home, into a huge ecosystem inspired by underground rivers and crustaceans. Disconnected from the ori of *Biscuit*, Seyitan (and {soapstone}) became planetary guardian, taking bird's-eye tours of Milk in an aeroplane built from the remains of the oriship. They would often come across the larger oxygen masses that lived in the higher altitudes, watching them writhe and bloom and make a music of atoms.

2. Like a platinum moon, the ori of the *Biscuit* was set free to roam. After it routinely beamed images, audio and other media of the vistas of Milk back to an unresponsive Council for Starward Expedition Hub, the perfection of its Mind's sphere quit broadcasting and swam the skies amongst the slick, dark Offspring in mass flight, an exercise they claimed kept them healthy and in clearer mental contact. It allowed itself to be held by them, even when there was no telepathy in session. It went dull as lead when it hibernated and vibrat-

ed deeply to communicate with the Offspring or the oxygen masses. It rarely ever acknowledged the human crew's existence.

3. Round and round they went, experiencing many orbits on Milk in the complex homes and cluster-families they had built for themselves, yet, they remained unable to undo a severe itch that filled their collective mind. Like a homing beacon it scratched and pinged, rushing in blinding crinkles across the secret garden of their tele-phasing brains, a whispering wind, a luminous vision of a before they never knew; the dreaming of a blue-green world that pulled at them, home to the living milks that brought their first cells to life. In search of origin and motherworld, followed by the freed ori of *Biscuit*, the offspring left behind the humans who had raised their bodies before the oxygen of Milk took over in elevating their spirits beyond any dreams of gods. Guardians held on to nurturers, fathers held on to fathers, mothers to mothers and caregivers to the wise, as their Offspring took off for a forgotten home, shooting up into the eternal blue of Milk's skies, leaving behind nothing but vapor trails.

Convergence in Chorus Architecture

One

I
Struck

In escape from sword and fire of war, Osupa was born.

Osupa was the sixty-something members of various tribes that had escaped from war in the city of Ile-Ife. Osupa was the land on which they survived and thrived. Osupa was a perfect rectangle on which fourteen circular huts made of solid sunbaked mud stood. They were all roofed with dense layers of dried banana leaves.

At the center of Osupa was a shrine – a large box of mud with a roof of thatch, supported inside with the trunks of many young trees. This was where the Awo Meta (Fatona, Fagbeja and Awojobi) lived. The mud walls of the square hut, were covered in chalk drawings of the moon and three orisha; Esu, Orunmila and Obatala, each bearing various objects in their arms to depict their roles in the machine of the oracle of Ifa. The oracle wasn't depicted because you would meet it if you walked inside the shrine.

They had found the smooth hard land of Osupa hidden behind a wall of trees and bushes full of thorns in which babies cried under the glare of a full moon, the bombs and fires kissing the sky behind them.

Ifa had been the one who had led them to Osupa, speaking guttural through the throats and seeing white through the eyes of the Awo Meta. The people had followed their calls and the sway of their white garb and pointed staffs through the night and into the teeth of the forest until they found the flatland which seemed to have been waiting, prepared. The Awo Meta had stuck their staffs into the earth at the center of the space and called it Osupa, moon.

As a sacrifice, the people of Osupa dug out the square for the shrine of Ifa that night before they all went to sleep, excepting the Awo Meta, who stayed awake enchanting and drawing a ring of aabo, protective light, around the land that they had claimed. This would make them invisible to the eyes of the demons, mercenaries and blood-drunk soldiers who would wander out of Ife in search of slaves and fresh kills.

Come morning, they showed the men, whose numbers were half that of the women, the breadth of the land, where the farm should lay and where the kitchen shed should stand. There was a lake just outside the ring of light abundant with mud. The men got to work cutting down branches and thatch to begin building. The women collected mud in the large open gourds that had held their clothes and other personal objects.

They forgot to mourn while they worked to build their new homes so after the shrine and the houses had been built, there was a loud weeping across Osupa by the wives who had lost husbands and the husbands who had lost wives and the mothers who had lost children and the children who had lost innocence.

The Awo Meta began to call meetings inside the shrine every seven days, teaching the mourners of Osupa songs of farewell to the dead, songs to heal and songs for the moon. Whenever this happened the great sound of their hearts would rise out of their mouths, through the black night, seeming to touch the starry firmament above.

Osupa grew into its rhythm in the space of three moons. The widows found husbands and sisters, and the widowers found new wives and brothers. The children were adopted by those who fell in love with them. There was bush rat and corn and yam and pepper and salt, and it wasn't rare to see the entire settlement of Osupa gather around fires to feast and dance and offer praise to Ifa and Olodumare for their survival. The aabo held strong and the war became like a bad dream that faded under the warm touch of a lover. Everything was going well. The people were in peace. The oracle and the three babalawo were joyous with their home and shrine.

Until Fagbeja threw cowries that flashed purple and filled the shrine with black smoke.

Until the storm came.

***

The Awo Meta did not tell the people of Osupa about the coming tempest. Instead, they told them that Olodumare was coming to visit. They made them wear white and smear the blood of wild duck across their foreheads and thresholds, then they made them sing to Olodumare, the Fount and Cradle of All.

The Awo Meta partially believed their lie and their best guess concerning the tempest was that it was a lesser orisha coming to cleanse their land through rain and flood. That night, enormous bulbous clouds rose black in the west, bleeding purple lightning and cold winds that made the forest howl. The people of Osupa curled up in their huts and prayed to Olodumare as the rain began.

***

The storm quieted just as dawn broke. Everything was heavy and wet, even the air they breathed. The water had risen to their knees and broken into their huts to carry out clothes and baskets of food. It had caused the roof of the kitchen shed to cave in. Some huts had been moved and lay half crumbled a distance away from the line in which the other huts stood.

The people of Osupa began to fish for their belongings in the water. The shrine was unperturbed, probably because it had been built on a foundation of stones and sticks that were three feet deep into the earth. Awojobi who was the oldest of the babalawo, tall with long hair plaited all back to his neck, eyes laced with venom and kohl, called all the youth together and told them to go check the damage done to the farm. The older men were going to rebuild the broken huts. The aabo had been broken during the storm and the Awo Meta were preparing to cast a new one.

The clouds that had brought the storm remained giant in the sky, casting a quarter of the morning in their shadow. There were about twenty young men and women in Osupa. Most of them were orphans who had found new parents.

The quietest of these orphans was a young man named Akanbi, who never went anywhere without wearing a gold and green abeti aja that his father had given him on his head. It was woven with a rare heavy thread that made it stand firm.

Akanbi led the party of youth towards the edge of Osupa where the farm lay. The twins with voices like heavenly trumpets, Gbolahan and Gbemisola Olohun followed immediately behind him, walking side-by-side. The rest were a distance behind carrying baskets and hoes. No one really spoke to each other, even when they were in Osupa, except those who had fallen into co-dependent relationships by virtue of shared loss. The only thing that brought them all together were the nights of praise when crop was abundant.

Akanbi walked to the edge of the farm and stopped. The lake had burst its banks and submerged the farmland which lay down a slope. Only the tips of ripe corn poked above the still water like lumps of tangled light.

"Olodumare is angry at us for escaping our fate in the war." Gbolahan Olohun was melancholy in the only way someone possessed of so much beauty could be.

"We are lucky nobody died." His twin sister echoed, "I think what the Awo told us to do helped. The duck's blood...we are safe. Thank our Fathers and Mothers Past." The remainder of the party arrived behind them and gasped. Some swore against the orisha and Olodumare beneath their breath.

"Bring me baskets. And any one of you who can swim follow me, please." Akanbi spoke, with a deep voice that always surprised because he was so small and had clear shy eyes. He was ridiculously polite and told great stories about orisha and elemi, the spiritseen, punctuating the most fantastical and horrid episodes with a coy smile and a twinkle in his eye, swearing he knew because he came from a family with an ancestral braid that lead straight to Orunmila.

Akanbi took the basket and walked into the farm, slipping under the water with a silent splash, basket trailing the surface like a ritual boat. Three other swimmers followed after. Gbemisola could swim. Gbolahan could not and he was secretly sure that when he eventually died, he would drown. He stood at the edge of the farm with the others. Beside him, two girls spoke excitedly about the rage of the storm and the power of orisha. It began to sprinkle light rain. The swimmers broke the surface near the middle of a row of cornstalks.

The stormclouds drifted; growing and stuttering, all lightning no thunder.

***

The baskets slowly filled with wet cobs of corn and big red peppers. The swimmers drifted languorous through the submerged farm, rising to take breaths before sinking back into the underworld of water and wavering green stalk. The morning light was milky above, coming from the side of the sky not shaded by the storm clouds. Light was nearly non-existent beneath the surface, but it was clear enough to see and pluck the softened harvest.

The storm clouds leaned into the morning even more and rumbled with new thunder. The boys and girls on shore began to call to the swimmers to return. The light rain was about to become something more. The light grew dim and the air became cold again like it did the night before. The four swimmers began to approach the shore with three full baskets between them, kicking their legs and supporting the baskets with one arm while paddling with the other. The storm continued to roil, eating up the rest of the dawn without letting loose.

Lightning flashed and for a moment, everything seemed made from white stone. The returning thunder caused the earth to tremble and made most of them duck against their will. Gbolahan Olohun called for his sister to be faster. They still had to walk up the slippery underwater slope to set the baskets down before they could come out completely.

Two of the swimmers, tall brothers who had lived close to the River Osun before the war, came out first. Akanbi and Gbemisola waited in the water to support the baskets from sinking. The brothers stood on solid ground just as the patter of light rain stopped. The remaining light took on an electric texture and the youth on the shore of the drowned farm wondered if their skins were glowing in the night that the clouds had brought.

A fork of lightning fell onto Osupa from above, pure and effervescent. The reporting thunder shook the earth deeper and all those standing fell to the ground, shivering from the sound. The baskets and the swimmers holding them slid back to the bottom of the farm.

Witnesses say they saw slow lightning touch the heads of Akanbi and Gbemisola Olohun with small bright hands.

***

They carried the lightning-struck and the dripping harvest to the village, running without a sound to conserve energy. Gbemisola and Akanbi's bodies were limp and their eyes had rolled back to reveal only white. The swimmer brothers and Gbolahan carried them into the shrine and the presence of the Awo Meta who were deep in a singular act of divination; the flat wooden tray before them was covered in fine white sand in which single or twin marks lay in vertical rows that told of many futures. They sat at its angles with bodies held erect and eyes lowered.

Gbolahan was the first to shout for help, and his voice was so keen in its terror that Fagbeja and Fatona fell out of concentration in shock. Awojobi rose to his feet in one sleek motion and was beside the tangle of bodies in a blink, asking questions. The brothers lowered the bodies of Gbemisola and Akanbi to the ground and stood back. Gbolahan shivered as he threw himself across his sister, caught between sobbing and silence.

"What happened?" Awojobi asked. Fatona and Fagbeja had recovered and were standing by his side. The three of them looked indestructible as a unit, as they had ever since the day they found Osupa together. Their eyes were hard as they stared at the situation before them.

"Lightning struck! It was lightning that struck them. When they were in the water. Aaaaah! Please help." This was said by Gbolahan who Fagbeja, a small but mighty man with white hair everywhere was pulling off Gbemisola and giving several small slaps to the face. Fagbeja wiped Gbolahan's tears away with his pure white wrapper and told him to toughen up. *S'ara giri!* Gbolahan swallowed the coming waves and yelled with panic, "Don't let her die, Baba!"

Awojobi was already in a crouch, laying his long-fingered right hand across the heart and temples of the fallen two. Fatona was just as tall as Awojobi but had no single hair on his head. He pulled the swimmer brothers aside and asked more questions about the quality of the light and the air before the incident.

When they responded, his mouth dropped open. He turned to Awojobi, who nodded in confirmation. The rest of Osupa was already gathered around the entrances to the shrine, some peeping in and others speculating away.

Their work done, the stormclouds were now dissolving to let the late morning sun come down and burn away the rain that had soaked into everything.

Akanbi's guardian, the old woman who he had clung to and helped as he ran away from the war wormed her way into the shrine and limped towards where he lay. She put her hand to her mouth and stood as she watched Fagbeja send the people away from the entrances to pull down the white sheets of cloth that served as doors.

"What happened Baba Awojobi?" she asked quietly as she watched Fatona and Fagbeja layer mats and old cloth on the floor to make beds.

"Nothing, Iya Akanbi. The children have just been called to see. They're dreaming vivid." Awojobi said, as he chewed a bitter root and his mouth turned a dark green. The two babalawo lifted the limp bodies of Gbolahan and Gbemisola and placed them on the two lengths of cloth.

"Dreaming?"

"You wouldn't understand yet, Iya." He put his hand on her shoulder and guided her towards the billowing door, where Gbolahan stood riveted, eyes on the prone body of his sister.

"Please tell the boys to bring us any dry firewood and oil and leaves that they can find." She nodded, still confused, and then walked through the cloth door. Gbolahan stayed. Fatona and Fagbeja had begun to lay out strange powders in lines around the beds they had made for his sister and Akanbi.

"Go and help them find dry wood, Gbolahan." Awojobi spat the bitterness from his mouth to the floor. "You cannot be here."

***

In one of the futures that the Awo Meta saw for Osupa, there was an exodus. In another, there was an expansion. They never saw the birth of two elemi, stripped of their skin by lightning, then called into the mind of Olodumare to see.

The three men, weary with worry over the fate of Akanbi and Gbemisola, walked around the fire that they had built near the heads of the dreaming ones. They had not slept all day and now the night was here. They could see the lanterns of the people of Osupa parading outside their shrine. They could hear people greet and console Gbolahan who had stayed outside since he and the boys returned with some dry thatch and wet wood.

The moon was a sliver in the night above.

Fagbeja, who was an expert alchemist and brewer of potions was boiling something sweet and acrid in a black pot on the fire whose warmth had managed to stop the random shivers of Akanbi and Gbemisola. Awojobi and Fatona were taking off strings of charms and singular object-potencies from around their waists and the nooks of their bodies. They washed their mouths and armpits and faces with saltwater before wrapping their bodies in spotless white wrappers, their heads and shoulders in shawls of knitted white aso-oke. Fagbeja was already prepared and draped, his face covered completely in a mask of liquid chalk as he stirred and stirred his distillate of dream.

Awojobi painted a circle around his left eye. Fatona drew twin lines from the center of his head to his jaw, slipping two fingers over his nose. They both came and stood by Fagbeja, who put his hand into the red coals, picked up the pot and placed it gently on the floor.

"This is the strongest one I've made yet. One large gulp and the spirit will forever be trapped outside the body, suspended in many dreams. We must take only six drops each. Enough to get us to them but also not too much that we all can't return home, to our bodies."

Awojobi, the oldest, was the weaver of light and the one who lived in constant trance already. He went first and lay on the bare ground opposite the fire, with his hands atop one another on his stomach and his eyes shut. He opened his mouth and Fagbeja placed six drops on his tongue. The distillate was terrible in its bitterness and the old priest's face crumpled as the liquid seemed to turn his tongue and throat black and sticky, then his face relaxed. His stomach filled with warmth and his tongue began to leak spittle sweeter than honey. He drifted to sleep.

Fatona was the healer whose body was sensitive as spider's web, he lay down to the right of Awojobi and took the drops on his tongue. Bitterness darkened his insides and in his sleep, sweetness bloomed.

Fagbeja went last, laying down and placing the pot next to his waist before taking the six drops onto his own tongue. His chalk-whitened face wrinkled and he too went to sleep at the sound of sweetness.

***

Midnight crept by on long hushed toes. In the shrine, five bodies lay prone. The boy and the girl lay to the right, three days asleep and covered in lengths of warm adire. Next to them, coals burned in a shallow pit. They cast a glow of tender sunset across the bodies dreaming. The babalawo lay to the left of the pit, stiff as three logs on the bare earth.

Everyone in Osupa was asleep as if by some transference. Even Gbolahan Olohun slept beside the door where he had stood all day, waiting for his sister to awaken.

In the sky above, three owls circled under the smile of a new moon.

II
In Exhumed Nightmare

Awojobi, who went to sleep first, woke in the shared dream last. He found himself and his brother-babalawo standing on an endless plain of sharply bright grass that seemed to flow in perfectly timed waves away from something that towered up ahead, at the focal center of the dream. Light sparkled around them, seeming to fall like dust from the cloudless blue sky above.

No birds called and no wind blew.

Fatona the hairless was already walking up ahead towards the thing that stood at the center. It was an immense blight, blotting out the bright fabric of the dream; throwing thrashing shadows, black and slick. It grew from deep in the earth, spreading as it made its way up towards the heavens. Right at its mouth stood Akanbi and Gbemisola Olohun, dwarfed into insignificance.

Fagbeja was close behind Fatona, an owl on his shoulder. They all wore fine heavy agbadas of white aso-oke shot through with silver thread. Awojobi followed his brothers, swaying through the grass towards where the two dreaming were like ants before the black thing writhing and splitting reality. He tried to remember if he had ever seen anything like it in his sixty years of trance but nothing.

Fatona followed the waves of the plain, his owl eye gleaming as the blight grew in size, polluting the blue above. As healer, he could sense that it was both wound and womb. A doorway from a distant place. Something began to push against the chaos of the blight. Its body flashed violet as it sluggishly began to distend the membrane of the dream through the blight.

Awojobi leapt and flew above the dream. He had gotten the wings of the owl. They flapped at their normal size a few breaths above the back of his agbada and helped him soar ahead of Fatona and Fagbeja to land behind Akanbi and Gbemisola. The two dreamers' heads were turned towards the blight, their necks bolted in place. Their toes were sunken into the soil and from the bones of their legs sprouted buds and leaves. Their eyes were black as pools of ink. Awojobi moved to touch them.

The membrane broke and a titanic object floated out; twisted, burnt black and heavy as old bone. The sparkling light and the lush green fields disappeared in its shadow. The broken membrane sizzled like fat in fire and from the point of the blight, the entire sky boiled into starless night.

Awojobi went blind. Fagbeja stopped moving, the owl on his shoulder was simply a tether and an advisor on how things were on the other side, where they lay on the ground in Osupa. Fatona saw clear as day with his owl eye, but he was still too far from where the two dreaming stood. He began to run.

Akanbi and Gbemisola opened their mouths at the same time. Akanbi began to speak incantations he didn't know and Gbemisola sang wordless from the bottom of her gut. Their voices reverberated, dissonant, through the air of the dream.

Turning his neck to follow its drift, Fatona saw with his owl eye on the body of the boneship, a living language, crawling and burning violet in the void of the night it had made. Awojobi followed the sounds of Akanbi and Gbemisola to reach where they stood, then he held onto their shoulders to keep them still till Fagbeja and the tether arrived. He immediately began to ululate and call to the boneship in an unknown tongue.

As the babalawo ran towards their patients and the boneship drifted imperceptibly to the center of the dream, camouflaged against the darkened sky, night against night – a guttural screaming began, random as birdsong, echoing from spots distant and near. Each voice allowed a scream to finish before the next rose with hair-raising pitch. They seemed to be screaming against the thing in the sky, yelling as if they were each about to be devoured in the slimy jaws of a great beast.

Fagbeja ran faster, prayers whispered under his breath carving open a path through the grass. The owl on his shoulder now flying low before his face, revealing the way to Awojobi with its body.

The first snatch occurred. A scream was cut short by a blaze of violet fire, as the body screaming exploded, up into the air, burning a trail thin as thread up from the distant plain into the gut of the boneship. Then the next scream was cut off, a body nearer to where the babalawo ran, ripped out of the earth, burning up as it shot into the boneship. As Fatona and Fagbeja ran, aided by the earth beneath their feet, the black sky in which the boneship now hung static exploded with violet missiles as bodies that seemed to be buried deep in the earth of the dream, screamed and went mute as they were ripped out of the soil into the sky.

Fatona reached where Awojobi, Akanbi and Gbemisola stood, making strange rippling sounds with their tongues. Eyes blind and riveted to the boneship. With his owleye, he saw violet streams rushing out of their lips up towards the boneship, along with the burning missiles of the stolen bodies. They were reading the living language.

He pulled a lodestone out of his agbada. It was a perfect cube of white rock.

Fagbeja and the tethering owl arrived. Fagbeja nodded to Fatona. Fatona threw the cube up and placed a hand on Awojobi's shoulder. The lodestone burst into white light and hung still as a sun but flashed like it was full of shadows of rippling water.

Fagbeja put one hand on Fatona's back and the other around the owl's feet.

The tether flew, lifting them up like they were the weight of dried leaves. It took them out of the dream into the lodestone.

In their absence, the nightmare continued and the earth was pillaged for her bounty of soul.

***

The cube of the lodestone opened up inside the shrine at Osupa. Forms slipped out of its blinding brightness, casting shadows against the walls. The forms were serpentine things, moving weightless and aglow with a shifting light. They swam through the air and slipped into the mouths of the five sleeping.

The lodestone collapsed into a sparkle, a point of light so bright it lasted in the air for the several breaths that Gbolahan Olohun took as he woke up and peeped into the shrine to watch the babalawo wake up and sit, each vigorously rubbing their eyes and back and ears as if to remove impurities. The sparkle vanished. A white owl flew out of the shrine.

Gbemisola Olohun and Akanbi stirred and moaned as they returned into the heaviness of their bodies. When they opened their eyes, their pupils were clouded silver with sleep and when they opened their mouths, nothing came out.

III
Herald the Masons

Three days passed before Gbemisola and Akanbi could stand up and walk around inside the shrine. They remained speechless. The Awo Meta consulted and divined every waking moment, taking turns at tossing opele on their oval boards and drawing lines in a circle of white sand. Ifa showed nothing, said nothing, but they continued to persist with the oracle and tend to their mute patients.

Awojobi knew exactly what was going to happen. A breach into this world, Ile-Aye, by something from another world, something powerful and hungry. Something beyond human understanding. He had touched Akanbi and Gbemisola's shoulder in the dreamscape and seen and heard as they did. He couldn't remember speaking as they did. The burning violet language was a message to open, a call, a courier.

Awojobi had never witnessed anything so strange in all his life as a babalawo jumping through space-time and seeing realms above and below. Awojobi also knew Ifa wasn't speaking to them three maybe because the two voices he had selected to use were currently muted.

Fatona and Fagbeja continued to work around the two when they tottered back to lie on the ground – Fagbeja with his herbal tinctures and dense aromatic submergence and Fatona with his cool hands and silent tears. Awojobi sat in the corner, draped in white shawls and stared into the firepit at the center of the shrine, seeing violet.

***

Gbolahan snuck into the shrine on a morning after a long all-nighter by the three babalawo over Gbemisola and Akanbi. Through the night, they had tried to get them both to talk, to explain what they had all seen in the shared dream.

Was the boneship coming for the settlement of Osupa alone or the entirety of the world as they knew it? Was it the war and bloodshed of Ile-Ife that would draw this hungry thing into this world?

Gbemisola had just stared at them with eyes like a newborn, a strange amused smile on her face, while Akanbi returned to his bed and slept so well he was curled into a fetal position.

By sunrise, the Awo Meta were also asleep around the firepit in the center of the shrine. Gbemisola was wide awake but unable to speak. She tried every other moment to shout and say something but all that came out was an airless whisper. Her pupils were blown wide with what she tried to speak of.

Gbolahan woke at the first crowing of the cock and saw that the Awo Meta were drifting to sleep, while Gbemisola stood up awake. He was overjoyed at seeing his sister live and move again, that the babalawo had barely begun to snore before he ran into the shrine and threw his arms around her. Gbemisola went still and then began to struggle out of his arms. She succeeded. They both stood apart and stared at each other with similar eyes; Gbemisola's full of terror and Gbolahan's loving and tired.

"Gbemi! It's me your brother. I was...so afraid. I thought you would never come back from your sleep."

Gbemisola turned away, arms wrapped around her chest. She looked at Gbolahan over her shoulder. Gbolahan walked over to her and tried to place a hand on her shoulder but Gbemisola moved before contact.

"Gbemisola? My other from the womb of our mother till now. We are here. Speak to me." She walked away even deeper into the hut, closer to where her bed lay beside Akanbi, and where the Awo Meta were knocked out, catching their first sleep in days. Gbolahan stopped moving towards her and she stopped walking backwards.

Gbemisola pointed to the thatch sky of the shrine. She began to walk in a circle, then she stopped for Gbolahan to understand her. Gbolahan did not understand and so he did what he always did when they had a fight and struggled to communicate.

He kept his voice low as the song spilled out of his lips, pleading and embracing in deep warm tones.

Sister. Tell. Where did you go? What did you touch? Did you see the gods all lined up in a circle in the sky, welcoming you into the chaos of their forever? Sing, sister. Tell.

Gbemisola watched and listened as Gbolahan sang, modulating his voice to not wake those asleep. Two of them stirred but went back in. Akanbi could have been a rock. Her eyes widened as memories flooded her mind. Their first language as barely speaking children had been song. She turned and ran towards the billowing curtain door that led to the back of the shrine. As children, whenever they sang and it was her time to respond, she always found a way to run, to lead Gbolahan out of his safety into a space where she could shine.

The center of Osupa was full of people in morning rhythms of cooking, gossiping, cleaning, kissing and eating. A hush fell over them as Gbemisola Olohun ran out of the shrine into morning light. Roasted yam fell back into palm oil and teeth-cleansing herbs fell out of mouths. Gbemisola looked at the people around her, dressed roughly in morning wrappers, their cheeks marked, their noses bold and their eyes expectant. She held them in anticipation as she looked around, finding herself in a place both familiar and alien. She wanted to see Ma'ami most, but none of the women here was her.

Gbemisola looked up, her twin's song still echoing in her ears and down into her heart. The sky was clear with trails of thin white cloud whose tips glowed with the pink of a rising sun. The black boneship hung high, small as a hawk and casting no shadow because none could see it but her.

She opened her mouth and sang – *to the door, to the door was where they birthed us. Two without skin. One the clarion, the other the salve. Obatala and the other, coming thief, held us between each other and waited, waited till the thief began to reap us out of our ancient home. Where the harvest goes, it will know no peace, only din, only monument, only sand, only –* her throat went hoarse and she began to choke.

Gbolahan ran towards her and she came out of coughing speaking a hoarse tongue that caused her eyes to roll back and all those listening to want only silence. They covered their ears quick. Gbolahan staggered back doing the same. As she continued to speak, the earth beneath her feet began to swell and relax like it was the belly of a sleeping man, lifting her up gently and setting her back down. Her blank eyes were set on the thing in the sky only she could see. Her neck was clutched in her hands like she wanted to stop the sound from pouring out of her. An object-potency came flying from the direction of the shrine, shaped like a rabbit. It struck her in the shoulder and she went still, then stiff. Gbolahan caught her before she hit the ground.

The Awo Meta walked towards the twins, eyes heavy with sleep. They collected the girl and carried her back into the hut, where Akanbi was still sleeping the sleep of the dead.

High up in the sky above, no one saw a blight the size of an eye close.

***

After the incident with the song, Gbemisola Olohun (and Akanbi) slept for seven days without water or food. The Awo Meta were reluctant to go into their dream again on a rescue mission. They tried with all their power, casting spells and laying hands and slipping bittersweet potions between the teeth of the sleeping, but the most that happened was a jerking of the limbs and mumbling. One time, Akanbi sat up, still asleep, and said, "I can't dig myself in any deeper."

The Awo Meta switched their approach and decided that protection would be the next step to take, until the thing that held them was done with their dreams. They cast a second line of aabo around the shrine, warding off all unwanted spirits, human beings and creatures. Even Gbolahan Olohun found it hard to stand inside the shroud of circling mist that surrounded the lower-half of the shrine.

The people of Osupa were grateful that there were no more rains. Their clothes and huts and crop had dried up fast under the sun. The two slept deeper and the Awo Meta stayed close by. Gbolahan spent his time apart from the people of Osupa, in the branches of trees, pondering the lyrics of the song Gbemisola had sang back to him. They had scared him.

The Awo Meta, who only heard the tail-end of Gbemisola's song, wondered about what they had seen in the dream they shared with Gbemisola and Akanbi. Although they were used to experiencing strange realms and objects and skies often, this one made them feel uneasy. Especially the parts where there was a taking of bodies.

They did not speak about it among themselves, though they knew that the symptoms that Gbemisola showed when she finally made a sound were those of a herald. Usually, heralds would precede the arrival of orisha or other beings from realms above before they came down to the earth. Heralds didn't have to sleep for so long. They simply fell into trances of song or dance, and sometimes intricate handwork. They didn't make the ground beneath their feet beat and swell when they began to speak in other tongues. Nor was their sleep filled with repeated cycles of a singular nightmare.

The Awo Meta continued to ponder the boneship and the parts of the song of Gbemisola as they sat sleepless around the two. They also began to worry for the future, anxiety filling their chests in slow gradual spikes.

One of them was full of guilt and regret for leading his brothers into establishing Osupa and bringing the people he had thought he was saving into a conundrum that could soon be worse than war. He wondered the best way to escape being sucked into a corruption into the sky.

Another thought of his inability to adapt to new spiritual spaces without first breaking out into a mental rash and experiencing bouts of raw madness. He hated coming that close to chaos within and so he began to keep a pod of poison in the folds of his cloth, ready to burst it in his cheek if the real sky above his head broke open as it did in the dream.

The third wondered what the owner of the coming boneship could want. Was it Olodumare in disguise, testing their settlement of refugees before gifting them a better future than they could ever imagine, if they passed said test? No. Not after all they had seen in the shared dream. Olodumare would never corrupt his creation to pass a message or bestow a gift. The girl was right, it was a thief coming.

The third babalawo decided he would wait, to see what would happen.

✱✱✱

The thief came at the witching hour.

Gbemisola Olohun awoke, eyes flying open. She began to cry, calling (every three breaths) in elongated tones to all who could hear. *They have come.*

The sky above Osupa surged with faint violet light. Awojobi and Fagbeja woke next, after Gbemisola. They moved towards the girl who seemed riveted to the mat, screaming on her back, her body stiff as wood. *They have come.* She continued to announce the arrival. Awojobi went outside to see if what she spoke was true, covered neck to toe in dust-stained white, his head bowed to the ground. When he looked up and saw a shapeless hole rippling with violet light, growing across the sky, he turned his heel and walked out of Osupa. *They have come.* He was never seen again.

Fagbeja was able to move Gbemisola Olohun to stand to her feet. He didn't know what else to do, another object-potency striking her flesh might do permanent damage. She stood but did not stop crying at the top of her lungs between moments of utter calm. *They have come.* Fatona stirred at her sound, waking up. Her eyes were wide open, staring hard at the air, blind to his presence. *They have come.*

Fagbeja walked outside to see the people of Osupa sleepwalk out of their huts as behind him Gbemisola's clarion call increased in volume. In the sky he looked to, he saw as they had in the dream, a blackness staining the night, the emergence of a void in the flesh of reality. *They have come.*

The violet light radiating from the core of the void increased in intensity. Fagbeja could finally hear what was wrong. The night was quiet as a stone; no insect or frog or bird made a peep. Only, *They have come.* He turned and walked to the lake, out of Osupa, his head and heart beginning to boil over with the always unfamiliar static of madness. He put the pod of poison in his teeth and crushed it, swallowing as he walked into the lake, to sleep beneath pale waters the color of corn cream. *They have come.*

Fatona watched as Gbemisola walked out of the shrine, her head locked into her shoulders with the intensity of her screaming. She did not seem to be losing any steam or power and her voice showed no signs of cracking or fraying, instead it seemed to grow stronger, resonating down the length of her body and out into the air around her. *They have come.* Fatona shuddered. The time had come. There was only so much he could do.

He turned to Akanbi, who remained asleep still as a rock and checked with his fingers if he was still breathing. He was, but strangely, exhaling once for every six breaths Fatona himself let out. Fatona covered him with a piece of white cloth and followed Gbemisola, who was making her way slowly out of the shrine, *they have come,* through the billowing doors of cloth into the night.

Fatona stepped out of the shrine behind Gbemisola and beheld the people of Osupa, standing and waiting, sleeping on their feet. *They have come.* Awojobi and Fagbeja were nowhere to be found. He turned back into the shrine to look and know if he was seeing right. His brothers were gone.

"Wake up!" he said as he ran into the midst of the sleepwalkers, panic settling into him. He clapped his hands and shook the shoulders of Gbolahan Olohun, and slapped the faces of the swimmer brothers who had brought the two to the shrine on the day that they were struck. *They have come.* Nothing happened. "Wake up!" Fatona screamed again, and Gbemisola, whose voice had become an essential part of the tone of the air, shut up.

Fatona looked to her. Her face was turned upwards to the widening void in the sky. The brightness of the violet light was now rippling off the earth and the huts and the bodies of the people of Osupa, like midnight sun off water. Fatona watched as all the people standing around him, sleeping, lifted their heads up to look at the sky with shut eyes.

The prow of the boneship broke the surface of the void in the sky as Fatona watched. Just as in the dream, it sailed out, the color of raw charcoal. Titanic and weightless, graceful and deformed. Every inch of its surface was engraved in the language that he had seen in the shared dream. The symbols of this language burned and sparked with violet fire in rapid winks and flashes. It made no sound, even the burning of its symbols was soundless. Fatona was wide-awake. The void that the boneship sailed out of continued to shimmer with violet light even as the language engraved on the body of the ship, began to glint and flash faster.

The people of Osupa opened their sleeping eyes to behold the behemoth and the screaming began. Gbemisola Olohun was the first to catch on lilac fire and shoot into the belly of the boneship. She did not scream like those who were looking at the ship, unable to move their bodies or shut their eyes, trapped. She sailed up silently. Once she entered the ship, all the symbols on its body exploded in unison and sent a wave of light across the sky before dying down into nothing. The ship was now black as a cold coal.

A single symbol lit up and another person screamed as they were ripped out of their world into the guts of the ship. The symbols began to flash haphazardly, as people caught fire and flew up into the boneship. Some of the people of Osupa combusted with the beautiful fire and turned into ash without flying to the ship.

Fatona watched as they all went up, high into the gut of the boneship trailing threads of faintest light. Everyone stood and looked. A single wail leaving their mouths just as their bodies caught on fire and they ascended into the black body of the ship. Women who had escaped war and men who had refused it and children who wouldn't know its scars until later in their lives. The boneship showed no discrimination.

Fatona staggered backwards away from the harvest, his mind deciding too late that he should have done as his brothers and escaped the moment he realized what was happening. Awojobi had always said his heart was too soft to belong to a babalawo. There were three of them left behind – Akanbi's guardian, an orphan girl who loved to mold clay heads and talk to them and him. He watched as the girl screamed loud enough to cause his ears to ring, then her body caught on the hungry fire that was white inside and purple outside. She rose into the air and vanished into the boneship. Iya Akanbi raised her hands up in praise. She screamed as the fire engulfed and pulled her up.

Fatona looked around at Osupa, emptied. A sadness filled him. He was afraid. He did not look up. He spun around in a circle, riveted. The boneship remained silent above him.

He remembered Akanbi and moved towards the shrine doors, which were motionless in the stillness of this arcane robbery.

It bloomed in his stomach and flowed up to his heart; a water-fire that was both cold and hot. It surged out, sank into his skin and wrapped around his long white toga. He threw his head back and screamed in ecstatic agony till his throat seemed to tear.

Everything went numb and in his blindness, he felt himself become nothing.

Two

I
Sleepless

Akanbi's eyes flew open.

He rolled over on the bed of layered cloth and saw that he was alone. The firepit burnt low, the coals going to sleep under a blanket of ash. The air was completely still. Akanbi heard breath as it slid in and out of his body. He tried to remember what had made him wake up. He last remembered the black bone in the sky eating more and more burning bodies. Gbemisola had left him alone in the flat green place. He had continued to look and see and call alone, even as the dream cycled back to the bright spotless plain again, and the big man in white stood in the sky and looked at him with pity in his eyes, his cloth bright as a sun, then the big man would disappear and the winds would begin to ripple out and the blackness of the void would start to stain the fabric of the dream.

Gbemisola returned one more time but by then she no longer sang, instead she wept as the bodies burnt and rose into the bone. She disappeared in a blink as the nightmare reached the point where the black bone returned into the wound and the wound closed up. Akanbi had noticed her vanish but he couldn't turn his head until the bone was gone.

Akanbi sat up in the shrine and every bone in his back cracked in a chorus. Sharp pains shot through his stomach and up to envelop his head. He groaned and remembered. The big man had finally spoken to him, his deep voice circling the flat sky and plain in reverberating echoes. "Wake up, Akanbi! You must follow your people immediately."

He stood up with great difficulty. His head swam with a migraine that nearly sent him back to the floor. He leaned forward and retched. The white wrapper that Fatona had placed on his body remained on his shoulders. Akanbi began to sob, the discomfort in his body unbearable. The earth rumbled loud and brief, like a herd of elephants had suddenly run through Osupa with the speed of a bush rat. He stood up, all pain forgotten. It was still dark outside. He walked forward over Gbemisola's bed, tottering and swaying, drunk on fatigue.

Akanbi knew that Osupa was already empty, but feeling it in reality made him want to go back to sleep. The night outside yawned with uncertainty and this...this new trembling outside. He walked across the shrine, one unstable step after the other.

The shrine was hung with various strips of white cloth, horns and teeth in strings. Bundles of object-potencies made from wood, limestone and mud swung in pouches from the roof. He walked past the altar which sat at the center of the shrine – three different statues of pale gold, black and dark red wood stood in a triangle on a layer of wood-shavings, around their knees more object-potencies stood, a golden pyramid and several cubes cube of white marble. The statues were carved bluntly, exaggerating the features of their owners and beside them was a gourd of chalkwater. Behind the altar, a white cloth hung covered completely in cowries. Akanbi's pointed cap was beside the altar. He bent and picked it up. The cowries rattled in the breeze that was now blowing through the shrine. It smelled sweet, of unwashed body, rotten fish and soil after rain.

Akanbi tottered past the altar and towards the billowing door of cloth. He stopped just before it. The cloth blew around his body as his heart beat hard in his chest. He wondered if the big orisha in white was protecting him. He prayed for strength, shut his eyes and walked forward into the night.

When he opened them Osupa was empty as he expected. The huts in a circle around the shrine, hollow and void of firelight and the chatter of people. Looking closer he saw that there was something different in the low light of the waning moon above, Akanbi saw what had caused the brief rumble of the earth. There was a pit in the ground. It looked like an open mouth because it was red and black and slippery inside. Something heavy began to rise up out of the mouth. *Thud. Thud. Thud. Thud.*

The last thud of her small feet brought the ofiliganga out of the gut of the earth where she and her sisters lived. Akanbi took three steps backward as she walked onto the land of Osupa properly. She was tall as Akanbi five times and thick as a full grown tree. Soggy skin the color of overripe oranges hung in fatty layers around her wide body. She was naked as a worm. Every inch of her body jiggled gently as she finally heaved her bulk to a stop. Her head was bald. Eyes and full thick lips took up either half of her face and her nose was a small nib in between.

Akanbi didn't know what to say. They both stared at each other for what seemed like forever, so much that Akanbi could now tell that dawn was on its way. Her eyes were clear pools of shifting black glass. They unnerved Akanbi. He held on tighter to his cap as new waves of hunger surged through him. The ofiliganga lifted her arms and spread them out on either side of her body, still looking towards where Akanbi stood. She brought them together with a clap! The air shuddered. Akanbi's bones seemed like sand and he fell to his knees.

"Boy. Nla Nla calls you." Akanbi stood back up to his feet and bent over. His stomach was going to eat him before he understood anything that was happening to him. "Do you hear me boy? Come down now." Her voice was deep and husky and made him feel suddenly surrounded by smoke.

Akanbi nodded. She turned back towards the slick red mouth in the ground, swinging buttocks each the size of a boulder over Akanbi's head. "Follow me." Her voice echoed into the pit and she thudded back down inside.

Akanbi followed, sliding his abeti aja over his head. He looked back at the empty land of Osupa, before he slid down, following the ofiliganga into the sticky warmth within the belly of the earth.

II
Boneship

The stolen bodies from Osupa numbered a total of fifty-five. They each lay fetal, entombed in clear eggs that hung in the void of the belly of the boneship. Each egg was streaked with veins that glowed like trapped lightning. All the veins led into the throats and circled the heads of the catatonic human beings, pulsing as it nourished or fed on them. The clothes on their bodies were disintegrating slowly, dissolving into clouds of color.

The people of Osupa neither slept nor dreamt as the boneship streaked through an endlessness of stars, planets and moons and swirling eyes made of stardust. It shuddered as it broke through wave and portal, a grain of sand in an ocean of process and disorder, chance and order. It rode currents made by the sinuous bodies of suneaters and passed beneath wars flashing silent in systems beyond.

Eventually it started to move so fast that it seem to have stopped moving altogether. The black coal of its body began to burn, heating up to an unimaginable degree in the span of three breaths. It vibrated white hot in the spot it seemed to be in, although it was now moving at the speed of light, then – it disappeared, or rather it moved, forward from the speed of light into that of thought. All of the cosmos stopped as this happened and the path of the flight of the boneship ceased to be linear. It spun with dizzying speed, carving circles of white fire in the void of the cosmos. Its motions became more ragged and haphazard, as it swam through the body of the universe, traversing the breadth of twenty galaxies in mere blinks.

After a while, the boneship winked out of existence, into the unknown.

III
Akanbi in the Nest of the Ofiliganga

The ofiliganga thundered down the throat inside the earth. The air became more humid and dense with powerful smells as Akanbi slipped and slid after the running giantess. The earth beneath his feet was red, slick wet mud. The ofiliganga reached the end of the tunnel and jumped. Akanbi's mouth fell open as he slid down the slope after her just in time to watch her fold into a ball as she fell down inside a vast well that made her large bulk seem inconsequential. He followed, slipping off the edge like an object flung, falling into the nothing.

Akanbi did not scream but he wanted to. The feeling of falling into a hole in the earth made his belly feel hollow and cold, scraped of all its soft warmth. He held on to the abeti aja on his head as he fell head down, his heart beat slowing, the sickening cold in his belly growing. He heard a thud that reverberated through, what he realized by the echo that widened forever, a cavern. The ofiliganga had landed on solid ground. Akanbi tried to turn around or twist his body but the speed of his fall was immense and afforded him no extra motions, except to put his hand on his head. After falling for another eternal moment, Akanbi suddenly felt the ground rushing up to meet his face, it was the head rising off it that made him know. He started to scream, loud and unstable but he barely got any sound out before he collided with a mound of softness that shut him up.

The mound drew him slowly into what felt like a pool of deep, warm dough, softer than fresh mud. Akanbi was plastered on all sides by it but still sinking slow, not yet done falling. Then he stopped. The thick warmth still covered him on all sides. He heard a familiar sound begin to surround him. dim.dim.

dim.dim. dim.dim. Heartbeats. As the mound started to affirm, causing him to rise back up to the surface, Akanbi realized he was surrounded by skin and sunken into the flesh of a great body. He struggled to sit up but it was no use. The body he was inside was too soft and his legs gave before he could even kneel properly.

A hand pulled at his waist and he was lifted through the air and placed on hard solid ground again. Akanbi wobbled and then stood still. His eyes adjusted to the lightless pit that he had fallen in and he saw a host of very dim fires burning inside sleeping bodies all around him. They beat dim.dim dim.dim. A nest of ofiliganga. Their massive voluptuous bodies rose in furrowed hills and valleys and layers dark and fair around him.

"Boy, come." The ofiliganga that brought him was standing right in front of him. He could barely see her apart from the mass of bodies lying around. Her voice was even deeper down her inside the earth. "Boy don't make any sound or the sisters wake and you no like that." Akanbi nodded. "Boy look where you put your feet."

He checked his body, which was adjusting to the warmth of the bodies around, for wholeness. His abeti aja was in place and the white wrapper that he had woken under the cover of in Osupa was still around his neck and shoulders.

"We no see toy in longest time." She said as she began to walk forward, swinging her body like a cat down the path that the bodies of the sleeping ofiliganga created. Her footsteps were completely silent. Akanbi followed. The bodies rose around as he made his way through a maze of rippling flesh. There were hundreds and hundreds of them. To the one who brought him it was a normal situation but to him it was like walking through a dense forest made of limbs and buttocks, a house of sleeping skin. After a while, Akanbi could feel the motion of their warmth past him like an invisible river, he could see little details and tell if he was looking at fingers or toes or shut eyes. Then, he could see bellies moving and hear breath hissing.

The ofiliganga stopped moving. They had passed through the long winding path that the bodies in the nest made and entered a clearing. In this circle, the arrangements of the giantess' bodies had become even more ordered and clean. There was an orange fire going dim.dim, dim.dim, being passed between of a gang of five ofiliganga, all with skin black as coal who sat right in the center of the clearing. The giantesses were hugging and kissing the fire that they held in their hands like it was a bouquet of flame lilies, then handing it to the next in circle. They were all twice the size of the ofiliganga that Akanbi followed and their bodies seemed to be firmer and softer at the same time. Their skin didn't pucker or freckle or crease. Just perfect smooth hairlessness. The ofiliganga that brought Akanbi walked into the center.

"What you need, small sister? You know better than to break a circle during Warmth."

"I have bring boy, from up."

"Where is he?"

Akanbi walked over to the center of the clearing where the skin of the giantesses gleamed as they continued to pass around the fire.

"Come closer."

He moved till he could see the fire in their eyes.

"Sleeping boy. Your father waits inside the earth. You cannot run from this one. Go in and seek him. Use our body." The fire vanishes between lips, a bite, a moan. Passed around. They eat the fire.

Akanbi moved forward, pulled by something he couldn't see, until he was between two hips, tall as huts. A small cave of blackness opened where they leaned against each other. Akanbi knelt down and crawled inside the emptiness.

The ofiliganga ate their fire. Akanbi fell into a hole.

IV
The Mute Thief

The black boneship slipped out of thoughtspeed into an infinite ocean. The ocean was still and white as purest sap. The boneship ceased to move with any precision and began to drift and spin slow. Nothing moved in the whiteness. There was no sound.

At the center of the white ocean stood a circle of eleven bodies made of rough serrated bone that ended in crowns like dead trees at where the head should be. They had no faces. Instead there was a hemisphere made from long spikes worn masklike beneath their crowns. Inside these spheres pulsed bright violet light. Where chests should be small blinding suns sat, their light also of this ultraviolet hue. Their arms and legs dangled useless, covered in big bony plates and a proliferation of spikes and scales.

These were the Mute Thieves and the white ocean was their mindscape.

The boneship drifted for eternity before it finally got pulled into the only motion under the ocean, a spiral that circled the Thieves. It swam around the thorny towers of the Thieves' bodies, an eighth the size of their heads, before it slipped into their center where the eye of the ocean rested. It became still as an image, suddenly riveted.

The vertical hemispheres of the Thieves' faces began to flash rapidly, each Thief creating its own pattern of blips and longs flashes. They were speaking to themselves and to the boneship. The boneship's skin began to freckle with the glowing symbols and glint in response to its owners queries.

The faces of the Thieves stopped flashing and the boneship broke, into eleven pieces. The eggs in which the human beings of Osupa rested in catatonia slipped into the milk of the ocean. The pieces of the boneship drifted off in eleven directions, each slipping where a mouth should be in a Thief's face.

In the ocean, the fifty five eggs gathered around themselves, sticking one to the other like magnets to metal, forming a cluster. The Mute Thieves began flashing their faces again and thin beams of pure light shot out of their chests and covered the eggs in a final fire.

The eggs broke open. The human beings slipped out, still in a cluster, floating boneless and naked as newborns. Their eyes remained shut. Gbemisola Olohun drifted out of the human cluster towards one of the suns that burned at the hearts of the Thieves. She grew smaller and smaller as she drifted closer to the sun, until she was but a grain, and then nothing, swallowed in the ultraviolet.

***

Gbemisola Olohun sat on a cube that floated in a blue sky.

There was nothing below, just aquamarine all around. She remained naked but she cared very little about that. Her eyes were fixed on the flow of an approaching cloud. It was a thin, long cloud that seemed to dance like a snake as it approached. Every time she blinked it was closer, until finally it was before her and then its clean mist was washing over her being. She shut her eyes and felt every cell and nerve in her body sing with bliss. When she opened her eyes it was like she was staring into a mirror.

Gbemisola Olohun sat on a cube that floated in a blue sky.

"Where do you think you are?" Gbemisola asked herself. Her voice was quiet and her gaze serene. Gbemisola knew she looked more tired and older than she saw.

"I don't know. Last I remember I was dreaming. Then I woke up and the sky opened and ate me. Is this another dream?"

"You are in Canetis Nix. We are Canetix Nix. We require use of your bodies and that is why we have brought you here."

"What? What does that mean? Brought you here? Is this not a dream?"

"You are far from home, youngling. We require your throats, out from which come what you call sound. We are unable to create this sound ourselves."

"Let me go." Gbemisola whispered to herself. She tried to move her body but could not. "I need to understand what is happening please."

"Much has happened before now and much will happen after. We chose you for the power of your song. We tried to get you to see, through a dreamstate what we required you to do, but we were obstructed by the presence of a radiant entity indigenous to your world."

"Akanbi?" Gbemisola realized she could still remember the dream that had kept her hostage for all those days. She could remember the boy she shared them with, things started to get blurry when she attempted to cast her mind back to what had happened before she began dreaming.

A place called Osupa. Had she always been dreaming? How did she even come to be in a body?

Across from where she seated, she watched her mouth move again in the sky where there was no sun but the light was clear as day.

"He is of that entity, yes. The entity chose to make physical contact with him at the very moment we attempted to do the same with you."

"Why?"

"We require your voice, voices. We have found a peculiar world, perfect to store our menagerie but it is formless, full of only dust. Only this sound can make it find form again."

"Voices?"

"Other members of your species are present. We require more than one tone to reshape this world."

"If we help you, will we ever get to return home? Or are we your slaves now?"

"What a strange word. Canetis Nix do not operate under such laws. Think of your work as that of an organ borrowed. You will be returned when said work is done."

"So you have taken us against our will and desire to use us as you please."

"We have taken you because you are a leader in convergence and where your voice goes the rest will follow."

Gbemisola Olohun felt a knot of emotions tangle up in her chest. Her face remained placid as that of the thing before her, mirroring her. They both sat with legs hanging off the edge of the cube, hands covering breasts placed on heart. Their backs were stiff and their eyes wide; one with confusion, the other with a cold intelligence.

"Please, let us go. We do not want to be here. Please -"

"How do you know where you want to be? You haven't seen it yet. Not felt the power in this sound of yours. We are giving your young species a chance at purpose beyond the dreams of your creators. We are creating with you and your fellow human beings, a new form of architect."

The reflected Gbemisola Olohun stands up on her cube saying, "Come with us and know glory." She falls backwards and takes the blue of the sky with her.

V
The Orisa's Gift

Akanbi crawled down a cold, mud-sticky tunnel in the earth that he opened up with his hands. In the lightlessness, his fingertips were numb as they sank into the tenderness of the subterranean ground and ripped it apart. He could see the perfectly fat ofiliganga talking his destiny over his head as they passed around the flame. Their round cheeks announcing that he had to save the people taken. Telling him to go deeper into the earth's belly if he wanted to survive, if he wanted to begin the rescue mission.

He stopped, out of breath. His lower body was covered in the sokoto he had been wearing the night of the storm at Osupa. His abeti aja was gone. He found himself dozing to sleep, digging more, dozing, digging, and soon he was breathing in rhythm,

Akanbi fell.

Out of the tunnel into a large white room that had always been there since Olodumare made Ile Aye, the walls covered in bleached spines from various species of men and animals in a serpentine pattern that fooled the eye with motion. A purple mat swirling with nebulae sat at the center of the room.

There was a mountain of stiff white cloth burning with holy fire. Holy fire is blue like water.

Akanbi jumped out of his nap when his skull hit the white gravel that flowed across the lower part of the room in clean waves. He rose to his feet, from beneath a covering of clotted soil, cold shivers tore into his spine and belly.

He took three steps towards the radiance and collapsed to the floor. A shadow swung about the room, like an arm in a single wave and the radiance opened. Something moved inside the burning cloth and through slats in the stiff cloth, forms passed - a sliver of black flesh, an eye, blue and gold with god, a hand trailing cloud.

"Akanbi." The voice whispered. The fiery cloth pulsed with the deep rumble. "Wake up, Akanbi. Stand up. We have work to do." Though low and deeper than lion's cry, the voice remained warm. Akanbi opened his eyes and stood again. The shivers returned. He could feel his every breath struggling to stay in his lungs. The room swirled and the spines slithered.

"Take palmwine." Akanbi saw Obatala's eye and followed it to where a fizzing horn hung black in the air before the orisha. He pulled himself, panting, up to the horn and then he placed his lips on the rim and pulled till a hollow rang in the white room inside the earth.

"See." The orisha was standing behind him. He turned to look as the palmwine surged warm as love up and down his insides.

Obatala's hand came down and touched Akanb's cheek. Akanbi looked into the orisha's face and saw himself. He saw himself on a coal-black eshinemi, galloping across a sky full of stars, streaking the air gold.

"You are to ride Ronke to the white place of our thieves. There you might break the chains of your kind."

Akanbi nodded furiously. The orisha's fingers on his cheek had put him into a stillness that unmoored him. He felt himself possible again. Maybe the fires of Ife had brought him here, into the presence of an aspect of Olodumare whose hand was grazing his cheek and filling him with emotions that had no sound. Akanbi asked about Ronke.

"The eshinemi? She is a being beyond your understanding. Ride her well and don't run when she starts talking."

"Why me?"

Obatala's hand left his cheek and the white room with the spines and the mat and the radiance were gone. Akanbi stood in a tunnel tall enough to hold an iroko.

In his palm, a statue of whitestone rested and in the far distance, fields of fire burned.

Three

I
Songstress

Flown out of the ocean of thought in which the Mute Thieves dwelled, into the black glitter of emptiness and stars, the fifty five from Osupa floated out of the boneship that took them from Ile Aye into the atmosphere of Canetis Nix. They all stood dazed and naked on a circular bone that spun slow as it descended. Around their heads grew translucent membranes, bulbs with a rainbow sheen, to help them breathe and amplify their voices.

Light on Canetis Nix was alive. The rippling mists that filled the atmosphere seemed to be sheets of pure light that drifted in circles. The bone dais stopped one foot above the ground.

There on the floor, it was like being on the shores of an endless white beach that was attached to an ocean of even whiter sand. A silence pervaded the air. This silence it seemed, also controlled the wind because no breath moved down on the ground, though in the upper stratosphere there had been some cool and a distant roaring like a wave crashing without ebbing forever.

Gbemisola Olohun alighted from the bone dais first. Her body plump and her skin smooth as skinned bark. On her back, where shoulder bones met, something like a spiked crustacean made of finest limestone was fused into her spine.

Twenty-four long segmented appendages follow the flow of her ribs and hipbones, slipping stingers half an inch beneath the skin where they stop, in a pointed oval that starts at the throat and ends inside the groin. Two of the appendages pinch above the collarbone, just beneath the voice box.

As Gbemisola walked onto the powders of Canetis Nix, feet sinking to the ankle with every step, wondering as she has since the lightning struck if all is dream, the *olorin* on her back, tightened its grip across her body.

Gbemisola staggered and held her midriff. Something was trickling into her, building inside her, the poisons that burned at the tips of the stingers inside her body were releasing their toxins. The trickle poured out of the *olorin* into her bloodstream and Gbemisola felt it flow through her, the tingles in her skin and then her bones. The collecting of that ache into a point made to escape, made to draw across all space a new thing. The toxins crested in her chest with a flush of euphoria that resonated across her entire being.

She began to sing of bliss, and the upper atmosphere of Canetis Nix was resonant.

It responded to Gbemisola's clear, long voice. The way she pulled at the song from inside her belly instead of her throat. In the air, around her body, vibrations began to collect and when Gbemisola reached the tonal nadir of the song, the vibrations opened into the air and the remaining fifty-four could see as tendrils of fine sand began to swirl around her, showing the outlines of the sonic sphere she stood in, ten times taller and wider than her.

The powdered white around her feet sank, forming a circle wide as the bone dias that brought them.

Rising out of the low note, Gbemisola flew to the higher reaches of her register, like a bird approaching death. The particles of sand followed the hum and sound of her voice, up, clinging and rippling and twisting like muscles around the vibrations and also the feeling of the song.

Gbemisola finished the song. It continued to echo for what seemed like forever. Behind her stood a spherical structure, like a hollow ball made of strings and thick muscle.

The architect remained standing. She turned and looked at the structure. The bliss in her blood made her smile, even though looking at the sphere she just stepped out of, she had a strong sense of being outside of herself.

The forty-four all understood as they watched. Sound and the matter of this place were like magnet and iron, hand and mud. The *olorin* in their backs squirmed and poison-ecstasy filled their bellies. They alighted from the bone dias, which slipped away into the atmosphere with the speed of air. They walked over to Gbemisola Olohun, who was standing staring at the structure, reading of herself in the sculpted sand.

The circle formed around the convergent and the first chorus began.

II
Ronke

By the grace of the palm wine he had shared with Obatala, the fields of blue fire that led to the center of the earth did not scorch Akanbi but he still walked through them fearfully, placing his feet on the shattered coals that covered the ground like they were going to burn him. All around him it roared. There was nothing for miles but fire like grass, rising out of hard black rock. Above there was no sky or cloud, only the returned glow of the fields below.

The fire gave off no smoke.

Akanbi got to a river of molten lava and the statue in his hand buzzed. He began to follow its flow. Past rows and rows of hot tongues licking, seemingly planted. The river ended in a lake of fire that split off into a rash of smaller and larger pools up ahead. The lake was placid, like a spill of yellow and red soup.

The earth around it was dead black, no smolder.

This was how Akanbi saw Ronke, staring from the shore, her hooves submerged. She stood two times the height of him, white as coconut flesh with one pair of snake eyes, high on either side of her head. Beneath the snake eyes, were two moons, sunken into the long skull but Akanbi was riveted to what shone at the center of her head, like a diamond sparkling.

Akanbi moved closer to her and she walked up from the lake and bowed her head till he could touch it. He pulled the statue out of his sokoto and placed it on her tongue.

She began to crunch it like it was sugar.

"Hop on my back" Her voice came into his head unannounced. "Let me take you to the whiteness. I can see your friends. They are building cages."

Akanbi walked over to her middle and found that his head only reached her belly. She lay down flat, white belly over black soil, and he climbed onto her back. She stood and Akanbi had a vantage of the fields of fire and the pools in the distance.

"Grab my neck." Akanbi slid forward and grabbed as much of her long neck as he could. She was cold like a fish, with flat scales like calcified feathers across her body. Akanbi shut his eyes. He had nothing to think of or wish. He was only following instructions in which the only thing needed was his faith.

As the eshimemi, began to gallop into the air, flying over the night above the fields of fire, he found out that he had a desire to be told of as a story.

III
Chorus Architecture

In the millions of seconds that the fifty five sang, they raised over five thousand of their indestructible spheres. The spheres peppered the surface of Canetis Nix like nests from an invasive species, all varying in size and pattern but remaining within the form of the sonic sphere that drifted around them everytime they sang the structures up.

The olorin were growing deeper into their bodies and their bliss was getting stronger. They usually needed screams and shouts and roars to push the structures to be bigger. The olorin made sure they felt strong enough to break their throats.

Soon, the Mute Thieves themselves appeared, distant in the always-day skies of Canteis Nix like halved samurai.

Gbemisola Olohun and the fifty four sport breastplates the color of olorin and throats of hard red stone when they come. Their symbiosis with the euphoric was almost complete. It has reached into their bones and turned them into hyper-vibrating elements, made their ribcages into colossal echo chambers and their throats into weapons.

They knew how it worked. They wandered the powders of Canetis Nix looking for points of convergence. Only Gbemisola knew these points, where air and sky and sand found equilibrium, equilibrium enough to be shaped with song. Once found, they stood as symbol. Circle and dot. Chorus and convergent. Then the olorin flooded their blood with bliss and their wordless songs rose, followed after by the powders of Canetis Nix.

The sands rose like smoke into the air and became steel at the end of sound.

To make the sand flow ornate they used melisma, for flair they roared like beasts, soprano brought finesse, bass built foundation and pitch increased density.

They were a machine by now, their olorin growing tentacles that linked them mind, body and voice. They wandered Canetis Nix, building with voice, soaring, lost yet found.

After they built their last structure, the Mute Thieves appeared, sending thousands of boneships of varying sizes. Out of these ships came a zoo – smaller versions of the Mute Thieves with the same spiked bone armor and violet auras, leading and lifting and carrying abominations stranger than the eyes of the Convergent could believe.

They put the creatures in some of the cages that the fifty-five had built. Afterwards, with a brief passage of voice, the cages were sealed.

Then, the Mute Thieves left the fifty-five alone on Canetis Nix, not to die, but because they too were creatures acquired, never to be let go.

IV
Resonance

Ronke and Akanbi galloped up, with a sound like a shot, out of the darkness under the crust, onto the glazed deserts of Canetis Nix. As far as the eye could see rose spherical sculptures, layered and built like nests. Ronke zipped through this odd farm.

Akanbi still gripping her neck, squinted through his eyes to see. He snapped up when Ronke stopped as if hit by a wall.

Twenty man-sized eggs lay in a depression in the ground of Canetis Nix. They pulsed and a fleshy redness squirmed behind their translucence.

"We are too late." Ronke said inside his head. "They are in metamorphosis."

Ronke knew too much. Akanbi suspected she was just Obatala in another form. He climbed down her cool body onto the heat of Canetis Nix and moved closer to the pod of eggs.

"How?"

"The time it took to get here might have seemed like a few days to you, Akanbi, but it was nearly a decade to them. They must have merged with the thieves and entered into this state."

The eggs were arranged in a spiral. The large thorny spheres that covered the surface of the white desert around them seemed immovable. Akanbi was unaware of all the cosmic life contained in them: hungry, thrashing, sleeping and calling to lost homes.

Akanbi stood by the eggs feeling futile.

He could tell that his people, the people of Osupa were there. He could feel their hearts beating and smell a bitter-sweetness in their blood. There were faces behind the sticky rainbowsheen of the eggshells. Gbolahan. The twins. Fatona.

He knew no one of them even though they had been recovering from their shared trauma as a collective. All his life he had been alone. He had failed those who sent him and now he was lost on another world.

The strangeness of the situation hit him and Akanbi turned away from the eggs towards Ronke.

"Ronke, can you take me anywhere I desire?"

"No. We are here to take these people home. We have to wait for them to wake up. Come, rest on my belly." Akanbi saw that the eshimemi was lying on the heat of the desert, joyous. He went over and lay on its soft cold belly in wait.

After an eternity of dreamless anticipation, the eggs opened.

V
Convergence

The olorin and the human being have fused into one being against the predictions of the Mute Thieves.

They emerge from their pods, new soldiers of tone. Their backs serrated and their eyes pools of nothing in which sound can be seen. Their tender throats have become split red things like sliced fruit and their heads are covered in plates of a porous tomato-red shell, as are their chests and thighs. They are beautiful, fleshless beneath these shells.

No more human.

Akanbi staggers back as they slip out of the dripping eggs into the heat. They lay and dry in the permanent sun, while the largest egg seems to wait. Ronke says nothing.

Akanbi looks from behind her head. The eshimemi sits on her side and watches the birthing.

The born begin to sing, a sound strangely human, like a memory of human song. They circle Gbemisola, the convergent, unborn queen.

Her egg splits and she spills out. No shell, no spikes.

Akanbi thinks he is looking at the placenta or yolk when the queen unfurls into the air, a mucosal serpent of white noise.

Her motions set off melodies which the air sings to itself. She stretches tall towards the sun, her every atom blooming with harmony, long fins cycling above the ground.

Ronke stands up in respect. The chorus of nineteen, all turned male, look to their queen. She in turn looks beyond Canetis Nix, letting out a sound, like birdsong unraveled.

In the sky, a circle appears.

Point of convergence, here to nowhere. Here to everywhere. The queen sails into the sky, towards the Convergence, gentle as smoke.

Her chorus follows.

About the Author

Dare Segun Falowo is a writer of the Nigerian Weird, influenced by liminal spaces, local cinema and traditional cosmology. Their varied works have appeared in *The Magazine of Fantasy & Science Fiction*, *The Dark Magazine*, *Baffling Magazine*, *The Dominion Anthology*, and more. Their novelette "Convergence in Chorus Architecture" was longlisted for a BSFA in 2020. They are neurodivergent, and currently haunt the city of Ibadan. They tweet @dsfxyz.

Acknowledgments

This book wouldn't exist if I, from the start of my literary consciousness to this very moment, didn't encounter kinship + nurture friendships + recieve feedback, support and kindness from these beings:

Akosile "Sylven" Tobi
Aderounmu Adedeji
Adelekan Adetayo
My band-mates from "Pass the Salt" (Edwin Okolo & Oluranti Olaose) and all those who supported our play in the blogosphere with their joy and awe, most brightly,
Ogaga Okparavero.
Dolapo Ogedengbe
Kehinde Adigun
Adebola Rayo
Wole Talabi
Chioma Odukwe
Lekan Olanrewaju
Adeniyi Ademoroti
Binyavanga Wainana
Geoff Ryman
C.C. Finlay
Oghenechovwe Donald Ekpeki

Ogundiran Tobi
Joshua Egbiameje Omole
Chad Pirtle

I also want to thank those behind the scenes:

The makers of paper, the operators of printers, and those who layout the text precisely. Bieke Van Aggelen and Caitlin Farley from African Literary Agency for working with me to pull this together, encouraging me through fatigue and chronic bodily occurrences to keep pushing. Justine Norton-Kertson and Somto Ihezue from Android Press, Ray and Rosalie from Tartarus Press. Elnathan John for lending his dulcet voice to my weird tapestry.

And to you, out chasing emergent horizons through eternity, in migration somewhere only you know, marked odd for seeking the new in a dying world, walking above and through aged rigid, unimaginative structures, until you find that light that you can rest in.

www.ingramcontent.com/pod-product-compliance
Lightning Source LLC
Chambersburg PA
CBHW070446200726
48293CB00007B/2132